BEYOND

—— THAT ——

ROOM

Susie Ruth Powell

What People Are Saying About Susie Ruth Powell

"Your book springs from a very authentic place—your father's and your painful experiences under the unforgivable yolk of Jim Crow.

As you have painted such multi-dimensional characters, which the reader can really CARE about, you are helping the reader viscerally comprehend something of the injustices of that era, as well as the emotional (and generational!) trauma brought forward from those who suffered in the decades before your father was born—not least in that horrific Wilmington Massacre.

Only the brave find words for such dreadful events; you are not only a gifted writer, but also emotionally brave."

—Marcia Angle, MD

"Through memory and artistic imagination, Susie Powell weaves a vivid and lyrical recounting of the 1898 Wilmington Race Riot and its aftermath. A remarkable book!"

—Lois Deloatch
Musician & Storyteller

"Reading *Beyond That Room* by Susie Ruth Powell felt like stepping into a world both hauntingly familiar and profoundly moving. The storytelling is layered and intimate, blending history, trauma, and resilience in a way that lingers. Powell brings her characters to life so vividly—especially Rose and Rabbit—that they feel like people we've known, carrying the weight of family secrets and generational wounds. The hidden room as a metaphor for buried truth is powerful, and the emotional honesty throughout the book made it impossible to put down. This isn't just a historical novel—it's a reflection on legacy, survival, and the unspoken stories that live in all of us."

—Canisha Bryant
Children's Book Author

Dedication

To:
Isaac and Sarah Powell
Colonel Tee and Nora Alston
Samuel and Fannie Powell

Acknowledgements

SPECIAL THANKS to my father, Samuel (Sam) Powell, Senior, who in his early teens was sold into indentured servitude by his father, Isaac Powell, a former slave.

At age 18, in 1884, my dad was free. He went on to become a successful independent businessman, farmer, and landowner.

I also want to thank Kenneth Powell for his talented and visionary assistance in bringing this book to the world. And thank you to Elizabeth Ann Atkins, co-founder of Two Sisters Writing & Publishing®, for helping to edit and publish this novel, to inform and inspire the hearts and minds of people everywhere.

Contents

PROLOGUE

Shots.
Silence.
Two more shots.
A *signal, perhaps*, she thought.

The house trembled, sitting on stilts.

And her boy child spoke up from the breakfast table, after a made-up piece of laughter.

"I can still make it to school going the back way, not the shore."

Her girl child, older than the boy, answered, "Mama told us not to go out the house today!"

"Shut up, Rebecca. You ain't nobody's mama."

"And you don't even like school. You skip most days and pretend—"

She had had it with these two. But she spoke softly to make them listen.

"Hush, both of you, and listen to me." She went to the door and wrapped her thumb and little finger around the doorknob. She faced the door. And then she turned, facing her children as she grasped the doorknob.

Sitting in the woods one night, three days after the Wilmington Massacre of 1898 and the family's great escape from the city, Walter broke into uncontrolled giggles

Rebecca and Sarah startled, stared. It went on. The laughter. Inside, down deep, Sarah fought the dread at the thought that Walter was going crazy. People weren't just crazy; they *went* there. And he seemed bound.

Rebecca asked her mother, "What he find so funny?"

"Nothing."

"What he laughing at?"

"Ask him." Then Sarah added, after looking at the soiled clothes and the torn shirt on Walter, "He laughing at what he think he ought to have."

Walter's giggles subsided and came up again, and Sarah feared that he would turn to drink with his joy and out-of-controlness.

Rebecca said, "Is he laughing at his own self?"

"Probably."

CHAPTER ONE

November 10, 1898

A blindfolded mule carried a millstone on his neck, walking forever on and on, straight ahead his perpetual circle: again and again, straight ahead, and winding back around and around, blindly chasing and following the tiny slave girl Sarah. She brushed the grain to position it beneath the grinding stone that pressed it into flour, which one day crushed Sarah's three middle fingers while she struggled, unable to withdraw quickly enough. While she screamed and shivered and bled, the master lamented, "She ain't worth a penny now."

Now, more than a decade later, the three fingers missing from her right hand made it hard for her to lift the latch on the other inside front door. Even so, she opened it, stood within the doorway, changed her mind, and closed it again as she backed herself back inside the house. She tapped her foot. She listened to a sound from far away but close enough to let her hear the sadness. It reminded her of a blind mule walking, though yoked up to something. It was a train rolling along a track of dread.

Her own dread had little to do with trains, but it was a present feeling about this cold November day. What would it be before it was over? She wanted her children, Walter and Rebecca, to know how scared she was. Yet, she wanted them to know that she was strong for them, if maybe she was. When she walked back through the narrow, dark hallway of the little shotgun house, they were still where she had left them moments before.

"Y'all know what been happenin' round this here election for political office. You done seen all them signs the white people put up." She looked at Walter. She could see his frown. He rubbed his hand alongside his face. She looked at Rebecca, who nodded her head.

She knew that she was repeating things she had been saying for many days. "You want to know how we know something bad is going to happen today? They cannot pour they own drink or put they selves down in' a chairs by they self. So, we have people right here from the Brooklyn sector of Wilmington, always know what the white people do and what they planning. There is been meetings all over town the last few days. Planning. And even before now. And even before election day. Some of our men got wind of trouble and no Negro man was able to buy a gun or a rifle to use to hunt with. And that was something new. And some the men what work at the port of Wilmington where your daddy used to work. They told me that there is been shipments of guns coming in this city since September. Plus, all summer long, every chance they get, if a Colored man got a gun, they takes it away from him. And for some reason, the mens that works in the hotels and the stables, hang around the dry goods, they know. This is the day. They tells me something is going to happen today."

Rebecca stood in front of the pie safe. She nodded when her mother spoke the familiar words: "I'm going to say it one more time, to make sure. Walter, you stay inside this house today. Rebecca, you stay in the house. This is a day that they devil have sent." Then Sara tried to search the face that

Walter hid from her before looking at Rebecca.

"I will go just long enough to finish up a few things from yesterday and then come on home. Probably in no danger myself. The menfolk is what they is after." Rebecca moved to gather up the breakfast dishes while Sarah talked. "I will try to get back home before things get too bad."

She walked to the front door, and with that thumb and little finger, she opened it again and went all the way out, walking fast.

She would not have believed it if she had not heard it herself. A man as prominent as her boss, Dr. Russell Wilson, should not have been as threatened as he was yesterday when a group of white men came to the Wilson home at nightfall. Sarah had let them in. Offered them a glass of water. They had politely refused. They made her think of snakes shining in the grass, moving languidly and gracefully. She heard them from behind the door. They told Dr. Wilson to leave town. They gave him until today. She had to get to the Wilsons to help with the packing and receive her pay for the week before he left.

She hoped that she had not wasted her breath. She wanted to scare Rebecca and Walter enough to keep them inside and out of sight. She did not want to leave them alone in the house at a time like this, but Walter and Rebecca's father, a seaman, died in 1896 off the coast of Cuba, when the United States had defended Cuba from Spain, its ships anchored in Cuban waters, and in the process made Cuba into a colony.

And right then, a song came into her head. She did not sing it out loud, at first. She thought it. *I went to the rock to hide my face.* She walked briskly towards the home and the hospital of Doctor Wilson. The song played in her head. As she crossed the street, she began to sing:

"Went to the rock to hide my face. Rock cried out."

Young Rebecca Brake placed the dirty dishes in a pan. She slowly poured hot water from a kettle over them and looked down at the particles of egg and meat, thinking of a hiding place that her mother often sang about. So much fear rumbled inside her that she strained to keep down her food. She tried to move quickly with heavy arms and legs. She was in a panic about what her mother Sarah had warned. She left the house. She turned and reached for soap on the window ledge, when the slamming of the door brought her around to face Walter's empty chair at the kitchen table. She heard his feet racing across the porch, and she turned to see him outside beside her. Against all their mother's warnings, her brother had walked right out the front door. Rebecca looked at him and sighed.

"I ain't scared," Walter said. He frowned at the air, crossed his arms in front of his chest. And before Rebecca could move to grab him and hold him back, he was already-pounding across the narrow porch.

Walter leaped the rail and dashed madly toward the place where, unknown to him, a phalanx of white men was passing on its way to the Colored hospital, after having set fire to the Colored newspaper office. He would just miss them and not realize, at seeing the stragglers catching up, that it had passed by. Walter did not know that fires were being set in Wilmington, North Carolina, this morning, although the smoke from the first fire was already staining the sky.

Sarah, Walter, and Rebecca's house was a long house with its three rooms in a row, just on the outer edge of the Colored section of Wilmington, next to a Catholic Church. Rebecca walked back inside to the front of it and looked out the window to the open, quiet street. She could not see Walter or her mother. But she saw a sign, a leftover message that had hung for three or four days tacked to a tree, as though it had been placed so as to be framed by this window. The sign read "White Supremacy. Vote for Democrats."

The wind plucked at the edges of the sign. But it clung. Rebecca read the words and argued with herself until, after a time, she decided to go after her brother. But because their mother had been so worried, she would first go to Dr. Wilson's house and maybe the Colored hospital first to let her know. Then she would hurry through the streets until she found him. Sounds of anger and movement surrounded her.

❧

Walter moved along the street for nearly an hour, though enjoying the push of the crowd. The street noise buzzed around him, a welcome diversion, certainly better than staying in a dull old house. In front of a barbershop, he put his back to the building to let the crowd pass. Where in the world were all these people going? It was like market day. Well, he could sure have himself some fun with this many folk out, walking back and forth.

As he searched the crowd for anyone he knew, he noted for the first time the anger on the white men's faces. Angrier than usual. One of them poked a stick in his face, nearly jabbing him in the eyes, but he ducked out of the way and let him pass with the crowd, not paying it much mind. Whatever they were they doing, it was maybe nothing to do with him, no matter what his mother said. He was fast and could dodge anything. He finally spotted a familiar face. Caesar, sullen as usual, moving in his direction, walking zigzag to navigate through the wall of white men.

Caesar surprised Walter with a warm greeting, despite the grim look on his face. "Hey, Walter Brake! What cha know?"

Walter smiled at Caesar. Caesar was about 25 years old and rarely gave Walter the time of day, maybe a thoughtless slap to the back of head running by but little else. Caesar was always working, too busy to chew the fat or make a joke. Because Caesar worked hard all the time, he was not Walter's idea of a model to imitate. Caesar never looked as though he was having fun. To see him standing so still was unusual. He always leaked sweat, was frayed and rough at his edges. Walter saw Caesar day in and day out, scrambling through the streets of Wilmington in gray dirt-colored rags that flapped about him, his feet wrapped with heavy papers and pieced-together bits of shoe soles. Many said that Caesar was touched about the head, the way he ran about with tongue out and swallowing dust.

But this day, Caesar stood still, one leg crossed in front of the other. Walter looked down at Caesar's feet and gasped. Caesar wore brand new, and shiny-black, high button shoes. Walter went close to get a better look. Caesar dropped an arm on Walter's shoulder, so that they now stood with the barber pole behind them. The throng of white men moved, some on foot, some on horse-drawn vehicles, some on horseback. One solitary car puffed by, scaring the horses and eliciting curses.

Caesar leaned down to wipe his shoes. Walter had never before seen a Colored man in worn-out dun-colored clothes wearing brand new shiny shoes. As he was about to ask Caesar about them, he stopped as he saw his nuisance of a sister, climbing down from Dr. Wilson's buggy.

From within the buggy, Walter saw Dr. Wilson point a finger to him. He was torn. *Rebecca will try to make me go home*, he thought. *I will not go.* The doctor looked at him and talked. He disliked the man, a Colored man with soft hands like a girl. He spoke crisp and sharply as he went about the city, caring for the sick in Brooklyn, Wilmington's Colored section. He had a few white patients, too. He went back and forth between his hospital and house calls, delivering babies, stitching up people who got cut in fights, injured on machines, or pulled behind horses. Rebecca loved the man. The doctor had treated her for a touch of the fever in '97. Now he and his wife regularly sent her books to read. He had the nerve to say to Walter, "Let Rebecca teach you how to read and write before it is too late."

Walter preferred to not let people know that words on a page were secrets he could not crack. That time when he had tried to run an errand for the doctor, the man had handed him a piece of paper with an address on it. That was why Walter hated him. Now, he pointed at Walter, who remembered that piece of paper.

Walter convinced himself that reading was something that he could function without. He could get around the city. He had left Wilmington many times, hiding on the train and making it back by remembering signs by their design and shape, along with landmarks. That was enough to get him where he wanted to be. He was relieved to see the doctor hurriedly click his tongue to the horse and continue on after Rebecca stepped down. It would take her a while to get through the barricade of people between them.

Just then, while still standing next to Caesar, Walter now saw a white man bring a whip down upon the back of a Black man. Other white men cheered with each lash. One or two Colored men seemed to try to get themselves lowered to the ground; their walking looked like crawling, getting distance. Walter shrugged. He was out here now, and he certainly was not going to let anybody know how scared he was. He wondered what it felt like inside to be grown up. However it felt, he did not have that feeling. He looked up at Caesar. Caesar didn't react for Walter to see. Maybe Caesar was relieved to not have his own back whipped, or perhaps he really was a little touched like Mama said.

In the meantime, what was most urgent for Walter was to know where Caesar got those handsome shoes. His own shoes were sturdy but scuffed and turned up at the toes. He curled his huge feet inside his scruffy, no-colored shoes and looked up at Caesar.

Just before Rebecca crossed the street, he shouted, "Where you get them shoes?"

He had to shout to be heard over the noise, a nuisance of cheers. Another scuffle broke out several yards away, but a crowd circled around the fray so that Walter could not see what it was. If he had seen, he'd have known that a group of Black men was refusing to submit to a pockets search.

Scared as he was, Watler paid attention only to Caesar, despite his annoyance at seeing his sister coming his way, trying to cross the street. Walter was bumped and jostled while he waited for Caesar's answer, but with the barber pole behind to lean on.

"Ha, ha, ha, ha. Well. You see. It was like dis. I walked over 30 miles to get here to Wilmington. Walk the shoreline from Smithville. I ain't want nothin' but two thangs in my life. Not to be whipped. And to git my new pair shoes. Just mines. Nobody wearin' them but me." He uncrossed his splendid pair of feet, still standing. "I heard dat dis here city had in it Negroes who could read and write. I thought it would be nice to live round dese peoples."

Walter listened.

"And, we is got doctors, lawyers, blacksmiths. Our own newspaper. Our own hospital. Of course, I can't read it like them, but I feels good knowing. And dem mens who runs the city, some of dem is Colored. Make me feel real good."

He asked Walter, "Is you seen me running up and down the streets, running errands rushing like a fool?"

Walter nodded. He looked at the crowd, unused to thinking about what they were doing and trying not to realize that the street atmosphere was different and dangerous.

"I bees busy holding horses' reins whilse white mens

dashes into they bank, the barbershop or a poker game. I carries they boxes and barrels. I hauls things strainin' sometimes at the end of a wagon tongue like a mule. You seen me."

"You be like the whirlwind," Walter said. Rebecca was coming at him, but Caesar was taking all the time in the world to answer the question.

"I done save every penny that was throwed in the air at me. I sleep in doorways and keep myself out of long relationships with husband-hunting women. I put all self too wards my mission. T' not be beat and to own one good pair of brand new ain't never been wore shoes," he said. "I is had piss throwed on my head out of windows, snuff juice spit in my eyes. But I toted boxes full up. I climbeded telephone poles and cleaned out chimneys. I done everything, even things I'm not proud of, to save me pennies and buy me these brand new shoes. And now, I rest cause I free. I got my shoes, I happy and I intend to never more be beat."

"How much they cost?"

Rebecca stopped in front of Walter. "You left the house again t'out tellin me where you was goin. Why leave t'out tellin me?"

Just because she was older, she thought she was the boss of him while their mother worked. She was always pushing into his business just because of that. She leaned in to shout in Walter's ear, raising her voice above the crowd so only he would hear her, "You see how dangerous the street is getting? Now, Caesar ain't got good sense, everybody know that. Come away from here and go home."

Walter resisted. He flapped the air next to his ears as if to swat away a flea. He turned away from her in his heart, taking in Caesar's dreams. "Tell me. You ever gone work again?"

"I doubt it." Caesar bragged, placing a thumb against his tattered shirt. "I may run just enough errands to get me some money to start gamblin'. Think that's what I going to do now, cards and dice."

Rebecca held her arms akimbo, anger and fear rushing through her as she looked from Walter to Caesar, and back and forth between them. Out of her sight behind her, a white man had stepped down from the stopped buggy. At first, she did not see him take notice of Caesar. The man held a horse's reins. Caesar paid no mind when the man tossed the reins to him, and they flopped to the ground, just as the white man ordered: "Hold my horse, boy."

Caesar had to have heard the man, or at least seen the reins, but he leaned down to wipe one of his shoes, ignoring the command.

Both Walter and Rebecca watched wide-eyed when Caesar made no move to pick up the reins from the ground.

"Naw, hell no," Caesar said. "I ain't holding no horse."

A moment passed before the man put his hand behind his suit lapel, drawing out a small silver pistol. He raised it to chest height and fired toward Caesar as he wiped his other shoe. A single shot pierced Caesar's chest.

The sound of that gunfire was ignored by a roiling mass of white men and was not the only shot to be heard. A crowd of protesters rushed, unconcerned that a bleeding Negro man was falling into a sitting position, blood oozing from his chest. Caesar's feet inched out as he landed with his back against the barber pole. Blood gushed from him, seeping into the ground.

"Niggers, beware!" the man shouted. "We taking back this town"

Another white man yelled, "Hell, we taking the whole damn South!"

He joined other men heading in one direction, as though they were going to a meeting. They may have been strangers to each other, but they were now united to overthrow the results of the Civil War. They were mostly Southerners who had never owned men, women, and children, but had been promised rewards for fighting. Some wore red shirts.

One called out, "Yeah, Dortches, you can kill one for me!" At the same time, he shot a blast into the sky.

Dortches, as he must have been called, replaced his gun into a pocket behind his lapel. Before he walked behind the barber pole into the barbershop, he leaned down, picked up the reins, and threw them to Walter, repeating the command: "Hold my horse, boy."

Walter caught the reins, and Dortches repeated himself: "You then. You Boy, hold my horse."

Rebecca coughed up pain, vomiting on the front of her dress. She reached for the ground to steady herself. Walter stood straight, looking helplessly back and forth from the reins in his hand to Caesar.

A strange thought entered Walter's mind, a thought to escape from the terror he felt. A thought that Caesar would want his shoes to not get dusty as people shuffled past. Rebecca reacted when, reins in one hand, Walter leaned down toward Caesar and called his name, as though waking a sleeping person.

"Don't touch him, Walter. Leave him alone."

"Wish we could get the doctor."

Caesar rasped, answering the question. "Three dollars. Cost me." His last words were, "Take them, y'all," and he stilled as the blood flow stopped.

Walter bent draw and loosened the shoes, still holding the reins and seeing them through salty tears.

Rebecca stood up. "Walter, we need to leave."

"I'm scared. If he come back and I be gone, bullets can reach. He see me cross the street and shoot me, too."

They froze, making their own stillness in the chaos swirling about them

Walter held Caesar's new shoes under one arm, with the reins in the other hand.

Rebecca whispered, "Don't nobody see him. That man almost stepped on him. They ignoring a dead body. He is dead, ain't he. When mama talk about slavery when she was a girl, it was like this?"

Did they think he was a drunk? No, surely they saw the blood. But they saw them through white people's eyes. But before now, some white people had been nice? Wasn't they. He is the garbage that they let pigs loose to clean up or get licked by a mangy dog.

Dortches came back, jerking at the reins. After tossing a penny to Walter, he leaned heavily on the boy's shoulders as he climbed into the buggy and clicked his teeth. He struck leather against the horse's rump and sped away.

CHAPTER TWO

October 20, 1906

Little Ida Harrison blew her breath on the train window, rubbed at the fog she had made with her little finger, and looked out. She turned to her mother. "Mama, what Souf Boun' mean? That man who keep walking up the aisle, he keep sayin' it. 'Souf Boun'.'"

The train rocked along. Houses bounced past, stores shook along, towns swayed about, fields wobbled, and crossroads pitched, all to the delight of Ida.

She had on a blue serge wool coat and a matching hat with white trim. The trim was long and tied under her chin and itched, but she did not mind, because people admired her and told her mother so. Her mother never said what the words "South Bound" meant. Ida would know later. That day, she had carried a doll for her arms and a rabbit fur muff around her hands. If she had had the least idea that was the last time she would see her mother, she would not have sat looking out the train window, watching and showing the dreamy cows to her doll.

Years later, and particularly on her wedding day, Ida would remember and thank that she had sat back from the window that day so long ago, and that she put her face to her mother's fur collar and saw her mama wipe her eyes.

"You crying', Mama?"

That was even before they got to what the white conductor said was the state of Maryland, where the Black porter made them to walk out of the sleek shiny car, past all the white people's eyes, including the little girl who had asked her, "Does your color wash off?" to go to the Colored car. She had been scared going from one car to the other, seeing where the cars connected and how violently they bumped and lurched. When they got to their new seats, a nice lady changed seats so that Ida could sit by the window again.

Ida's mama said, "No, my eyes running water, that's all."

Ida wondered later, was her mother crying about her or about being put out of the white people's car on the train? But that was later; for now, Ida kept on looking out, even when it got dark out there and it was harder to see a town coming, and the fields and horses were hiding in all that pitch blackness. When daylight came back, she was ready and saw clotheslines with tiny clothes and big clothes and woodpiles and more houses and fields, barns and crossroads.

It was after the daylight came back when her mama had said, "Trip near 'bout over, now." She had sounded like she was waking up from deep sleep. It seemed like magic that mama knew and, soon after, the things outside slowed down. Ida realized that they were stopping in a town that was on both sides of the train.

She saw a horse racing down the street that day, chased by a man, and laughed out loud. Then she saw a wagon with a horse hitched to it and an old man sitting on it, looking at the train. Her mama didn't see him, and when the train stopped, Mama was looking around and then saw him. They stepped down and the porter helped them get the two suitcases off. People were racing toward each other and hugging and screaming. The conductor set their luggage on the ground and got back on that high-up train to lift Ida down.

The man Ida had seen across the street in front of a store still watched the train, but didn't seem all that interested, even as Ida and her mama dragged the two big suitcases, Ida holding her doll and helping as best she could with the suitcase nearly as tall as her. Ida realized they were walking toward him. But he wasn't moving. As they got closer, he lowered his head, and Ida wondered, *was he praying or what?* He was sitting on a board that lay across the two sides of the wagon, his head down like the horse. Ida told her doll, "Look, see, the horse and the man with his head down like a horse."

Mama said, "Not no horse. That's a mule."

Ida told her doll, "Not no horse, doll baby. Bees a mule."

The mule's head was down to where it pestered a hunk of grass. She got close enough to touch the mule and was not afraid while her mama tried to push the suitcase up into the wagon. The old man sat up straight. He was very tall, even sitting down. He grunted in a not-too-friendly way before he lay down his reins and took the suitcases one by one, lifting them high up in the air as though they were shoe boxes, looking annoyed.

"How many clothes is she got?" He looked at Ida and said, "Hey."

But Ida knew not to talk to strangers. He was a lot more scary than the mule.

"What your name?" He was still not too friendly, even when he lifted Ida into the back of the wagon. She flopped down on a burlap bag that had something soft inside to sit on. "You be Ida, don't you?"

Ida was surprised that he knew her name.

He said "Gee" to the mule, and he pulled the reins to turn the wagon all the way around after Mama got on board next to him.

"Yes," Ida answered.

"Yes, sir," he corrected. "I know your mama, she used to be my daughter."

Ida clung to her doll, pushing her doll's legs into her rabbit muff.

He was looking back at her, and something about his size and the way he looked made her still. "And that doll, throw it away."

He reached back and tossed the doll to the ground. Ida cried and heard him tell her mama, "We gone break her of that habit."

She was right to be scared of him. The wagon moved out of the town and Ida sat looking back at her doll, looking like a bit of cloth on the ground. She watched until it was gone. That meant she was somewhere else.

As time passed, Little Ida managed to hide from the two old people who pressed words about Jesus at her in measured doses. How much of herself had she kept out of their influence? She was aware of outgrowing all the pretty dresses that she had brought on the train in the suitcases, and she was gradually handed plainer and bigger ones. The heels of her feet stretched her socks until she was handed the rough, plain, cotton, woven ones, but they, too, were bigger and bigger. That was how she knew that she grew.

As she saw herself reaching beyond the little girl to middle and teen, she kept the inside of herself a place where she dreamed and wished and waited for her mother to come, or for her to be rescued somehow. She was sometimes ashamed that she wished the two old people were dead. When her grandmother sent her for a drink of water, she put her dirty finger in it. When her grandfather lay down his Bible, she tipped it to the edge of the table where it would fall later. In the days that followed, the old people beat her. The first beating, the first of many, was for her having let slip from her tiny hands a glass bowl. They forced her to stare open-eyed into a white light while her voice got in the way of her breathing, and she wet her panties.

Terror got inside her belly, and no matter how careful she was, she could not please the grandfather. He was convinced that she had inside her small body all the evil of the world, all the way back to Eve and the serpent. At his most generous, he instead said that she was not evil and was actually evil's victim, and that he was determined to remove it from her, lash by lash.

The ritual that hollowed her out the most was the preparation for her beatings. Both grandparents gravely sent her outdoors to a particular tree in the yard, with instructions to bring back a switch. At some point in her fourteenth year, she was amazed to find that when the grandfather came home broken out from poison ivy, she felt great sympathy for him and realized that she did not want him dead. But it was later that she discovered that she could hold poison ivy without incident, crush it in her fingers without the oozing sores appearing on her hands. After her discovery, whenever she was sent to fetch a switch with which to be beaten, she rubbed it in poison ivy before she brought it to the grandfather. His outbreaks of oozing sores and itching were frequent and debilitating, making her beatings almost bearable.

CHAPTER THREE

June 9
Rural Route 2, Griffinton, North Carolina

Dear Aunt Vate,

Papa say no I cant come to Rocky Mount to stay with you. He say 7th grade plenty enough for a farmer. And he say I don't need more school than Griffinton got now. Even my uncle Walter and his wife, he try to tell papa to let me go, but he still say no. Mama said tell you thanks. My best friend since I was little, Winston Lockheed, left last week, coming to stay with his people in Rocky Mount to go to the eighth grade and finish on up. I wish I could but Momma say God will fix things for me.

Your nephew, I thank you very much.
Kinchen Cobb

June 17, 1914
7 Thru Street, Rocky Mount, North Carolina

Dear Joseph,

Rebecca I no you read this letter to Joseph cause he cant read. Joseph, I so sorry that you cannot see the light. You no that Kinchen is a good boy and all ways done what he told. He wuld make a good school techer or could even go up nort and work in the Pos Ofice if you giv him the chanc to leve the farm and finis school. All colord peoples be better off when more of us got more edication. You gone regret. Give Rebecca my love. I do not no why she cant talk sinse in you. I'm just goin to pray for you myself. And, Joseph, see bout gittin Rebecca some glasses next time you come to town.

Your sister,
Vate

September 9, 1914
21 Nash Street, Rocky Mount, N.C.

Dear Kinny,

I started school here in Rocky Mount and that school is a bigger place than what we had in Griffinton. I do not miss milking the cow before I go to school. One class I don't like is shop but the teacher say if I want to be a doctor or a dentist I need to know how to use my hands. But I don't like it. It remind me of the farm. Is Carolyn still pretty? Keep your eye on her for me, your friend,

Winston Lockheed

September 14, 1914
Rural Route 2, Griffinton, North Carolina
Dear Winston,

Carolyn had to get married. She married Sack. She fourteen. He seventeen. I guess you know that. I see her since and she don't look too happy. She didn't wait long after you left I guess. I wish I could go to school too. You really think you can be a doctor or a dentist? Well, well, well.

Kinchen Cobb

> *September 21, 1914*
> *Rural Route 2, Griffinton, North Carolina*

Dear Vate,

    Rebecca writin for me to tell you. Leave my boy alont. I seen him talkin to you at Rebecca's mama's wake. I seen you try to git the farm outin him. Tellin him he ought go to school. You doesnt know no Negroes what need more edicashun than he got. I got some good hams if you want one. Smoked wit hickry. Come git it or I bring it to you?

> *you brother, Joseph Cobb*
> *wrote by Rebecca Cobb.*

The tall heavyset Griffinton sharecropper, Walter Brake, died in the predawn hours of July 11, 1917. He met his death before the alert eyes of friends and rivals, behind a tobacco curing barn two miles from where he lived with his wife and children. In the minutes after his death, he lay where he had fallen, face down in the dirt, the back of his skull an opened gash for anyone curious to behold. Living men surrounded him, some with sadness, others with indifference. A few groped the air with a "glad it wasn't me" attitude. Several set out to publish the news. Meanwhile, his killer looked for shadows and, in the growing light of day, went into hiding.

In the same predawn hours, Walter Brake's sister, the petite Rebecca Brake Cobb, awoke and sat up in bed, unaware of her brother's death a mile away. She slid her feet to the floor and got out of bed. Running anxious hands along her long white nightgown, she put her back to the bedroom and started out the door. Too late, she tried to stop the screen door's creak as she stepped through to the porch outside. The damp night air kissed her face. Behind her, her husband, Joseph Cobb, lay sleeping on his side of the bed. Their son, Kinchen, lay in the only room upstairs.

Rebecca looked up at the star-studded night sky, with clouds creeping across the face of the moon. The first signs of morning were stealing in. "Somethin' don't feel right," she said softly, to no one except what was left of the night. She flexed her toes, feeling the cool plank floor. A dog barked from far away.

"That dog is either comin' this way or watchin' somethin' come here. Wonder which one it is," she said. "Bark all you want to. You don't know how to dread anything or worry 'bout anything for all that noise you make."

She paced up and down the porch.

"I know sometimes, dumb animals can see more than people. Just dumb, can't tell about it. See more. I have heard tell of it. Bark all you want. Bark all you want. Try to tell it. But know this: even if you get scared, you don't know nothin' 'bout fear. You can't reason nothin', plan nothin' you can't worry 'bout nothin'."

She went on talking to herself. She wrapped her arms around a porch post.

"After all these years. You would think I could get used to it. I wish I had asked Walter something when he was here hours ago. He upset me so, though, going out of here, not on his way home, going in the opposite direction of his house. He put me between him and his house and my poor sister-in-law and those girls, heading off to God know where. All of them in threads for clothes. That house with barely enough to eat. Walt will work the fields, but will not even have a garden for himself and his household."

Joseph had told her many times not to worry herself about the things she could not change. Walter was a typical sharecropper; he gave his sweat to a system that furnished cotton, tobacco, peanuts, and grains to the rich people of the world. After the fieldwork, Walter was only good for drinking and gaming. Joseph said that he exercised the freedom to be as unaccountable as he pleased and was never challenged on it by his boss man. As long as he got to the fields on time and worked, nothing more was demanded of him. Because of his rowdiness, Rebecca used to worry about him getting himself lynched. It was Joseph who explained that Black men were not lynched for being wild and noisy. They could get lynched for trying to vote or for trying to get a living wage. Their father had died trying to work, lynched by life.

Rebecca felt her way to a porch rocker and dropped into it. Walter was perfectly safe. But, she nevertheless wished that he had gone straight home from here. She had the feeling that he had been looking for trouble when he left, because he had his work shoes under his arm and his good shoes on his feet. Few sharecroppers owned two pairs of shoes, but Walter insisted upon it. You couldn't call them his Sunday shoes, because he did not attend church. They were his gambling shoes, his funning shoes. He tried to keep them shiny. A man with five children, why was he always in a frolic? Although she loved his playful way with his girls, she hated that it often took drink to make him cheerful.

She always thought of him as their leader, as the little boy who led them out of Wilmington once their mother decided that they could not remain there in November of 1898. Even though their father had died in 1894, the elections had put so many Blacks in different offices, they made themselves satisfied and lived cautiously. That was why the two followed each other everywhere. Their mother did not want them separated from each other.

That year, 1898, two days after the election, the one that Colored people had been warned to not show up for, more Blacks were slated to have even more offices in the government places: more representatives on town council, one or two judges, magistrates. Two Colored men owned a newspaper just for the Colored. Its editorials on the days leading up to elections urged all able-bodied former slaves and descendants of slaves to vote as dutiful citizens. And Colored men voted, ignoring the warnings of the cowards who could not be seen tacking papers to trees and sides of buildings. The messages had winked in the daylight and dribbled inky blotches in rain showers. When had it started? The threats? August of the previous year? That spring? It was always harder to remember back without specific markers to pause for.

Rebecca remembered when they traveled away. Five of them. Moving sometimes in a phalange, like birds on a wire, side by side, sweeping forward and away, sometimes bunched up, running, falling, crying, arguing. They had journeyed away, mostly lined up, ducks in a row behind that young boy. Walter had known how to row across the Cape Fear River, how to choose a train, hop that train, and dodge the ticket taker. All five of them had gotten through the swamps. They were relieved that they did not have to contend with water moccasins or hissing snakes because they were sleeping underground during the winter, a time when the alligators were also less active.

They had been agreed on one thing: their fear of what lay behind them and their resolve to not turn back. They were Rebecca, then a girl, Walter, their boy leader, their mother Sarah, and two girls that her mother had grabbed by the shoulders and pulled away from where they stood staring, who became her sisters, Florence and Vate.

⁓★⁓

Griffinton, North Carolina

In that same November of 1898, three weeks later, Clementine—a white woman—followed her morning routine, staring out the window toward the woods behind her kitchen. She was alone. She was often alone. Her boys went off with their father to the seed and feed store when not in school. Sometimes they played for hours in the woods. She used her time alone to stare out. She sometimes stood at the window, pushing and rearranging things again and again in her mind. Things to fix. Things that could not be fixed.

Now there was the business of the thefts. There were clothes missing—shirts and two dresses—from the clothesline on different days. The evergreens in those woods held the secret, maybe? Tins of meat walked out of the summer kitchen. A hickory-cured ham had hung just inside the door of the smokehouse. Gone. First though, her husband missed the shovel. What would a low-down, probably Nigger thief want with a work tool? Another excuse for her husband and his pals to go awaken Black folk from sleep at night, shooting guns to put fear in the hearts of sharecroppers and make them mind.

She worried over his night rides. She fretted over his taking terror with him to make the world safe for her. No Nigger ever looked her square in the eye, much less offered her some dismal comfort.

While she stood holding a now-cold coffee cup, a Negro girl bounded across the yard on skinny legs, swinging skinny arms. Clementine could not see the eyes, but the movement of the head showed an animal vigilance; that girl thought she was not seen. She disappeared into the summer kitchen. Clementine quickly followed her outside to the summer kitchen door. The girl, a half-child, half-grown thing, dashed back to the woods and was taken in by the tall grasses and the trees.

Clementine saw her twice more. Once more that day, and then again the next morning. By that next day, Clementine had decided what to do, after having tossed in bed the night before arranging and rearranging her thoughts, so that the third time she saw the girl, she managed to see two or three gray shadows behind. Clementine dropped a shawl over her shoulder and whipped her horse and buggy into a fierce gallop to the farm of her Colored neighbor, Nick Cobb. She shortly after bounded back home with Etta Cobb in the buggy and they sat at her kitchen window facing the woods.

That was a long time ago, Rebecca thought, from 1889 to 1917. Another dog barked. This dog was closer than the last. Something was passing. Or someone was coming, on a course, steering steadily and purposefully forward. Rebecca imagined the sentinel at the houses along the way, lifting their heads at their stations by doors as the messenger drew near and passed by them before they lay their hairy heads back down.

She stopped rocking and let the chill air play on her face and arms. It would be a mild morning. A fine mist forecasted mild warmth to come after the sun was finished with opening the day.

She thought of Joseph teaching Kinchen to work the land. Day by day, week by week, Joseph drilled into him, the tow of them rising with the sun and working long after their clothes were soaked by the rain of sweat. Now, Kinchen's best friend, Winston Lockheed, was off getting ready to learn how to fix teeth. Joseph often reminded her that Winston's family were sharecroppers, not landowners like themselves. It was the land that Joseph used to hold, and it was the land that made Joseph feel separate and different from the others, except for the few other Colored families who had one way or another been deeded acreage. Maybe one day, Kinchen would appreciate the importance of the land for himself, this house, their history. For now, Kinchen moved through his days mule-like and lethargic. As for herself, the land, this house begun by the ancestor, did much to make her feel comfortable, but not quite enough for her to feel safe.

Joseph said that Wilmington taught them that for Black men, reading and writing posed dangers to life and limb. It had been a newspaper article written by a former slave that caused the white people to march into the Black business section of Wilmington in November of 1898. In her heart, Rebecca believed that the Colored newspaper was a handy excuse, when it had really been the elections. But she did not often argue with Joseph. Not about beliefs.

She wished that Kinchen could have become a university student, like the one who had stopped by one day to ask questions for some survey. He said that he wanted to interview former slaves and descendants. He said he was writing a paper. He was rather dull-witted, she thought. Not to be unkind, but he clearly could not tell the difference between a Jersey cow and a white face. Kinchen would not have been as stupid, even in a university. The student was the type that caused people like Joseph to dignify the work of their hands and to speak of the many ways to measure what was produced: acres of fields, bushel baskets of produce, sheets of cotton, baskets of cured tobacco leaves.

She had not been able to convince Joseph to let Kinchen go to high school, because she had been unable to say what education yielded that was measurable. Still, she wished that Kinchen had kept his enthusiasm about life, the enthusiasm that he showed in seventh grade. What she could say about him now was that he was nice. Not interested in much, but nice. She felt the absence of the days when he raced home with a borrowed book tucked under his arm, feeding the animals, stacking wood. She had not seen his head bent over a book for a long time. She herself did not read often, except for every once in a while, when she would take down the Bible and read a Psalm. But she liked seeing Kinchen read. It made her wonder.

She wondered what her son's future would be. He was older now than she had been when Wilmington fired up and her whole life changed as the end of the world had swirled around her. He did not seem bent toward changing anything in his life. There were one or two girls who seemed set on him, but she saw no sparks coming from him. She wondered if he had known a woman. Surely he must have. His father had probably seen to that. There were things that a mother could not know about the life she had carried inside her and brought into being.

Kinchen had filled the water bucket to the brim and placed it on the porch shelf. She filled the dipper and sipped. Inside the house, in another hour, she would light the cook stove. She would build her fire from the neatly gathered kindling and sticks of pine fatwood that Kinchen had gathered for her before going to bed. She never had to remind him to do chores, but she saw that he drooped under the repetitive rhythm of his life.

Maybe they would sleep a little past daylight. Today they were going to repair tools. They deserved a slowed down day, a day away from the jealous land. She was not sure what had gotten her up at a little before dawn this morning: a wakefulness, or the old dream. She sometimes dreamed of searching through a large house for something, she and her mother. She now watched the light change all around her, giving her a feeling of eerie peace. A light grey came out of the night sky and then shifted to light blue with a tinge of quiet pink, just before the sun began its rise. She saw the horizon getting dressed for the day, showing off the land.

There stood the cotton, not yet in bloom, strong and cleaned of weeds. Off to the side, almost behind her, lay the fields of tobacco, the stalks nearly three feet tall. She could smell the soil that Joseph and Kinchen turned for the last time in the season. They all—the cotton, the tobacco, even the corn—rested growing, laid by, waiting with her in the haze of dawn as she stood on the porch of the house.

It was a house that their ancestor built, started by Nick Cobb and added to by those who came after. Only the last two rooms were built by Joseph Cobb, and those rooms were built for her, including the tiny closet of a room that eased her mind about wanting a hiding place.

She was about to start musing aloud to herself once again when she saw a figure rolling steadily toward the house. It got closer, growing larger. It was not four-legged. It ran on two legs, along a path hidden by the tobacco that she could not see but knew lay there between the fields. Her Joseph and Kinchen had beaten the path down, and she had walked it, taking food and water to them in the fields. She could not see whether the figure was man or woman.

Then she saw him, and he must have seen her: Rebecca Brake Cobb in her white nightgown, her hair standing in spikes about her head, sleepless on her porch at daybreak. Not only must he have seen her, but he seemed bent on coming toward her. Sometimes the person's head bobbed nearly out of sight when the path wound through the tobacco stalks, but then it emerged again. He was definitely coming toward her. She took hold of the skirt of her long gown and tugged absentmindedly with her thumb and forefinger. For some reason that she could not explain, she did not go back into the house, though she was conscious of her nakedness beneath the gown and her bare feet. She touched her stiff hair and picked off a stray feather from her pillow and let it glide to the ground.

While she waited, she curled her toes and felt the splintery planks of the porch beneath. Had she gotten up, leaving the snoring husband in bed and her teenage son upstairs, just for the purpose of meeting this runner? Did she know somewhere in that spirit part of herself that he was coming? Maybe he had been on his way, running through the dark when she had been pulled out of bed and onto the porch? She stood up, moved to the edge of the porch and watched him come.

The runner turned out to be a mannish boy, the age of her Kinchen. He stopped at the porch just as the world was brightening in the harsh morning sun. She recognized him. She knew him by sight, but not by name. She had taught him as a little boy in Sunday School. Now he halted where the edge of the porch came below his shins; he was *that* tall. He bent over and hassled for breath, and in the rush, sucked the air with his mouth opened. He asked for water. She let go of the post, stepped back, not taking her eyes off him, reached into the water bucket and held up the communal dipper for him to drink. He drank, spilling some on the ground in his haste and seemed not the least aware of her wearing her night clothes.

"Miss Rebecca, a few minutes ago, not half hour passed since then, your brother, Mr. Walter Brake, he got killed. I was there. I seen him die my own self."

"How?"

"Hit on the back of the head with a shovel. He is as dead as dirt, sure enough."

Rebecca Brake Cobb accepted the empty dipper from his outstretched hand. She moved to replace that dipper inside the water bucket that Kinchen had filled before he went to sleep. But she missed it several times. The bucket pinged noisily, tin against zinc, each hit startling her, each bump causing her to shake. Her belly hollowed out and rumbled under her crossed arms. This was the hissing snakes and swamp rats she had feared all her life.

The runner ran on, carrying the bad news to other households in his path.

Before she could gain the inside of her house, a second runner appeared. He was the one who had grown on the horizon without her notice, though he ran the same path as the first, whom he had followed. This newer runner stopped at the corner of the porch, bounced from leg to leg and peered brazenly at Rebecca's reaction as he said out loud, "Morning, Miss Rebecca. I just heard 'bout it. Mr. Walter Brake. What ya think? Some husband musta caught 'im, musta got he throat cut?"

There was no answer given to this meddler. Her silence told him enough, as he stood only long enough to see her stumble. He then ran off to catch the first runner to tell him and others that the murdered man's sister was standing with her mouth open, arms out about the water bucket like she was hanging on the cross.

Before she pulled the screen door that gave metallic yawns in time with her trembling, Rebecca looked at the two runners' shadows linking up as they ran on in tandem, aiming for farmhouses along the way, spreading the bad news and its rumors, setting up a relay. But she did not actually see them. She tried to get herself back into the house through the screen door that she now let slam without noticing its racket.

Once inside, Rebecca's tears came so fast that salt coated her throat, so that the voice she used to tell Joseph was hoarse. "Dead."

"Who?"

"Walt."

"How you know?"

"Someone tole me. Killed. Hit on the head."

"Who?"

"I don't know."

Joseph sat up and hunched over on the side of the bed, rolling his great head in his hands.

"Now, what could be the matter?" Joseph asked. "Wonder was he killed by somebody's husband," but answered himself and reassured weeping Rebecca. "Naw. Walt always was a tough dog to keep in the house. But, he love gamblin' a whole heap more than women."

Rebecca did not build the fire in the cookstove that morning from the neat kindling pile that Kinchen had placed for her the night before. They all three struggled into clothes and joined the horde swarming for the Brake house a few miles away. They were in a dream where every footfall was muffled to the sound of walking in the woods, cushioned by pine needles. A woman shot a spittle of tobacco on the ground and told Rebecca that her Vera Brake fainted at the news of her husband's death.

They walked past a crowd on the porch of Walter's house. One man, Otto Davis, was hard of hearing and gave his observations at the top of his voice, a contrast to all the whispering. Rebecca put her hands to her ears on hearing that the body lay inside the house. As she reached for the door, she realized that the remains had passed her and Joseph's house, causing her to wonder how she missed seeing it and recalling to her mind the speed at which they flew from room to room before coming here.

Rebecca soon learned from many persons that her sister-in-law had not been awake, standing or walking about when news of her widowhood came. Widow Brake was sleeping soundly after having seen to her daughters' washing of the supper dishes. The last thing that she remembered before she awoke to the rough knocking on her door was lady asking, "Momma, can I fix a plate for my daddy in case he might want to eat whenever he get home?"

Rebecca learned that Vera Brake came out of her faint with her children standing about, rubbing sleep from their eyes. They took up their crying when she told them of their father's death.

Finally inside the house, all three heard the widow take up the tale. "Before I could finish telling the children what was going on, I looked out the window and seen all the peoples in the world pressing toward me. Behind that first flow, a wagon bringing his body. Before I could send the children for extra chairs from the tobacco barn, the people had invited they selves in my house with their curiosity and good wishes. Everybody taken they turn, trying to hold my hand and telling of they sorrow for me. But that was all right. What tore at me was that I heard one of them say, 'Likely not a jealous husband done him in.'"

The two women sat on the side of the bed in one of the bedrooms, all the rooms in the house being bedrooms except the kitchen. They rocked together, weeping upon each other.

Rebecca had fear to share. All her grownup years, she had kept an almost cherished anxiety, a premonition about a violent death to her brother, her husband, her son. Black men. It didn't matter that Walter's end came at the hands that had held a deck of cards and friendship, from a man who had sucked whiskey from the same Mason jar passed back and forth.

Lady said, "Auntie Rebecca? How come my daddy love shoes so? I asked him one time."

"Child. You noticed. I guess you couldn't help it. Me and your pa come here from Wilmington. He come here wearing his old scuffed-up shoes and wit a brand new shiny pair looped around his neck, kep' up out the way. The streets was burning behind us when we left there that day. My mama called it a devil-sent day. It was a day or two after the elections. And a Colored man had wrote an article in the newspaper sayin' that white womens was in no danger of bein' raped by Colored mens."

"'Scuse me, Auntie Rebecca. What that got to do with my daddy lovin' shoes?"

"Wait, Baby. I'm a comin' to it. Sit on down. We is got us a death in the family. We got time."

She sat on a three-legged stool, a milking stool owned by a family with no cow. She told of the days when she and Walter, her mother and Vate and Florence (who had become women by now) had traveled to Griffinton on the train, hiding and trying to ignore hunger and cold. When she finished, the girls shrugged. They had been too distracted, looking for the origin of the love of shoes, that they did not ask why a man would shoot another for refusing to hold his horse. Or, maybe they did not hear that part. They left the room. Rebecca sat, remembering a young boy who had asked a man, "Is you ever gone to work again?" to be told, "Naw. I think I'm gone to gamble."

On the evening of the day that Walter Brake died, Vera Brake received news of how he died, which brought with a modicum of relief. The truth had finally caught up, overtaking galloping rumors. A gambling buddy shamefacedly stepped forward to say that Walter died holding his winning dice in one hand and his won money in the other. The gambling buddy stated that it was his winning hand and his in-your-face attitude that got Walter killed. It was Walter's fault for winning and gloating. But, he was not ended by a jealous husband.

The man who killed Walter had been his closest friend. Just before striking the first blow, he had said for all to hear, "I can't take your mouth no more." He drew a shovel behind him for leverage and struck Walter on the side of his head, knocking him down in the dirt.

In life, Walter Brake had been a man of inferior standards against whom higher-minded residents of the community of Griffinton measured themselves. When the preachers in the churches called out Sin's name, even small children visualized Walter Brake, his cronies, and their women, the ones who would not be caught alive at a church unless they were selling whiskey on the grounds or attending a wedding or a funeral.

Griffinton, a tobacco and cotton farming area, was a large flat place of more than 2,500 acres of land and a small place with about one 170 households, 140 of those households inhabited by former slaves or their descendants. The houses were separated by stands of timber, fields of tobacco, cotton, corn, wheat, and peanuts, as well as barns and outbuildings with livestock of mainly cattle, mules, hogs, and a few horses.

Griffinton had no town center and only two general stores, a school that taught up to the seventh grade for the Colored (the white children went to school in the next town, all the way to the eleventh grade), one or two filling stations, and an unknown number of juke joints for the low-livers and the sinful. As a result, funerals, church services, school plays and recitals were the gathering places outside the home. The news of Walter Brake's death foretold one such gathering: a funeral.

⚹

Nearly every able-bodied Colored person in Griffinton assembled at the Paradise Sanitified Church for Walter Brake's funeral. One white person—Walter's former boss man, Sloane Smith—came with his two puppy dogs, who were trembling excitedly on their hind legs, balanced on the seat in the cab of his truck. (Back as a teen, Walter had known Sloane, along with Nathan, who had grown up to be bosses with the sharecroppers.) Sloane parked beside the road and walked up the path to the church, his puppies yelping at his back. Sloane Smith was there, he said, because he was in the mood for some Colored singing. Most people knew that he and Walter had grown up together after Walter came to Griffinton as a boy. Walter's and Rebecca's mother had worked for Sloane's mother Mrs. Smith, and it had been Mrs. Smith, along with Joseph Cobb's mother, who had coaxed the Wilmington refugees to come out of the woods for food and shelter in November of 1898.

The church bell tolled.

The blood relatives and the relatives by marriage and law marched mournfully into the church to sit in the reserved center aisle. Onlookers stared wide-eyed and vigilant from the outer aisles to watch the bereaved. The elderly and devout, the men and women who were regulars in church for services and prayer meetings, divided along the lines of sex—women on the left, men on the right—in the outlying parts of the church that formed the stretched out arms of the cross.

Vera Brake had borrowed a veil and dressed herself all in black. She sat on the first row of the pew, facing a rough new pine box that held her husband's remains. She wept copiously, helplessly, but quietly, surrounded by well-meaning and curious women. They were edged in between her and her children on the pew. They fanned her, dabbed at her tears, and tried in vain, without expectation of success, to soothe her. They whispered, "Amen," and "Lord Jesus," and caressed her neck and hands. Taking up the balance of the pew were her children. Huddled together, they were watched by other women who fanned and stood over them like shade trees, causing onlookers to keep moving from side to side to see. The trees swayed and fanned. The children leaned away from the trees and toward each other. They took turns crying. The oldest child, Lady, a girl in her teens, three years younger than Rebecca and Joseph's Kinchen, alternately screamed and stared angrily before her as though she saw things.

Behind Widow Brake and the children sat Rebecca, also draped in black but not wearing a veil. The onlookers sang,

"Precious Lord, take my hand, lead me on, let me stand,
I am tired, I am weak, I am worn . . . "

Joseph sat next to Rebecca, his arm draped about her shoulder. Next to them sat the adopted in custom sisters, Florence and Vate—whom Sarah had grabbed up while escaping from Wilmington as little girls, and their husbands, then a brother of the deceased's mother. On the next rows sat cousins, nieces, and nephews, to complete the family section of the church.

Behind the family, on the last pew, seven pews back from the casket, sat six of seven male friends of the deceased. They stared dry-eyed, looking at their hands or idly fingering and examining their soft felt hats and occasionally looking at each other. They had probably been with him when he died. They had not been chosen as pallbearers, as they might have if Walter had met a less exceptional end. The missing friend, the murderer, had saved the sheriff a trip from town by presenting himself at the jail. At the funeral hour, he sat in his jail cell, probably thinking of the funeral and the possibility of his sentence of road work for at least six years, the maximum for the killing of one Colored man by another Colored man in the white man's courtroom.

The Reverend Jonathan (pronounced Joe Nathan) Harrison opened his sermon by touching on his disadvantage at having never met the dead man face to face. He said that for many years, Mrs. Brake served her church, attending Sunday School with her children.

Hidden behind the drapery of black, the widow Brake's sobs grew louder, when Reverend Harrison expressed regret that he could not preach the deceased anywhere close to the doors of heaven. The onlookers called out "Amen." Few in that packed, hot church could fail to notice the preacher's glee at having the opportunity to hold up a real-life example of the wages of sin, a gambler struck down just after winning. There would be time to talk of that when they reassessed the funeral with each other over the next few days. For now, they answered him, "Praise be to God," and, "Blessed be his Holy name."

Reverend Harrison questioned whether Walter Brake was even entitled to a Christian burial, but hurried to say, "God is a forgiving God."

"Thank you, God," the women cried.

"Thank you, Jeeee-sus."

He stamped his feet, shaking sweat from his forehead and cheeks. He looked out at the gathering, where hand-held paper fans moved back and forth, back and forth, causing a gentle hint of an intermittent breeze to flow through the church. He announced that maybe, just maybe, Walter Brake had, in his last moments as his life slipped away, breathed out a prayer for his own soul. Sisters in the Amen corner jumped to their feet and offered:

"Praise God."

"Amen."

"Thank you, Jesus."

Rev. Harrison progressed. "If in his final moments of life, Walter Brake offered up a prayer for salvation, only God know 'bout it now. 'Cause God have the only eye that can see into the soul. Y'all hep me now."

The Amen corner sisters urged him on to his now almost obvious conclusion. "Yes, Jesus."

"If such a prayer was uttered, perhaps, Brother Brake was at the last minute SAVED from hell, fire and damnation. Praise God. Lord Jesus. Maybe he died BORN AGAIN!"

The children's sobs could be heard interrupting every heart that beat in the church. As the Rev. sat down, the widow stood up, stretching her arms toward the coffin, trembling beneath the black veil. Widow Blake waved her arms above her head, throwing away from her the clinging women. They righted themselves and stood up with her. Like gangly willow trees, the women swayed with her and "Amen-ed" with her.

Such a raw experience of grief made the eighteen-year-old Kinchen Cobb cringe, particularly in light of the fact that the service was not what the deceased might have wanted. Kinchen was embarrassed. He thought of how his Uncle Walter had once abruptly abandoned him to play cards, saying, "Hell, Kinchen, you not enthused enough to remember the suits."

In the hollow of the church, he felt the damp as though he sat in a watery cave moistened by women's tears, salty tears. In that cave, he remembered a time well before this day when the dead man had in life placed a hand upon his shoulder and said, "Don't make no difference no how. You never goin' to be cutthroat enough to be good at no damn cards. But just remember, in the game of life, it not how good a hand you have, but how good you play a bad hand."

But, more importantly, in life, the dead man had said to Kinchen's father, "This boy ought to finish school and you, his daddy, ought to see to it." Kinchen would always remember that!

Kinchen stretched to see better the pews up ahead and saw the back of Joseph Cobb. His father had a self-righteous neck on his shoulders, and next to him, his mother bowed her head. The nape of his father's neck seemed less arrogant in this place where women held sway. The grief belonged to the women. It was a frightening thing. Kinchen was nearly a man. He was no longer as skittish as when he had been 14. He hadn't figured out how to handle fear, though, except to sit perfectly still.

The women were using their time in the pause that death brought. Now they were past the stunning, the rumors: grief became theirs to exploit. As he watched them, trying to forget himself, he thought that grief resembled laughter. It came from the same deep place. It burst out the same way. One dragged both up out of a hidden place. He heard the cries and weeping of awakened dreamers railing at all that hurt them with his stretched-out uncle lying stilled as an occasion for the outbursts, while people deep inside reassessed themselves.

His mother's weeping harmonized with the sounds and heavy breathing from Aunt Vate and Aunt Florence, their husbands, nieces, cousins, aunts. He couldn't draw up feelings from deep places where the women plumbed. Maybe they were thinking of feeding molasses biscuits to the children when they ran out of meat. Their wailing felt like a forecast of pain, but he was sure that it was a remembrance, too.

Kinchen rocked himself. A cousin sitting next to him, another of the dead man's nephews, one of Florence's sons, placed a hand on Kinchen's back. Kinchen drew away. He breathed deeply, recovered himself and looked around. He had to get out of himself. It was always good to look out, for your own protection if nothing else.

That was when he saw her. He had seen her before, though Kinchen and his parents, Baptists, never attended Paradise Church, a Holy and Saintified church, but were worshipers at the Pleasant Grove Baptist Church. They, like most Griffintoners, were somewhat acquainted with her grandfather, the Rev. Harrison. She sat in the Amen corner with the elderly and the devout, next to her grandmother, Mrs. Jonathan Harrison. Kinchen felt his nature rising. He placed a fan on his lap. His cousin snickered.

The choir sat down. That meant that they had sung. Everybody all around them was standing. The Rev. was standing next to the casket intoning, "I AM THE RESURRECTION AND THE LIGHT, NO ONE COME TO THE FATHER, BUT BY ME . . . "

Several men positioned themselves and began to move the casket down the aisle and from the church. Women in crisp white dresses helped his aunt to stand up and then walk from the church.

She did not look much like a widow. Widows were old. She was the age of his mother, 48 or 49. Then, he took his mind from his aunt and began to watch *her*, the girl. She was standing straight and tall, perfectly still, two plain braids pulled forward and falling down the front of her bosom. He managed to make his way down the aisle between the hedge formed by the onlookers. She was not looking at him. He was disappointed and thought a curious thought for that moment: Joseph Cobb saying, "Time you found a wife, boy." Well, not right now, just looking.

At the cemetery, Kinchen saw the girl again. Just after the Rev. had committed the body to ever after and while people were walking away in the direction of the grave, the widow saw a gravedigger's shovel standing up, its sharp metal edge in the newly unearthed dirt. At the sight, she went screaming to collapse and was aided by a male deacon. Turning away from feelings too strong to endure watching, Kinchen saw the girl standing on the opposite side of the grave. She seemed to take no notice of him.

He lost himself watching her and the next thing he know, everybody was walking away, toward the church. He did not notice when the mood changed, but there came a moment when no one was crying or screaming or preaching. People talked, hugged, and soothed each other, and bits of laughter slipped out. Some blue-haired women who proclaimed they had come from New Jersey, hugged Kinchen, pinched his cheeks and tried to convince him that he remembered their having visited when he was a crawling baby.

But he watched her and wondered if he could guess her name, the lovely tall girl with dark coffee skin and deep eyes, who looked a tiny bit angry. He half expected her to turn away from him because he wasn't sure whether she really was angry or just scared, with her turned-down lips. Perhaps because he was one of the family of the bereaved, she felt sorry for him. He wondered what it would be like to see her with the corners of her mouth turned up. He crossed to the other side of the grave and maneuvered himself until he was behind her. He gained on her until they were back at the church yard. He startled her, asking:

"What is your name?"

"I'm Ida." What a name. He heard in it a piece of a sigh. He loved her little plaits, her long hair, her deep brown skin. Darker than brown sugar. "Brown Sugar." That's what they call such as she, looking like sweetness itself. He could tell, because she was not looking around, and her hips did not seem to have their own swivel. She was tight.

He knew the answer to his next question, but he wanted to hear her voice more. "Who your mama and daddy be?"

"I live with my granddaddy, Rev. Harrison." She twirled a braid with a little finger.

"Is that what you call him, he make you call him Rev. Harrison?"

She went from shy to bold in a second, "You foolish or what?" and he laughed, a loud deep laugh getting him out of the funeral mood. She smiled. He had done it! He had made her smile!

A shadow moved behind him. "My granddaughter, she not 'llowed to talk to young mens, Boy. She not but sixteen. Her grandmama and I done raised her to be a Godly young lady. I keep her away from temptation. Now, you, Boy, get away from her."

Kinchen ducked his head as he walked backwards, dipping with each step, looking at what he wanted. He collided with his mother and father, and the three of them rode home while Rebecca looked back.

"Lord, I hate to leave my poor brother behind in that graveyard. Why he have to die like that?"

"He was a good man," Kinchen answered. "Whatever they say about him, you know. He just liked a good time."

The two, his mother and father, his favorite people when he was willing to be around people over 20 years old, talked softly, intimately, as though they were alone.

"Did you see Mabel? Hadn't seen her since we was girls."

"Was Tommie there?"

"I didn't see him."

"I did."

"Lots of people."

"Yeah, Walter woulda been proud if he coulda look up and see'd all the folkses."

"Casket looked nice. Price done a good job with that pine."

"Say he worked on it into the night by candlelight. Started with a tree."

"He still wid Nora?"

"Naw, he done left her."

"You talk to Bob?"

"Yeah, he say he want you back in the choir."

"Wonder is Pope gone stay on where he is?"

"Jimmie was sober, I see." Kinchen heard in their voices the coos of lovebirds in the habit of each other.

He could barely tell one voice from the other. He knew little of the people they referred to, and he had little interest in knowing more. It was their past and present together. From the back of the cart, he faced what they were leaving all the way home. There came a moment when his father reached over and took his mother's hand. She said many times, "He don't even know he do it."

"After all, it was a nice funeral," they concluded in unison.

At the path to the Cobb house, Kinchen said, "Mama, tell me about that preacher."

"What you want to know?"

"He seem kind o' crazy. Is he?"

"Show more respect for your elders, Boy."

It was nearly dark, and Kinchen leaped from the wagon to change clothes for the cow milking ritual. He sat on the milking stool, took hold of the cow's teats with one hand, and with the other pushed the protruding bone above her flank to open her legs for easier access. The animal shifted first back and then forward, pretending not to understand and holding a closed position. He slapped her back. She swished her tail. The hairs burned across his face.

"Stubborn Tart!" he called out. Without warning and only when she was ready, she changed position, struck her pose and held it as he took her milk, squeezing alternately from left to right hand until his pail was full, the milk foam crackling on the top. The pigs in the next stall squealed jealously. When he removed the pail to a safe place beyond the stalls, he took armloads of feed and rolled them into the cow's stall, before he closed her in for the night to the tune of a pig's full-pitch chorus.

"I'm not gone move not one bit faster, so shut up."

At the pigs' stall, he emptied several baskets of feed, flinging ears of dried yellow corn before their frothing snouts. "Bossy things, we gone to make hams and shoulders and sausages out of you." The dry shucks of the corn rattled as the swine ate. He dismissed them with, "You sound like a funeral," and raced with the dark into the house where he could have his evening meal and think of Ida.

For the next few days, Rebecca walked about and talked to herself about her brother, her grief protecting her from the questions of her lovestruck son. In the days after the funeral, Kinchen heard her mutter and clear her throat. Twice he came upon his mother too quickly and found her weeping. What amazed his young mind was that his father was also subdued and seemed to be thinking about Uncle Walter.

During the months after Walter Brake's funeral, Kinchen made many trips back and forth over the four miles to the Brake house, with food and supplies for the widow and the fatherless children. It was on the first trip that he enlisted his cousin, Lady Brake, as his go-between with Ida. For two years, Kinchen secretly penciled letters to Ida, handed them off to Lady, the eldest Brake cousin, who delivered them one or two at a time. She slipped them to Ida in secret every Sunday, by innocuously taking Ida's hand while coming out of Paradise Saintifed Church. Kinchen was surprised that Ida answered his first letter right away, and then every letter after.

Four months after the funeral of Walter Brake, Vera Brake moved her daughters and herself to a house within a half mile of the Cobbs', after the landlord refused to pay her Walter's wages for the year's work on the farm, saying that he had no contract with her even though she and her children had harvested the crops. Vera Brake took up house-keeping jobs and was picked up in a car at her mailbox every day by a different employer.

❦

In the fall of 1918, the flu epidemic came to Griffinton. Vera Brake came down with the disease first. Next, the twins were stricken, one after the other. Lady nursed the entire family through the crisis, and when she then came down with the disease, the others were already recovering, though weakened. Lady, exhausted, was unable to recover with them, and she died.

It was also during the flu crisis that Joseph stopped going to church, and he tried to keep Rebecca from going too.

"The more we stay away from people," he said, "the better off we will be."

The following year, 1919, Rebecca slipped out of the house, leaving a sleeping Joseph and Kinchen, to attend a New Year's watch service. When the sun came up on the New Year, Rebecca said, "I am back in my church to stay," and attended her church from then on.

Kinchen suffered through 1918 and the loss of Lady. He gave notes to girls whom he did not know, and he stood on the church grounds as he watched them pass the notes to Ida. It was an agonizing two years. He was confused over his progress in winning Ida. Nothing in the letters reassured him. She answered every letter.

> *Dear Kinchen,*
> *How is you? Fine I hope. I hope this letter fine you*
> *alrite.*
>
> *Ida*

He copied poems out of books and wrote letters too thick for hiding in a woman's bosom, as his late Uncle Walter's oldest girl complained. Ida always replied. At the end of two years, he had nearly a hundred letters that all said, "*Dear Kinchen, How is you? Fine I hope. I hope this letter fine you alrite.*" Then, one day, it came to him. Ida was protecting herself: if ever a letter written by her fell into the wrong hands and her grandparents were informed, she would suffer consequences. The way Rev. Harrison had spoken to her just for talking to him made that obvious She was being non-committal and ladylike to be safe. He became reassured during the times—five or six of them—when he would venture into the grandfather's church to see her. He boldly looked at her and she returned his look, open-eyed and half smiling!

⚘

~ 1920 ~

It had been two years since the funeral services for Walter Brake, where Kinchen first sighted Ida Harrison and began his correspondence with her. Rebecca knew about their exchanging of letters. She had been privately applauding her son's efforts, taking care to not let him know of her interest.

One fall day, Rebecca had finished clearing away the dishes from the midday meal. She waited for the kettle to boil water to rinse the plates. The sun came in through the window, and she noticed that it slanted a different way. She thought that the earth had tilted again. That was one way to mark the passing of time. Then she heard his footsteps. Not her husband, Joseph. Her son's foot falls were lighter and stronger, while Joseph walked with a hesitancy on his right side. On the floors of the house, his movement was a slide step, slide step. This was the pounding, hurried step of her 20-year-old. She could tell that he was not just wandering in.

"I'm goin' to ask for my girl's hand, Mama." He bounced from one foot to the other. Then he backed up and set two pans vibrating on the table. He laughed nervously, and it seemed that his confidence was coming and going, right before her eyes.

"Is it Ida?"

"How you know, Mama?"

The kettle whistled. She lifted it from the stove to the side table and whispered, "I know you been tryin' to court that girl. I was glad because it gave you somethin' to think about other than school."

He stopped moving and looked at his mother. He hung his head apologetically to one side. "I never said I was thinking about school. I made up my mind to make myself satisfied." She waited. He tried to convince her: "I haven't said a word about it. I put it out of my mind. Why you think it bother me?"

"'Cause I know," she said. "I know you see what you missin'. Winston Lockheed, he come by here from time to time to remind you just by the way he walk and the clothes he wear, that he on a different road. You have to see. His hands not hard like yours. And I know for you, one day is no different from the other except, for the seasons of the farm."

The screen door creaked. Joseph came in through the door in his slide step movement. He looked from one to the other and said, "Huh? What you all talkin' 'bout?" He got no answer, but he did not seem to notice. "The man what killed Walter? I just heard. They give him fifteen months on the road gang."

"My Lord," Rebecca said. "It is been two years since we buried Walter. Lord, Lord, Lord. Why it take so long? And that ain't hardly no time at all."

⁂

In February of 1920, Kinchen turned 20 years old. In March of 1920, his beloved Ida became 17. One April day in 1920, Kinchen put on a stiff clean white shirt and a pair of brown linen trousers that Rebecca had starched and ironed for him. He was pressed and clean-shaven when he presented himself to the senior Harrison. His heart pounded, it being only the second time in his life that he had stood so close to the man who was Ida's grandfather. The man columned over him. Kinchen had trouble getting enough air in his lungs, but he managed to ask the Rev. Jonathan Harrison for Ida's hand. Kinchen cleared his throat.

The man was looking at him. He did not seem inclined to answer. Had he heard? Kinchen cleared his throat again, testing the silence. Just when he was about to excuse himself and back away all the way home, Rev. Harrison exhaled,

"Yes," which presented Kinchen with a problem: Kinchen had only practiced the apology he had planned to give when turned down, something about being terribly sorry to have taken up the precious time of a man of God. But he had not prepared for this. He struggled to think of something to say, until Rev. Harrison spoke again: "Take her, my boy. Be one less mouth to feed, praise God. Once she married, I'm sure she won' be like her mama, singing devil songs and dancing to the devil's music. The Lord be praised."

⁕

1920. The year that white women in the United States voted in national elections for the first time, but women of color in Griffinton raised not any eyebrow, except to wonder if Warren Harding could do anything to help Colored farm folk.

⁕

October 20, 1920

It was Ida Harrison's wedding day morning. A voice from downstairs called up to her bedroom: "Get up, Ida. Your bridegroom be here afta while. Want him to think you lazy, still in bed afta the sun done up?"

The footsteps came up the stairs to Ida's room. The women brought her breakfast of sassafras tea and biscuits and ham.

Three of her grandmother's friends raised her wedding dress above her head. The dress had a circle of crochet as the collar and crocheted cuffs at the sleeves that stopped at her wrists. The women lowered the dress over Ida's upraised arms. She wondered at the conspiring smiles on the married women's faces. When the 14 buttons on the front were fastened by the many clutching hands, they stood back to look at her. Several ladies put their hands over their mouths to cover giggles. Their eyes told her, "Just you wait til tonight," but they called her "bride."

She wondered if there should be someone in that room her own age, but her grandfather had reminded her that she was a preacher's grandchild. He had discouraged girls from coming to the house to see her. She missed Lady Brake. She had not been able to visit Lady when she was so sick. She thanked God that she had been lucky and missed the influenza of 1918. Before she left that room, holding her long dress up around her ankles, she closed her eyes tightly and wished for whatever was good, finally.

Once dressed, she went outside and sat in the porch swing, a piece of cloth placed underneath her to keep her white dress clean. In her mind, she was telling Lady, *"Thank you for bringing me his letters. I wish you were here. I am scared,"* while she watched people milling about her grandparents' yard and porch. They were all churchy people and addressed each other saying, "Greeting, praise God."

She looked at the smooth stiff white lace handkerchief that her mother sent her in the mail. She twisted it up and straightened it out. That day 14 years ago, her mother had not taken off her coat, the coat with the nice fur collar, at this house where Ida had spent the last 14 years. But she couldn't be sure, because as soon as they had arrived that day from the train station, Ida's grandmother gave her milk and cornbread and she fell asleep at the table, resting her head next to her glass. She seemed to recall her grandmother taking her tired arms out of her own coat, the arms that missed holding the doll. But she fell asleep anyway. That day, 14 years ago, she had heard her mother's voice floating upstairs to where she was lying in a strange bed where someone had put her.

"Can I at least write to her?"

"No. Not while you sing devil music."

Ida had sat up in that strange bed facing a wall of calendars and flyswatters. She dashed down the stairs, finding her way in the direction of the voices. She found the porch and saw her mother walking away from it. Her mother's high heels made crunching sounds on gravelly sand as she walked toward the wagon where the old man sat. Mama looked back, saw Ida, and blew kisses at her. Ida ran, but the wagon was gone before she could cover the space between them. When she realized that she would not catch up with the wagon, she lay down on the ground kicking and screaming.

Reverend Harrison performed the wedding ceremony on the steps of the Harrison home, uniting Ida Harrison and Kinchen Cobb. In July of 1919, the Reverend had been driven out of the Paradise Saintifed Church by a discontented deacon board, after he demanded a salary increase and a car like some of the white people were driving. As with most rural churches, the separation was like the storm in the breakup of a relationship that had begun with a long-forgotten handshake.

The bride's mother was not present. She had sent a lace handkerchief, the prettiest the bride had ever seen. After the ceremony, the bride's family and friends served fried catfish, baked sweet potatoes, and boiled vegetables, all prepared on open fires in the yard in wash pots. They drank lots of lemonade, because Reverend Harrison was opposed to strong spirits, and because of the Volstead Act, which made spirits a crime.

The wedding guests left in the mid-afternoon, as soon as the food was gone. A few complained of the need for strong drink. Before long, the Harrison house was down to six. The three men—the bridegroom Kinchen, his father Joseph, and Reverend Harrison—sat on the front porch. The Reverend quoted various scriptures that came to mind. Joseph reminded him, "We been to church, too. Heaven a big place, I expect."

The three women—the bride, her grandmother, and her new mother-in-law—went upstairs to fasten Ida's suitcases. They hesitated in what had just become her old bedroom, with Mrs. Harrison folding and unfolding towels, gifts from neighbors.

She said to Rebecca, "Ida is been with us since she was four years old. My daughter was singin', goin' round from place to place, and the lady she had been leaving Ida wid, she got sick and couldn't care for her no more." She looked sternly at Ida. "And she said the child was hard to handle 'cause she miss her mama so. My daughter was to go to Chicago to do some singin' and decided that she bring Ida to stay wid us. My husband said he was gone raise her up in a Godly fashion and make sure she not stray like her mama. But he put a condition on it. That once she brung her here, she not to come back for her. And that what she done."

Rebecca nodded and the two women looked at Ida who twisted her fingers in the fabric of her dress.

"Stop wrinkling your skirt. Miss Tab made her dress. Did a right nice job, didn't she?"

"Yes," Rebecca said. "She my next door neighbor, don't you know. She got a daughter-in-law 'bout Ida's age. Now I got me a daughter-in-law, too."

Rebecca smiled proudly.

Mrs. Harrison was dour, however, despite Rebecca's smiles. She turned to Ida. "Now you is leaving here to go become a man's wife. I need to tell you some things to start out. First, you can't come back here. No matter what happen, you have to stick it out for the rest of your life. Second thang, tonight, you gone have to git in bed and sleep with the man."

Rebecca, the other elder, grinned and put an arm around her new daughter-in-law. Mrs. Harrison continued, "Now, after he blow out the kerosene lamp, he gone act like he crazy."

Rebecca frowned and let go the girl. "I wouldn't say it like that."

"You will think he done mislaid his good sense."

Rebecca shook her head. "I wouldn't say it like that."

"Pay no attention. He gone want to do something nasty. Let him do what he want. It'll be terrible, but you lay still and let him."

Rebecca waited for Mrs. Harrison to hug Ida. She did not. The three of them stood terribly uncomfortably, looking at each other in silence. Then, Rebecca could not control herself any longer. She reached out and took Ida's hand, while Ida's grandmother picked up the suitcases. They walked single file behind her down the stairs, through the front room and out to where the men sat on the porch. The wagon had been brought up, the mule tied to a post. A calf was tied to the back of the wagon, the Harrisons' wedding gift to Ida, a heifer that would become a milk cow. The men loaded the two suitcases onto the wagon. Rev. prayed a final prayer that included a thanksgiving. "Thank you, oh God, that she not singin' the devil music like her mama."

Joseph, Rebecca, Ida, and Kinchen all got into the wagon, with Kinchen at the reins, and started for home.

⚬✦⚬

The newly marrieds were strangers to each other, with prenuptial communication having been limited to letter writing and glances across a church aisle. Nevertheless, Kinchen fully intended to enjoy himself between Ida's thighs. She fully intended to do as her grandmother said, no matter how disgusting his behavior, she would *let* him. Only problem was, she could not control the tingling of her body each time he looked at her. By the time they were behind the closed doors of their bedroom, she was a mass of coils and springs inside. A power raced through her bloodstream.

Sitting on the side of the bed, Kinchen removed his trousers and kicked them to the floor. While he was removing his shirt, Ida got up, pulled the door open and folded it into the room, leaving her room to undress behind it. She looked back and saw him plop down on the bed, leaning on one elbow. She flopped her skirt over the door, her blouse, then her petticoat and pantaloons. The door swung in protest and the pile fell on his side of the door. He laughed, a "ha ha ha" laugh.

"Ida," he called out. He thought he heard her trembling, as though her elbow was keeping time against the door. She came from behind the door wearing a long white gown with the lace collar buttoned to her throat. He said, "I hope you naked under all that."

As soon as she sat on the edge of the bed, his hand came across from behind, and he unbuttoned the top button of her gown. When he got to the second button, she buttoned the top and followed him down. While his fingers worked, and while she undid his loosing, he told her about spelling contests that he had won. Ida took one leg off the floor while laughing at something he had said, opening a shoulder to him. He began to unbutton her gown again. This time she did not stop him. By the time he was finished telling of the spelling contests he had loved, Ida had both legs off the floor.

He plumped a pillow at her back. He talked of teaching himself to swim in the creek. In a voice so soft, she said that she didn't know anyone who could swim. He took the opportunity to lean close to hear her. When he told of himself and Armand having been with Napoleon Alston when Napoleon almost drowned, she turned her face to him and looked at him. He moved his hand to her leg. He let it rest there a moment. Then he kissed her neck. He kissed her cheek and pushed her down as she lay, moving his hand under her gown, first up to her breasts, and gratefully felt a shiver go through her. Then he tried gently to spread open her thighs and when he felt her tremble, he told another story while gently prying her knees apart.

"Do you remember when you first seen a car? Traveling by itself, no horse or mule or anything? I do. It was on Essex Road. Me and Winston was comin' home from school and had sneaked off to the creek. We got scared. And after that, we seen plenty." He could feel her soft bush of hair. "Specially in town when we went on Satday. I 'member when Roxanne got hit. We was with her. A line of us walkin' the road. The Essex road. The girls up ahead, arms linked. Roxanne was the one close to the side the car come on, behind. It picked her up and tumble her through the air and kept on going before it stopped and the other three girls were screaming and crying. The car stopped and two white men got out and looked at her."

She said, feeling as his warm hands moved along her stomach, "I remember when I was little, the KKK came to my granddaddy church one night. Prayer meeting. The men folk blew out the candlelight and we all got on our knees in the dark. We see them out the window wearing them white sheets. White sheets shinin' in the light of the torches they carry. Scariest thing I ever see. It was the firs' time I ever really prayed in my heart. They looked like white devils and the torches made shadows. My granddaddy told me after, "'You always look at white men's shoes. They don't have sense enough to know that them sheets don't cover the shoes.'"

His hands were looking for her opening. She felt herself oozing wetness there.

"You can talk, can't you. You seemed so quiet."

"When I got somethin' to say."

"You gone have plenty to say."

And he kissed her for real, placing his mouth fully on her, keeping his hands beneath her. He lifted her gown and exposed her plump breasts. She lay, unresisting, quiet. He placed her hand on his member, even though she dared not look at it, but sensed that it was fully swollen. He tried to enter her. After one or two spirited thrusts, which must have hurt her excessively, he made no progress, but saw that she bore the pain, shown only by the tears that rolled into her ears. He kissed her tears. He kissed her mound of hair and treated himself to a full view of her cleft of flesh before him.

"Trust me, Ida, my Ida. I love you."

He was delicate at first in resuming his attempts. Then, he placed a pillow beneath her hips and again put himself between her thighs, resting her thighs upon his hips. He thrust in and out, and when he was in, she tried to inhale more of him, and when he was out, she yearned him back in. He lay back to get a look at her face and whistled softly. People often said that whistling was a dangerous attraction to snakes. She did not care.

Before he fell asleep, he said, "The scars on your back. You want to tell me about them?"

"I'd rather not."

Just as she fell asleep, he realized that her grandparents had not spared the rod. He promised himself that he would be her healing and fell asleep. She eased herself closer to his warm body, her soiled gown wrapped between her legs, and she threw a leg around him and clung to him in the night. He limply fell open to her. She hoped that in the morning, he would thrust into her again, although, in her soreness, she wondered how she could endure him. She wondered if he would always whistle when sexually satisfied. It reminded her of a teakettle. Over the years, she would learn that he did. For now, she hoped that the soreness would be gone by the next day and that she could get used to being loved and loving, maybe. She hoped that he would not ask about the scars again. After a time, she, too, slept and the two newlyweds began their life together.

CHAPTER FOUR

Joseph and Kinchen left the farm for town before Ida got out of her new bed and down the stairs. As she came down, Rebecca smiled up at her from the bottom of the stairs. Ida sat down to breakfast. Rebecca explained, "They taken the wagon. Got two shoats squealing they behinds off all that fifteen miles, probably. Takin' them to the stock market for to sell."

Ida wore an everyday dress. The day before she had worn a wedding gown. The old and faded, but clean and whole, everyday dress of blue linen felt new. She sat with her new self, looking around in the nice clean kitchen with its bacon and biscuit smell, and listened to Rebecca's plans.

"We go for a little walk in the neighborhood for you to meet people, your new neighbors. Most of them came yestidy, but I'm sure you don't remember the names."

At the first house, from the road, they saw into the backyard where a woman stirred a long stick in a steaming black pot. Ida and Rebecca walked the path leading alongside the gray, rough-plank, three-room cabin and were greeted with cackles of delight while the woman churned. At her feet on the ground lay a pan of rancid animal fat and drippings from fried meats. Under her arm, the stirrer held a can of lye. Rebecca took the can from under the woman's arm, saying, "Christine Lynch, you better be careful. It come open, spill out, wash down your side, take every bit of skin off down your leg to your feet!"

The two women laughed heartily and kissed the air near each other. Rebecca lay the can on the ground and took Ida's hand. "Meet my boy's wife. This Ida."

"Your Kinchen is done it, ain't he?" Her look felt like a bright light falling on Ida. Ida ducked her head to hide her own smile before Christine Lynch turned back to stirring in the violently bubbling steam. Ida felt Kinchen's warmth stirring inside her and instinctively placed her palm over her belly. Miss Christine winked at her the way married women would over the next few months, an acknowledgement of the initiation to conjugal activities.

The three women threw chunks of meat and drizzled drippings of bacon and ham renderings into the pot. They jumped back and forth to avoid being splashed. When Rebecca and Christine nodded to each other with a meeting of the eyes that it was time to add the lye, Rebecca pried the top off and turned the can upside down, letting the tiny crystal pellets disappear into the boil.

Ida whispered to Rebecca. "What is we doin'?"

But Rebecca did not answer. Christine Lynch snickered, "Makin' soap, honey. Didn't your mama never make no soap?"

Ida was about to say that she had no mother as near as she could tell, but looked at her mother-in-law, who was holding the lye can up close to her face.

Christine asked, "What's the matter, Rebecca?"

Rebecca shook her head. "Nothin'. Just this skull and bones put me in the mind of the handbills that was nailed all over Wilmington back when I was a girl."

On their way to the next house, Rebecca was quiet. They walked easily next to each other, Rebecca juggling her fears, Ida basking in the ease of her new life.

They walked to three other houses that day. At the second house, three old people lived, three siblings who had never married and talked to each other in Ida's and Rebecca's presence about an omniscient "Momma and Papa." They were two women and one man in their sixties and seventies.

Rebecca whispered, "They momma and papa been dead for over thirty years, poor dears."

It seemed that there were two nephews from a deceased sister, the only one in the family who had married. Rebecca explained later that it was those nephews, who performed the bulk of the farm labor. Ida was able to relax in the house. The inhabitants were shy and quiet people who made no reference to her bride status. In fact, they were deadly serious in talking about crops, weather, and gardens, quite formal for farm folk.

On the path to the third house, Rebecca explained that Kinchen's childhood friend had grown up here, but that he had moved on to the city to finish schooling. His name was Winston. There lived two Lockheed women. They explained that the children of the younger woman were at school for the day. Her husband, and the father of her children, was away in the United States Army. He was Joe Lockheed, Winston Lockheed's brother and the elderly woman's son. At the Lockheed house, they talked of the 1918 epidemic. Ida thought of Lady Brake. The older woman, Miss Liza, had lost a husband and two daughters in the influenza epidemic.

"I scared to death that my son gone to bring back some horrible disease when he do return from overseas." During the 40-minute visit, Miss Liza washed her hands seven times, each time making Ida and Rebecca leave the front room and follow her to the kitchen where she filled a basin with cold water and soaped herself to the elbow. The younger woman, the daughter-in-law, Pearl, who was probably in her mid-thirties, vigorously chewed gum. She always remained seated and was still there when they returned from the washing trips. She smiled sympathetically at Ida but seemed impenetrable and disinterested in anything her mother-in-law said.

Rebecca asked Miss Liza about Winston. She shook her head, as though being reminded of someone who was as lost as an influenza victim. Rebecca explained on the walk away from that house that Winston was away in school getting ready to learn how to fix teeth. Ida tried to figure out why a mother would be disappointed in a son who wanted to become a dentist. Rebecca had no answer, but she speculated that Miss Liza was fearful of being left behind somehow.

The last house was the one closest in proximity to the Cobb's. As they entered the yard, several dogs barked and ran to meet them, circling back to the house and out to the visitors, shaking their tails hard enough to twist their back-sides toward their snouts. The old woman, Tab Cobb, said, "I seen you go by and wondered was you gone to bring this pretty bride here to see me."

Tab had made Ida's wedding dress and was acquainted with Ida's grandparents. They embraced warmly.

"Oh, Miss Tab. I loved my wedding dress."

"And you looked mighty pretty in it. That muslin bleached up real nice. I bleached it and boiled it white and then ironed it up good before I cut it out. It was my pleasure."

It was there that Ida finally met someone close to her own age. Tab's daughter-in-law, Doll Amos, age 19, was pregnant and enjoying the joyful uncomfortable part of her pregnancy, in which she had trouble sitting down and get-ting up and walking. She said, "Hello. I sorry I couldn't get to the wedding. Scared to go too far from home."

Ida's eyes were glued to her belly. Doll noticed and laughed, reached for Ida's hand, and placed it beneath her breasts, and they all four stood still and silent while Ida felt the baby's moves, kicking life in that hidden place. Ida left that house promising to come back the very next day just to talk, and she left there thinking for the first time about babies of her own.

All her life she had been warned not to get pregnant. Her grandfather had condemned illegitimate births and made allusions to her own birth having been without a responsible father. But now it was okay.

Those first days, Ida kept on her guard in her new home, where no one yelled or cried out except to express joy or surprise at something. She heard no loud prayers from the head of the household like there had been in her grandparents' house. Joseph chuckled a good deal, was always trying to be funny in some cornball way. There was no spur of the moment sermons. Every night, her husband got into bed anxious to hold her in his arms, and when he was spent, he fell asleep whistling. He often went about with an offbeat out-of-tune hum during the day. When he fell asleep whistling, lying on his back, she was the vine that wrapped around him.

During the day, she tiptoed about, alert to see signs of dark ugly secrets in the house. So when she often saw Rebecca on her knees, praying but with no sound, she tensed up. This one prayed in secret, and said a quiet blessing over the food at every meal, not like grandfather, who raised his voice for an audience, standing, arms extended to make himself in the shape of the cross. She saw Rebecca get up, smiling and talking to herself about being blessed in so many ways. Finally, after about two weeks, she said to her mother-in-law, "No secrets in this house."

It was not a question, but Rebecca treated it like one.

"Oh, yes there is. The hiding room."

Rebecca sat down. She twisted the rag between her hands while she told of Caesar and his shoes. "Before that day, November 10, 1898, we get up every morning and see new handbills flapping on telephone poles, warning Negroes not to vote. And there was a group of white men and boys, called themselves the 'Six', and another group called the 'Red Shirts.' They wore the shirts colored of the name. They seem to be walking the streets, patrolling and scaring folks. And rumors they are pulling men out of houses, taking them off and beating them.

"All that stuff come here with me when I come and haunted me in my dreams so that I couldn't help but cry out at night. I waked up 'fore I cried out, I get up and walk the floor just as scared as if a mob was outside the door. It was the darkness that scared me so. They build me a room to hide a man in if I ever had to.

"It the size of a tiny closet in case a man get in trouble. Of course, they could burn the house down on him, and I think of it, it don't make much sense, but I age 19. I didn't have any idea how young I was til I got older, raised my son and got some wisdom from seein' and thinkin' and bein' responsible for somebody."

Rebecca laughed. Ida didn't quite believe her because of how Rebecca laughed, and Ida got distracted in thinking of the house that she was coming to love, and said, "I love this house," leading Rebecca to think of other things.

"This house and this place got its own story. The ancestor, Nick Cobb, he was give this land in 1867. His real-life daddy was a white man, the doctor in these parts. Nick Cobb had received the 29 acres of land as payment for his slave labors from the rich, white doctor father after the great War. At first, and for years, the house was one room. The room that Nick built for his bride. My mother-in-law. Then a second room was added. When I come here, a third room was added, then a fourth, and finally, the upstairs room. The Cobb house was built with the owners building in stages, with each owner addin' rooms."

✦

When Ida spent time in the Amos house next door, she heard other parts of the family history from Miss Tab. That the doctor committed suicide on the Stagecoach road, and that his horse stood in the road all night until he was discovered in the morning. That all the Negroes knew that the Black slave mother had switched Dr. Cobb with the master's wife's baby, and that Dr. Cobb had truly been a Colored man who remained afraid all his life to marry a white woman, for fear that his passing would be found out in children with too much color and too many twists in their hair.

Ida went home with questions. "Miss Rebecca, what happened to the Cobb man who was white and thought he was Colored? The one they say ran away and went off to Ohio and Antioch College?"

"Call me Mama."

"Yes, Mama, after college at Antioch in Ohio. Was that the white doctor who they say killed his self in his buggy on the Stagecoach road? Did the doctor find out he was Colored? Did the Colored son graduate of Antioch find out he was white? Is there some white people name Cobb runin' around thinkin' they is Colored? Is there some Colored ones don't know they white?"

Rebecca laughed. "Don't rightly know. What difference do it make?"

And they went back to peeling potatoes. In good weather, it seemed that everybody touched down on the Cobb porch: the Lynches, the Lockheeds, the Amoses, and the Webbs, as well as people from farther away came to visit. They dropped by to laugh, complain, and to eat whatever Rebecca had warming on the stove. In that house and on that porch, Ida could pretend that she was not a girl who had been brought to Griffinton on a train by a mother who left without taking off her coat. And, when Rebecca looked straight at Ida—not side-long passing by or reaching for something, when she looked *straight* at Ida—Ida wanted to pretend that Rebecca was her mother.

In the kitchen of the Cobb house, the mother-in-law and her daughter-in-law shelled peas side by side. Rebecca boiled potatoes and Ida mashed them and put in a little bicarbonate to make them fluffy. They washed dishes together. Rebecca measured and cut shelf paper that Ida held, and it was Ida who stood on a chair and pressed it in place and then lovingly put back the glasses and plates on top. Rebecca beat the cake batter, Ida oiled the pans and handed them to her, before she then raced across the kitchen floor and opened the oven of the cook stove.

The closeness was the kind among women where, when their hands open and close over their joint projects, their freed-up minds run off and they would be reminded of things. They would find themselves saying every day, at the clothesline, in a bedroom on the opposite sides of the bed sheet flung and popped between them, "That remind me of the time . . . "

One of those times came when Ida, popping string beans, forgot herself, slipped up and said, "The wind blew haaarrdd last night. Remind me of one of the nights when Grandpa made me pray on my knees all night . . . " She caught herself and stared into space.

Rebecca did not hesitate. "I have wanted to ask you. Did they beat you?"

"Oh. My granddaddy, he said my mama was bad and he want to make sure the devil left me alone. My grandpa, he say his beatin's would teach me the right from wrong. He beat me if I drop somethin'. He beat me if I forgot to do somethin'. He beat me first time Kinchen spoke to me at his Uncle Walter's funeral when we got home."

Rebecca faltered, stepping away from dishes soaking in hot, sudsy water. They were both quiet enough to hear the suds peak and fall as the water cooled as Rebecca sat herself down in a side chair in that kitchen. The kettle's hissing came on and was unheeded. When she had let her mind turn over what she had heard, Rebecca held out both hands to Ida.

"Your mama was not no bad person. Singin' and tryin' to bring joy to people is a good thing." Ida showed surprise. "Lord child, everybody know your mama is a Blues singer. Sometime she be in the paper. Everybody know, too, that your grandpapa done disowned her. Ain't no secret. They say he tell it from the pulpit every chance he git. You ain't never need all that anger you been taught, not to be pure. Try to get out of it in this house."

Just as it was time to set the table for their men coming in from the fields, Ida said, "It's different here. Nobody fussin', accusin', testin' to see is somebody livin' right. I am glad to be here."

She had grown up in a house where every word that was said was harsh and intended to make tough-minded, judgmental Christian imprints.

"My job, I believe, is to make you forget. Pretend like none of them pages in your life ever was."

Soon, Rebecca announced at church, in the seed store, passing another wagon going to the market, "We is havin' us a baby!"

Ida swelled to ripening in the months to come, and Rebecca said, "I believe it be a boy, carrying low like she is."

"I'm so glad . . . "

Next door, Doll's new baby was starting to walk, and she had another biscuit in the oven.

In December of 1922, Doll Amos wrote to her sister, who lived in South Carolina:

Dear Kiza, It not quit as lonsome now. The people on the next farm, the boy Kinchen marri a girl my age. She name Ida. She pregnant. She not always frinly but she company anyway. We made some peach presarves.

your sister, Doll

Just before Ida's baby boy was born, Ida noticed that Rebecca sometimes seemed blocked in her passage among the furniture inside the house, and she realized that Rebecca's light was dimming. Ida said nothing while standing close at Rebecca's elbow, memorizing her recipes. She tried to duplicate the fists of flour and half fists of sugar, the proper shakes of salt and pepper for seasoning, even holding her tongue between her teeth as Rebecca did. As they did chores together, she kept a corner of her eye on her mother-in-law.

When Ida's baby boy was born, in 1923, the one who would earn the nickname Rabbit, she studied the way Rebecca talked to him, sometimes sending messages to the other family members through her conversations with the baby.

"Yes. Yes. Grandmama can't see you too good, but dat's alright," planting kisses on his face and in the air around him. Ida mimicked Rebecca's warmth. It was not that she would not have felt it herself on her own, but watching Rebecca helped her share it with her baby in that house where voices were most often raised in laughter. By the time Hart Lee was born in 1923, Ida doubted whether Rebecca could see anything but his outline.

When Rebecca could no longer see well enough to push thread through a needle's eye, she took up every loose rag and twine that she could find. She twisted these findings into rugs. No bit of large-gauged thread, no piece of grass, no corn husk or loose half-living grapevine escaped her bending them to her will. She discovered the art of basketry. She twisted and wove quietly, almost stealthily in a searching way before she had faced the darkness sufficiently to simply sigh about it. By then it was twilight the full day long, and when she accepted the dimming, she rediscovered her pride and went back to doing what she pleased, openly, almost defiantly, only differently. Her new occupations were done by fumble and touch. Out of that fumble and touch came baskets of every conceivable size and shape, filling the Cobb house to overflowing. Before long, the family had a sense of time by the proliferation of the baskets. In a single week, she could turn out perhaps 10 or 12. Every kitchen utensil and nearly every tool had a pretty resting place in one of Rebecca's baskets.

On June 19, 1924, two days before the end of the spring by the calendar, Rebecca told Joseph in the morning that she had a taste for new potatoes, and that she intended to dig underneath the potato flowers where she would find some tiny juicy pellets. Minutes later, Rebecca picked up the older grandson, little John Rob—who would later be crowned with the nickname Rabbit—from his crib in Ida and Kinchen's room. Rebecca walked, carrying him to the outside. Joseph saw Rebecca carrying the baby child in one arm. She walked across the porch and into the yard. She held a basket in her other hand, one made of grapevine wound and braided around pine needles. The pine needles closed the cracks, making it nearly watertight. The basket was surely deep enough to hold many more potatoes than she expected to find so early in the season. She expected to find one or two.

Joseph sat on an upturned tall basket under the chinaberry tree. He guessed that she was headed for the white potato patch. He sat, pretending to pay her no mind. He was sure she could not see him. He knew she hated having her vision reduced to outlines and shadows, and that she was dogged about navigating for herself. Barely breathing aloud, Joseph crouched on the basket, hugging his knees and touching the tips of his fingers together, holding quiet. The truth of the matter was that she could not see the baby she held. It was her habit to finger the infant's face, tracing his features and measuring his growth.

She perched the wiggling creature high up onto her shoulder off to one side, his fat baby legs pumping next to her face but with all the movement, hers and his. She kept her balance as they went along. She balanced the wiggling baby to one side high up, the basket off her arm held low and outward so that she seemed to paddle it like an oar through the air. The baby tried with all his might to kick his toes into her mouth and giggled after each try.

Joseph watched her bound away toward the fields. He was still watching before she stopped and then bent down holding the baby aloft. He had noticed that the sun was bright. The air had not been as humid as it could have been. He was sure that the bright yellow sun made a halo behind the house and wondered if Rebecca could see any light from it. It seemed that she walked into it and on beyond. Maybe there was even a halo encircling the tree where he sat. Spring was always a trickster, making him want more warmth with him, still fresh from surviving winter cold with its chores of splitting logs, hauling firewood inside the house, keeping fires in the fireplaces ablaze, and trying to keep Rebecca from building and tending fires herself.

She nuzzled her face into the baby's leg. Just before, she paused. Maybe she cooed against the baby's skin, priming the baby for laughter. Was it after that that she bent down? Had she worn blue? Or was it green? He thought later that maybe it was a greenish colored dress, a long dress that fanned out over the long stick legs that she tramped about on. Joseph was shorter than his wife and hated for her to know that to match her stride he had to push his legs.

She had never simply walked anywhere. She marched, beating her feet on the floor or ground. She could find her way through the shadows by herself to the field, sit down on the ground and fumble into the earth, digging, pushing the dirt aside, daring it to get in her way until she found a tiny pebble of a potato. He wasn't sure what she planned to do with the baby. He was too big to fit into the basket while she dug. He was almost ready to walk, just learning to stand up, too frisky to stay put on the ground. It never mattered because she never made it all the way. The basket dropped. Rebecca stopped in her tracks. When Joseph saw Rebecca standing still reaching down, he stood up thinking that she had lost her balance. He realized later that she dropped the basket on purpose. She said later that she reached down to pick up a piece of rope in her path. The rope whipped up into a coil and nicked her hand. She said that at first, she didn't believe it had struck, she took a step toward it, and so it sliced a second time. By the time Joseph got to Rebecca, he saw the tail of it streak away into the grass.

For the rest of Joseph's life, he would wonder how in the first moments, she had disregarded the venom burning in her hand in two places. She attempted and succeeded in sitting down gently with that baby in her arms, that infant John Rob. She did not fall. She did not scream. She was determined to protect the baby. Joseph raced with himself and when he got to her, he was sure it was only seconds later. The baby laughed, slobbered and plucked his fingers at Rebecca, mistaking her low moans as an invitation to play. The venom must have begun to moved up her fingers, but she clutched the baby in her good hand before Joseph picked her up. He carried them both toward the house.

He cradled Rebecca. Rebecca cradled the baby. Kinchen met him and took Rebecca from his father's arms. Rebecca said, "Snake bit me."

Ida pulled the baby from her free stubborn arm with some force.

While Joseph and Kinchen were carrying Rebecca through the house toward her bed, she said that the thing struck twice. A neighbor said that for a snake to bite two or three times, it would probably die its own self, like a wasp losing part of itself in the stinging. Joseph did not believe that.

They drove her into town to a doctor two days after they had tried everything anybody suggested, cutting into the fang marks and trying to wash the venom out by flooding it with soapy water and squeezing, irrigating and soaking with turpentine, stuffing the wound with sulfur while she screamed to be touched. The doctor said that all the things they had done were wrong, and he alienated them all with his clinical detachment. He told them that if it appeared some venom had moved and caused nerve damage to the fingers, that they had been correct to keep the arm below the heart. It had been a bad idea to try to suck the venom out, that it was dangerous to the person sucking in the event of a sore or broken place on the tongue.

Most importantly, there was nothing in the mouth to direct the sucking in a stream so as to separate out venom, which as soon as it was injected, began to seek the bloodstream. They kept telling him that no one had done that. They had tried to put things on the fang marks that would draw out the venom. Then, as he examined further, he realized that they had cut tiny pieces of flesh around the fang marks, causing more area for infection and certainly more area that needed healing without eliminating the main invasion. He gave her some pills. He did not say what they were. They paid him and carried her to the car.

What did a white doctor care about the discomfort of one old Black woman?

The doctor stood in the doorway for moments as they left. He realized that Rebecca's wound had not been cleansed of bacteria. He thought of the fact that the snakes' fangs were probably septic from the meal it had eaten, if it had eaten that day or that week, the kind of uncleanliness that mere soap would not wash away, and such that would attach to living flesh and grow. He thought of the venom causing some damage to tissues, but the possibility of infection festering was more likely. Well, she was old, anyway. He was amazed that some of the things they had poured on the wound—including iodine and Watkins Red Oil, known as snake oil—were likely to have killed a germ or two. Well, they would bring her back if she worsened. There was always amputation.

Soon after the doctor visit and back home, Rebecca stopped talking to anybody about anything and kept to her room, sitting in a rocking chair with her arm resting on the armrest. The neighbors began to visit one by one. Mrs. Lockheed offered to wash the wound every day with soap. As it began to swell, she said that the soap would kill the teenie little living things that were growing inside there. And, she said, this reminded her of the 1918 influenza. She even predicted that Rebecca would become feverish.

Mrs. Lynch chanted and wondered if some lye soap tied to the wound would help. Miss Tab put a necklace about her throat, made of leaves that, as they dried, fell away in a powder. They seemed not surprised that Rebecca was not talking. But Tab also, like all the others, tried to get her to say something:

"Rebecca, pick up. Fight back. Don't let this take control of you, woman. Speak up."

Ida wanted so badly to cure her mother-in-law all by herself. Despite the traffic into and out of the house, Ida was convinced that she was alone with this problem, and that she had to cure Rebecca all by herself. For the women, Joseph and Kinchen were nuisances that they had to put up with. Ida found them useless in this calamity. Joseph wanted to go sit and look at his ailing wife. He never offered to wash her face. The days invisibly marched by. Rebecca weakened, Joseph saddened, and spent all his free moments in between feeding the livestock and doing farm chores watching Rebecca, who stared straight ahead or took long naps. Soon, Ida found him an annoyance as she cared for Ida. How could she wash between that sweet lady's legs with that man sitting, looking, his lips hanging loose. Kinchen ran in and out of the sickroom like a hot toad trying to cool his burning feet, bouncing in and out. His visits were frequent and short.

One day when Joseph left the room, just as Ida was about to bathe Rebecca, Ida locked the door behind him. She was able to dust powder on Rebecca's behind, comb out the tangles on her head, massage her scalp, smooth her cheek. Then, after the sick woman was in order to Ida's satisfaction, she opened the door to Kinchen and Joseph.

Joseph demanded to know, "Why you pin her hair up like that? That nightgown, she don't want to wear that now, do she?"

"But she won't talk to tell me, how do I know?"

"I'm her husband. I know what she like," Joseph insisted, though they all could see that Rebecca was losing interest in everything. They had long ago begun to talk about her in her presence without expecting her to react.

Ida had decided, however, that to get anything done, with a baby at her knee and another in her arms, she had to do things, her chores, over and over, the same way each time, the same time of day. The imposition of her own order set her racing back and forth all day past the two sad men. In all that order, Ida was sure Rebecca could get well.

The doctor came when called in the second week, when Rebecca's arm had turned dark and the swelling had not gone down. The arm by then looked like a tire, dark and rubbery. Although there were many tales of people dying of snake bites, no one in Griffinton could name one. The doctor said that although the snake may have been venomous, it was the infection, the blood poisoning, that was the problem. Initially, Rebecca's arm remained swollen, stretching the skin to look like the hand and arm of a fat circus lady, something grotesque and ugly.

After three weeks, the doctor spoke the word amputation. He warned that the longer they waited, the higher up the arm the amputation would have to be.

Rebecca finally spoke. "Why? I'm old anyway."

They had tried all they knew: minced tobacco leaves, kerosene, salt pork, garlic.

Rebecca's sisters came from the town. Florence and Vate smelled of store-bought soap and feigned fear of flies. "Let us take her with us to the city and get a white doctor to amputate her hand and get her back in shape."

For the second time in weeks, Rebecca spoke. "Why?"

"Else you gone die. Tole you to leave this jungle of a place, hot sun, snakes and white people and hard work."

"White people don't worry Negroes what got they own land like we. You cookin' and cleanin' for them. What's the difference? But, tell me, how do I make baskets with no hand or arm?" She fell asleep and awoke in a coma, reliving the event that had her to demand that they build the secret room.

Female delegations lobbied and whispered. Some bowed down and tearfully turned to a confused and pathetic Joseph.

Joseph said, "You right," and shook his head all at the same time, so that even they could tell that he had gotten a ringing in his ears. It was at that point that Rebecca beckoned Kinchen to her sick bed. With her good hand, she pulled him with the roughness she would have used with a plow line. She didn't let go when she had got him, his face in hers, he trying to find footing, twisted half on, half off the bed. They were eyeball to eyeball when she reminded him that she forgot to count the diapers she had changed on his behind. She threatened him that she could, if she needed to, pull him down to that bed and whip him if necessary, with her other hand. Then she made him promise that no one would amputate her arm. She let go and lay back, and they were not sure how long after that she went into a coma.

She had said all she had to say and they were coming and going, moving her this way and that. At some point, one of the ladies said, "She still breathin', but she don't even know we here."

In August of 1923, the fervor of summer made waking and sleeping unbearable. Grown people and children alike felt racked by the heat. The women from the neighborhood took their turns with Ida, wetting Rebecca's feverish brow in a vain attempt to keep her cool. From next door, Doll Amos and her mother-in-law, Tab Amos, came every day, several times a day to help. Rebecca by then was like weather—she had chills and fevers. She was nearing the end.

In her mind, Rebecca tried to remember, had she told Ida. That room if it was ever needed, it would be a woman's job to use it, to hide a Black man from the terror of the night riders. She was unable to get out of the fog to find out.

They whispered to each other as she slipped farther and farther away. "She's dyin', praise God."

And they went on accidentally dripping their own sweat on her, but they were relieved that no harm came of that, the dreary women who gathered in the sick room.

They greased her lips and mopped her brow, each woman taking a turn and staying as long as she could stand the smell of the blackened hand wrapped in salted pork. Oh, the swelling was gone. It was rotting and shrinking. They were resigned to not being able to do anything about the stench of her gangrenous arm, except to sprinkle herbs about the room and wait.

When Kinchen argued for her, "I know. I know she will die, but I promised her and if you cut off her hand, you got to go by me." And to Joseph. "Papa, it seem like to me, you have made every decision for you and Mama that was ever made. I may be wrong. I just don't ever remember hearin' you ask what she thought. You just went ahead and done what you always thought best. This one time, this one time, you let Mama decide."

And he thought of how their voices could sometimes merge.

The knee baby, John Rob, crawled like a squirrel with his all fours not splayed out but holding himself with his rear end in the air. And John Rob cooed and cried for "Gaaamama." They took him into the sickroom in vain attempts to interest Rebecca in this world. The women friends ruminated together and lifted little John Rob in the air for Rebecca.

"If you die, see what you miss? Look, see? Doctor say you die if he don't cut that arm off."

When they held the two babies next to her, she seemed to almost rally and then change her mind, even with the two flapping tiny fingers in her face, even touching her and slobbering on her.

While Rebecca lay dying, Joseph took to sleeping fitfully, napping, sitting upright in a chair in the corner of their bedroom. He left the room for meals and trips to the outhouse.

After Rebecca began to go in and out of consciousness, Ida told Joseph that he would be more comfortable sleeping on a cot in the hallway. Ida latched the door from the inside if he stepped out for a moment, saying that she was bathing

Rebecca or changing Rebecca or fixing something personal on Rebecca. Joseph hated having to knock on the door for admittance to his and Rebecca's bedroom. He fussed. Kinchen turned away, giving them his profile.

Kinchen became two people: the one who pleaded for her change of mind whenever he thought that he saw focus in her eyes, and the other, who dared anyone to touch her with any intent to separate her rotting limb.

In September of 1925, Rebecca Brake Cobb died. Finally.

CHAPTER FIVE

Ida hated how reminders stole upon her: the day that she thought she saw her doll lying in the yard, the doll her grandfather had made her throw away when she was four years old. On another day, she thought she felt the gentle hand of her mother-in-law resting on her shoulder. Finally, she dropped a glass because she was handing it to somebody who was not standing in front of her, but was resting in her mind.

She missed Rebecca terribly. Her grief, along with all the reminders, kept creeping up on her, forcing her to become armed and guarded for the balance of her days. On one particular day, she wrapped her arms around herself and promised that she would guard against seeing things and remembering. She unclenched her fists in order to see her hands. She had to drag those hands over something, didn't matter what, hard or soft, wet or dry. There were beds to make and supper to fix. There was a Dominique chicken shut up in a floored pen waiting to be made into supper. She had already built her fire under the iron pot outside to heat water to scald the feathers off. Her hatchet stood tall, way up, the blade dangerously down. She left it and opened the slammed door to make her way to the outside.

In the yard where there was no doll lying on the ground, Ida walked purposefully to the chicken coop and reached in to where supper's main dish nervously tramped the ground and nearly speared her hands with its horny feet as she reached for it. Ida swayed and waved her hands in time to the pullet's moves and, when the moment was right, snatched the bird into both hands. She readjusted to a one-handed grasp of the head. She began to rotate the bird. She swirled it, turning its head against the weight of its heavier feathered bulk of body. She heard the neck snap. She wrung, unmindful of the blood, until the head was off. The headless creature danced in a circle, spurting blood and making a border around itself. Ida chuckled hoarsely and with a measure of triumph. She needed no axe or hatchet or any other tool.

She waited while the dancing chicken died. Her boys and her Kinchen loved themselves some chicken and dumplings. Ida thought of herself, learning to make it. She mixed the lard and flour, rolled it out using a glass jar. She remembered how Rebecca had cut the squares. Ida dropped the squares into the broth and how Rebecca had determined when it was done enough.

Ida's water boiled hot on the fire nearby. She spread open a newspaper on the ground. She dunked the chicken in and, without regard for the burns to her fingers, began to pluck the feathers and drop them in clumps on the paper. She squatted down to her work. She plucked hard and furiously, trying to keep her hand moving.

The day of the doll sighting was the same day that the baskets got in her way. Ever since Rebecca died, Ida hated the way she could turn a corner and step on an empty basket, anywhere from the size of a quart milk jar to a double bushel. When she bumped the things, she remembered having seen those brown hands with the knotted knuckles that twisted and plaited grasses, twigs, and pine straw into the many containers that littered the hallway and corners of rooms. The filled ones were okay, though; the filled ones reminded her of the posture of open arms holding things. The filled baskets paid their own keep, holding quilt scraps waiting to be sewn or sweet potatoes waiting to be roasted. It was the empty ones that angered her and slung her from a neutral, dry contentment back upon that burning grief that hung low in her chest like a Christmas ball on a string. It dangled against her as she walked.

Comforted by the smell of chicken and dumplings that simmered carelessly on the stove, she went to check the rooms of the house. Her little men had gone with Kinchen to the store and were probably stealthily licking hard candy and giggling, out of breath like they stole something, with her not there to protest against all that sugar. She started for the grandfather's room. When he was away from hard work, out of the pull of the fields, he let the boys do whatever they had a mind to. Only once in a while did she have these moments of walking the hall without tiny feet hitting her heels. And, even now, she had to remind herself not to go looking for them up at the roof or the low hanging limbs of their favorite trees.

In the hall, she bumped a basket. Empty. Round. Big. Arms big enough to encircle her.

They had a life, these baskets. They seemed to have multiplied long after Rebecca stopped wiggling her fingers to shape them, even after the total blindness and after the serpent's prick. They were everywhere. These were the baskets that Rebecca's hand had made, taking straight and dry twigs and lines and coiling them. That was partly because, even after the funeral, several marched out from under the beds, stirred by the intrusions that the death watches brought. They should have been given away, but Joseph would not hear of it. They reappeared everywhere each time Ida put them away, despite her efforts. She had finally decided that "away" was Joseph's room. They were out of the path in Joseph's room, and Joseph was only there early in the morning and at night. He never sat there anymore. He rested there and came out of that room to live.

She bent down to pick up the stray. Some nails fell out. This all had Joseph's hand near it. She was standing there with the basket, looking for where to put it, there in the hallway that did not have its own light or its own sounds.

The baskets. The empty-armed baskets. She was in the habit of gathering them in from their wanderings and putting them in a decorative fashion in Joseph's room along one wall, some hanging on nails above the window. Every day she went in to make Joseph's bed, the baskets, the hanging ones, all sizes of them—pint sized, quart sized, bushel basket sized—stacked on top of Joseph's bed. This day, she opened the door to Joseph's room. Sure enough, again, he had gathered them around him in the night. For a moment, she realized his pain. That realization weakened her, so she brushed it away as she would flick a braid from her face.

She intended to throw the stray baskets into the room from the doorway. But, the familiar sight of the unmade bed stopped her to stand and see the sheets wound in a huge rope in the middle of the rumple on the bare mattress where she made it up neatly for him every single day.

This had been Rebecca's room, too. Ida once locked Joseph out for ten minutes or so, just to bathe her mother-in-law in peace. She probably shouldn't have. It was after the locked door that it seemed Joseph always looked at her slant eyed. That was okay.

The room was a mess. Baskets piled on top of the twisted sheets. Clearly, he was sleeping with the things. Reaching in the night, perhaps, for what she had touched.

Ida made several trips, fast enough that she felt a swelling in her ankles by the time she had gotten the baskets out of the house and stacked on the porch. Maybe they would rot in the rain and sun and disappear back into the fields where they came from.

Some hours later, Ida was unaware that Joseph stood in the doorway watching her methodical moves as she placed a stack of plates alongside each place setting of the table and moved the pile along the places.

"Why you take my wife's baskets out of my room?"

He had not asked why she put them there in the first place, but that was not the matter.

"You hear me? Why you put my wife's baskets on the back porch to get rained on and dried out in the sun?"

Ida never looked up. She never stopped her two hands moving. She placed a plate, then a knife and fork on each side of the plate and moved the stack, progressing along the table. He hated how at each place she did it in the same order, always holding the remaining cutlery in her fist. When she answered, it seemed to Joseph that she barely changed her intakes of breath. "I put them stacked up on the back porch out of my way."

"I seen that, but WHY?"

"They was gatherin' dust. In my way." She placed the butter dish off-center in the middle of the table, and a short knife down beside it. She snapped her fingers and said aloud but to herself, "Got to churn a pat of butter before dinner time." She must have promptly forgotten because she made no move toward the butter churn in the corner.

"Put them back where they was."

She gave no answer. She was holding back. He felt her holding back, he felt her not caring about him and his. She went on her noisy way, slamming through what had been his house, the house built by his father and to be passed on.

"All right, Miss Boss Lady."

She gave no sign that she heard the words, words that floated with the aim of a dust mite as far as she seemed to be concerned.

It hurt to think that the baskets could be rained on. She could have at least stacked them, smaller ones inside larger ones. She was careful how she made a bed, set a place. After he had the dreams that drove him to the baskets, he had made sure every single night of his life to tear up his bed and twist the sheets into a rope. Every next day, she made up that bed so tight that one could bounce a dime off the spread when she was finished.

Before it could rain on his Rebecca's precious baskets, he loaded as many as he could at a time on a wheelbarrow, five or more trips it took to get them to the tool shed. The tool shed was kind of a lean-to, one wall and a roof overhang. Long and narrow. Though he met her there one time, she was going to the henhouse and another time coming from the clothesline, and though he cleared his throat each time, she didn't say a mumbling word.

At first, Joseph went to the shed each day to think. Sometimes it felt like someone was there. It was the swish of a woman's skirt-tail sometimes, a skirt-tail just leaving. By the first anniversary of his wife's death, he had enclosed the two ends, window at the end that overlooked the fields, the end away from the house, a roughly finished room as a result of tinkering a little every day. Kinchen laughed at the old man and noted that it looked like something that needed wheels and a pile of hay, the mishmash of nailed boards. It didn't matter; by then, the thought of missing Rebecca had become a dull ache that Joseph could manage.

After Ida exiled the baskets, Joseph ducked his head where Ida was concerned and salvaged his feelings by throwing daubs of laughter at Ida's back. Over the next four years, he made fun of her at least once a day. When she was fast walking and fanning about, he would say, "Miss Boss Lady, is you got some important business appointment somewhere that you got to git to dis morning?" and snicker. "I hear tell war is gone break out again. Better ask my daughter-in-law, she know everything," followed by a slap of the knee and deep-throated, derisive laughter. She pretended not to notice and did seem unaffected by him and his foolishness. She viewed him as an aging old coward. He was relieved that she never answered and puzzled that she could ignore every single attempt to break down her guard.

Rebecca had lain in the grave for four and a half years. The little boys were then ages seven and five. Just after Kinchen told his daddy that the third baby was forming in Ida's womb, Joseph said to Kinchen, careful to be loud enough for her to hear, "Them eh some strong boys, my grandsons. Them eh little mens. They gone to be real mens one day. I sure do hope this next one that she is carryin'. It be a boy, too."

Kinchen shot him a warning look. "Daddy, don't say that. We be glad to love whatever come. You hear me?"

But Ida said nothing.

At the end of that day and in the privacy of their room, Ida bore upon Kinchen, he first sitting on the side of the bed and then lying with one ankle crossed over the other. How many times had she said to him already, "A girl got a heap more complicated body than a boy. Now, when you carry a boy, the midwife tol' me, you get a heap more morning sickness. But with a girl, your body much more out of harmony—"

"*Crock of hog slop,*" Kinchen thought. "*If the girls' bodies so complicated getting formed, that would make the mother sicker. A crock, indeed.*" But he didn't mind.

" —cause she is a machine what is being made inside of me. She be born with all her stuffed inside of her, ready to hold life and carry it and hug it. Not no innards hangin' out. I ain't thinkin' 'bout that old man, pretend like if I have a girl, he goin' to do somethin'." She lowered her gown over her head, giving him enough of a glimpse of her flesh to keep him awake and wish he was the gown whispering down over her. He leaned toward her, ready to reach for her when she finished.

Ida looked at Kinchen. He looked as though he was listening to every word she said. She appreciated that. In fact, he was looking at her shape through the gown and noticing the swelling of her waist and thinking of the months ahead of positioning himself around the obstruction of her belly.

"The girl, the girl woman, she is the door that life pass through. And it don't make no difference—"

Here it comes, he thought.

"—what the menfolk say, not one of y'all come in this world 'cept through that door."

As soon as she shut her mouth, he would enter that door. He needed to get in and out before one of the little buggers dragged tiny footsteps sounding outside the room. That would be followed by "Momma, Papa, I want water," or "I'm scared." If those little feet got outside the door before he climaxed, he might hear, "Momma, what'sa matter with Daddy?"

⁂

The new year, in January of 1926, brought Ida and Kinchen a new baby. They named her Lenore. Joseph stepped up on the porch to get a peep. Ida came to the door, held up a tiny bundle, lifted a blanket flap from the little face. Joseph leaned down and whispered, "Little baby, hope you not got lancet tongue like your mama, else we menfolk goin' to have to get up and get out of here." Ida opened her mouth, sighed, changed her mind about answering him and turned away.

Joseph worked at installing a window in the shed where he had walled up Rebecca's baskets. As Ida walked by one day with Lenore in her arms, Joseph looked up from nailing a board, and with his arms upraised, called out, "Now that won't nothin' but worry some man to death. What you say her name was?"

Ida shot back, "Yes, but she gone be able to feed herself, she might decide to go to some college. Be a schoolteacher don't ya know," and walked down the path, across the field to the Amos house. Doll Amos' baby girl, Rose Amos, had just been born, two weeks younger than this brand-new Lenore. Ida and Joseph needled each other, and the needling became more pronounced each day. They both knew that someday, something would have to give.

⁓★⁓

On the morning of the day that Joseph moved out of the house and into the tool shed for good, he came upon Ida shouting to Kinchen. It was the winter of 1928. He often said that he had known six years of the "reign of Miss Boss Lady." Robert Earl was six and three-quarters, Hart Lee five, and Lenore two.

Ida stood next to the porch talking to Kinchen, waving her arms. "Your daddy, that man is a dirty dog!!! Killed my cow!!"

"Now, Ida, I don't think you should call my daddy names in front of the children." Kinchen held two fingers in front of his lips and pointed to Robert Earl, Hart Lee, and Lenore.

Ida pulled Lenore protectively in front of her and grabbed her hand. Robert Earl stood on one side of her, Hart Lee on the other. Ida lowered her voice and repeated herself, pushing her words though her teeth. Then she said:

"That maggot. Your daddy done killed my cow." She raised her voice, pleading, "Don't you care?"

Kinchen looked over her shoulder at Joseph.

Joseph rubbed his scalp with the balls of the fingers of both hands. *When had he last seen the woman's cow?* he asked himself. That silly cow that had been tied to the wagon with a rope on the children's wedding day seven or eight years ago. Earlier that day? Or was it the day before? What day was it? He had thrown away some bean hulls after shelling butter beans. He looked at Ida and then at the children. The six-year-old Robert Earl stood looking from his mother to his father and then over his shoulder at Grandfather Joseph. Five-year-old Hart Lee was, like John Rob, moving only his shining, snapping pairs of eyes. They both waited. Joseph thought they looked like they were watching some kind of show. Only Lenore ignored the fight; she straddled Miss Boss Lady's hip, concerned with only her world, chewing her fingers as though it were work as serious as cooking or sewing.

Ida spotted Joseph. She turned. "You short, sawed off—"

"Not so loud, Ida. The children."

"Well, they got a stupid granddaddy. I don't see how we gone keep it from them. The bowlegged midget. You done killed my cow." She walked. Her two children trudged behind. She bore Lenore.

Joseph thought about the daughter-in-law who, as a bride, had not come into the house making a racket, but six or seven years later made the rafters rattle in time to her step. He decided that, by the time that woman got back from her walk, he was going to have moved out of what had become her house, the house that his father, Nick, had built. The house that he was going to leave to Kinchen anyway. He did, at least, have the tool shed. He would go there and live with Rebecca's baskets.

She turned back to Kinchen and, as he was coaxing her to calm, managed to explain, "He dumped a pan full of butterbean hulls on the ground, next to the fence. All the cow had to do was stick her tongue through the space in the fence. My cow ate every one of them hulls she could reach.

Left enough for me to see. All that green fiber and all the gas in the world. Enough to fill up a barn and bust open a cow's stomach. The cow ate the hulls and got a savage thirst like eatin' salt. But then, all that gas buildup."

The child, Robert Earl, stifled a giggle and wisely covered his mouth with his small hands. Ida snatched him by the shoulder getting instant quiet out of him. "That cow broke loose, runnin' for water, broke her chain and galloped off to the drinkin' trough where she drunk nobody know how many gallons of water. Made her bell swell up to twice its size."

Robert Earl broke in. "Yes, Daddy. She laying out there next to the fence her stomach swolled up grreeaattt big." He made a circle with his arms. "Mama say she dead."

Ida pointed a finger in Joseph's chest. "Yes, and the somebody that killed her was you and you can't deny what I say! Tell me it was not you dump them hulls!"

Kinchen thought for a moment and said, "Well, I'm sure Daddy didn't mean to, did you, Daddy?"

Ida did not wait for an answer. She grabbed little Hart Lee's hand and said to Robert Earl, "Come on, y'all," and tramped off toward the road, probably to visit Doll and tell her of her newest troubles.

"What you lookin' at me for, Papa? Don't worry, Ida always go off, and she will calm down later. Just stay out of her way for a couple of days. She'll forget all about it."

"What do you think I is? In my own house, too. I shouldn't have to hide from no dress tail woman."

"Well, Papa. What you want me to do? She mad at you, not me."

"I see."

"Well? What? You want me to go gainst her? You always say, husband and wife s'posed to be a team."

"Yes, but the husband s'posed to decide for the team, not

some dress tail woman or other. Your dear sweet mama," Joseph saw Kinchen roll his eyes. "My Rebecca, she never crossed me."

"Is that what you and my mama had? A team?"

"I don't like the sound of your question. It is got something cunning and sneaky in it." Joseph waited to see if Kinchen had any more to say.

They had all the time in the world, standing on the porch with Ida and the babies growing smaller in the distance. Flies buzzed noisily. A Rhode Island red rooster strutted up, halted at the sound of snarling voices. He walked hesitatingly by. He passed and rotated the eye that sighted Kinchen and Joseph. Then he dipped his head with each step, step, step, step. When he was past, he resumed his strut.

"Let's take for instance. When my mama wanted me to go to stay with Aunt Vate in the city so I could go to high school, you decided that I couldn't and you made her back up. You was a team then, was you?"

"I made you stay here because of the land. This land. Our land. My grandfather give it to my father, and it go from me to you and then to your boys. And now, you think if you had went, you'd be off in school still like Winston Lockheed? Think about it. He ain't got no land. Just a whole lot of books, I 'magine." Joseph went into the house, collected his things in baskets and boxes, and moved into the shed.

He vowed to never set foot in his ancestral home ever again and experienced two whole days of hunger while Kinchen negotiated with Ida to prepare the old man's meals and let her precious willow patterned plates be taken back and forth across the yard three times a day. Ida had given in fairly early on letting Joseph have his separate meals, but she said that he could use two battered tin cake plates that the children had warped in their play. Kinchen quietly insisted, surprising Ida with his resolve in his refusal to have his father eat off anything other than plates, like a man who was respected in the family he had chosen to move 25 yards away from.

⁓★⁓

In 1929, the Depression hit, just after Ida's remaining cow went dry. They would later remember that that was the year they spent no money on anything. They were glad to have a farm and farm animals and garden vegetables and their own canned goods. While in his first year living in the shelter, Joseph lost his nest egg of $400 when the Rocky Mount Bank went bust.

⁓★⁓

Someone sent Joseph a postcard from up North.

Dear Joe, Times is bad. The bars is closed. Cant even git a legal drink of whisky. Wish I could git a god piece of smoked Ham.   Love, Juju

⁓★⁓

Ida became heavy with her fourth child. Millie was born in November, 1930. In the year of Millie's birth, the price of tobacco plummeted to 15 cents a pound. T and the car and truck remained parked due to the cost of gasoline. Some neighbors hitched oxen and mules to pull gas operated cars. Hoover cars, they were called. In 1933, Ida was told that someone had heard on the radio in Sloane Smith's store that 13 million Americans were unemployed.

CHAPTER SIX

The wind was fretful on the day that Sloane Smith carried a ladder to the rooftop of his house. He placed the ladder against the stout brick chimney, climbed half-way up, and paused for a moment to look around. He saw the pines trembling where the wind ran. He looked up at the sky in anticipation of the rain that the wind was dragging from beyond the forests and fields. He swayed to the beat of the pines and lost himself for a moment.

The next thing he knew, the ladder was going down, collapsing from under him, pulling him with it. The ladder crashed through the roof and through the ceiling of his parlor. His weight dragged him helplessly behind. He and the ladder made a hole in the roof and he was pulled part of the way through. When he stopped, his pain was unspeakable. Thousands of splintery pints of hot cold light. It was nearly a minute before he was able to call. He hoped that the foolish woman would hear.

Inside the house, Clara Smith was already on her way in response to the crashing sound in the parlor. She heard her husband bellow and saw his feet and legs in the ceiling above her head. She trotted in place for a full minute before whirling herself to the outside of the house. She flagged a driver on the road and sent word for her brother-in-law, Nathan, as well as Cecil and Gator, her husband's two farmhands.

"Somebody, tell them to come right away."

Cecil and Gator left their homes to go do a job they didn't want to do, whatever it would turn out to be. Word was that the white landowner had been drinking in the morning before he climbed the ladder to his roof. Cecil and Gator wanted somebody with them who didn't work for Smith and wasn't beholden to the man and his mood swings. A stop at the Cobb place was in order.

Ida Cobb climbed into the truck with Kinchen, in preparation to follow Cecil and Gator's truck to the Smith house. She was dying of curiosity, and this would be a good way to maybe see inside the Smith woman's house. On the way, she wanted to talk to Kinchen about his night meetings.

She was not happy. Kinchen was attending meetings at the county courthouse to hear the deliberations about a proposed high school for the Colored children in the county. She refused to go. The meetings were in the court room. The Colored sat in the balcony. She had been told that at the last meeting, he had risen to his feet and spoken out. She winced at the thought of him having his say in front of all those people, he from the Colored section of the balcony of the court room speaking to glassy-eyed white men. With the white people turning those eyes way up and back, her Kinchen spoke about the educational needs of Colored people and their desires to read newspapers to know when to list taxes and where to take the dogs to be vaccinated. They told her that he had told them how his father, Joseph, paid taxes to the county and worked hard. Had stood up and said it out loud. Ida worried about what she had heard of those meetings. In the truck, she looked at his strong neck.

"Kinchen, you worry me. You so hard-headed. I don't like

you arguin' for the new school. It not safe. Next thing we know, there be a cross burning in our yard."

He held the steering wheel. He had beautiful hands, even the callouses, nice good-sized brown hands. He said nothing while she looked at his hands, sitting beside him where they faced the same way together. No one knew what Kinchen thought very much, unless he decided to tell them. No one decided what he would tell. And this day, he turned her no answer. That was an answer in itself, the refusal to dignify her comments with so much as a twitch, much less a word.

"Kinchen, did you hear me?"

"Yes, Ida. I heard every word you said," he chuckled. "I heard some you didn't say."

She sighed and tried to put her mind on something else. He was the strongest man she knew. *The person who stood up to her but never insulted her*, she thought. They drove into the Smith yard.

She had never actually met the Smith woman, though they passed each other in the seed store and each could identify the other. She was a bent and apologetic woman with watery eyes and trembly fingers. Ida saw from the truck that the woman waited on the porch, waving her arms in the air.

"His brother came and got him. Taken him into town to the doctor. His ankle is swollen up real bad. Got a big old bump on his head. And he bruised and got splinters all over him practically. Is a wonder he didn't kill his self."

Ida wondered why the woman sent her husband off and stayed behind. Clara Smith looked at Ida. "I should have went with him, but it look to me like rain and I got a big old hole in the roof, big enough for a cow to drop through. And besides, I don't do too well round him when he drinking."

She led them into the house and through the hall. She, at every step of the way, wiped her dry hands on her apron. Ida followed at the back of the line, behind the two farm workers and Kinchen. As she walked, she looked about in the long hallway with its huge walnut table piled with magazines and books. They went into the parlor where, in a corner on the floor, lay a broken lamp. A small table stood with its top gashed. The ladder lay above, caught in the hole it gouged open enough for a ten-gallon bucket to sink through sideways. Debris from the roof covered a grape-colored, overstuffed velvet chair next to the table below.

"It was my fault. I want to get far-away stations on the radio. He was putting up a radio antenna I ordered out of the Sears and Roebuck Catalogue. But, I didn't tell him to try to kill his self." She crunched ceiling plaster under her shoes as she pointed up to the peek of sky. The two workers stared hard at her while she talked, but when she looked at them, they each looked down at their own feet. Kinchen looked at her shoulder. Ida looked straight at her face, noticing how lines gleamed around her mouth as she talked.

"I've got to do something tonight before it get dark. Probably all the snakes in the world will want to crawl in here. Or it will rain me out, one or the other." Mrs. Smith turned and looked at each of the three men, one at a time, beaming her helplessness at them. Cecil and Gator looked at each other.

When Kinchen and the two workers climbed the roof, Cecil and Gator whispered to him, begging him to offer his help and leave them out.

"If we have to do it, we don't get paid since we belong to this place. You do it, they will pay you," and then, derisively, "You get to act white, yourself. Everybody talking 'bout you standing up at the courthouse, speakin' out last week."

While they picked up broken splintery chunks of roof, broken poles and piled slabs of tar paper, Gator explained to Kinchen how he and Cecil took great care to not let Sloane Smith know that sometimes they could think and solve problems when they were of a mind. Gator said, "No matter how hard we worked, we ain't gone to prosper."

"Yeah," Gator said. "We even pretent to not know how to read one day, and on another day me and Cecil pretent to misunderstand when Mr. Sloane Smith tol' us to bury some gasoline for safekeeping 'cause of rationing, see. We know full well he meant us to bury the cans with gasoline. We didn't want to dig that deep. We poured it in the ground. That was one way to bury it. He he he he he he he." He stopped to slap his leg, stood up, and fell into another fit of laughter.

Kinchen said, "That is funny. You ought to stop cuttin' the fool. But, I think black folk will suffer more if you really convince white people that we just one step above the animals. All that head scratching and foot shuffling, that is gone come back to haunt us one day. Y'all need to stop." Then he laughed.

When he straightened himself up, he became very serious, for that was when, while Gator went around the house to relieve himself behind a tree, Cecil said, "Don' stop goin' to those meetings. I want my children to have a chance. I want them to leave here and not face a life of sun up, sun down dirt seat and poor. We can't speak up like you. We dependin' upon you."

❦

Ida never did see the radio that Mrs. Smith talked about, but while Kinchen, Cecil, and Gator were covering the roof hole with a tarp wagon cover, Ida idled about just inside the front door. Some white women were funny, and it was their call, not yours, whether they talked to a Colored woman or not. Many were relaxed and friendly as one pleased, as long as no other white people were nearby.

Mrs. Smith suddenly turned to Ida inside that house, smiled, and said, "I hate it happened. It was all my fault. My brother-in-law say if I get the antenna up on the house, I could hear Chicago real clear. That radio keep me company. It talk to me in a house that would be silent except for the breathing and an occasional dog bark. My husband got his books and articles. I am not a reader, myself. I listen to the NBC symphony of WPTF. We protect the family. And then, there is *One Man's Family.* Every day at six o'clock. I stop and sit down."

"You don' think the waves will make you sick?" Ida had come full into the parlor and perched on the corner of the chair nearest the door.

"No worse than smoke from the fireplace, I expect."

"What about when it thunderin' and lightening strikin'?"

"Can't hear above the static in a thunderstorm, that's true. But I don't think it can hurt you. This morning I heard somebody on the radio said that the United States was making a '"marked extension of public secondary education.' I guess it's true, with the county talk' 'bout buildin' a Colored high school."

Ida was careful not to answer.

The day darkened. The rain came. Kinchen offered to return the following day with Joseph to effect a permanent repair to the roof, assuring the hand-wringing woman that she would be fine for the one night.

In the truck on the way home, as the rain fell noisily on the cab of the truck, Ida said, "Her house not clean as mine. All that mess and piles of papers and books all over the parlor and in the hall. Nice furniture. Under all the dust. She don't take care of it, though. Look like ain't been polished since she had it. But one thing for sure, I want me a radio one day."

She sighed and leaned her head back against the window behind the seat.

Kinchen thought about the two Black men telling him that he was almost white, as brown as he was. He thought about the measurement taken by men who were unwilling to allow for any differences, though he felt scarcely different from the two of them. And then, one had gotten him off and apologetically expressed ambitions for his children. He often hunted in the woods for squirrels and deer with Gator and Cecil and, during those times, he had a drink or two out of the same fruit jar, but they in their hearts saw him closer to the white men because of that little piece of land that Joseph owned. Then he asked himself, would he change places with them? Told himself, "No." It was too much to think about.

The next day, in the late afternoon, Kinchen and Joseph got out of the truck in their home driveway. They had spent the day repairing the Smith roof. Joseph carried the tools toward the barn. Kinchen walked slowly, daydreaming it seemed, and suddenly began to whistle a tune. In her mind, Ida rendered the words.

Some glad morning when this life is o'er
I'll fly away.
To that place in God's celestial shore,
I'll fly away.

Then, in the middle of following his mood, she suddenly stopped to think. Kinchen pointed his foot for the porch. She frowned and remembered something. The whistling. Ida walked toward him as though to greet him, raised her arm, and brought her hand down across in a slap to her husband's face. Kinchen unpointed his foot, dropped it, unstretched his reach and touched his thumb to his face. He chuckled and walked backwards, reorienting himself toward the front of the house. He shook his head, but he held his hand to his face and disappeared into the house.

Joseph looked back just in time to see. He dropped his tool bag on the ground and strode fast toward the shed house. He scooted inside and pulled shut his door. He hesitated a moment on the verge of saying something but could not think. This was not a laughing thing.

Millie called from inside, from behind the door of the big house, her head just visible to her mother. "Mama, why you slap my daddy?"

"'Cause he tryin' to get his stupid self killed, that' why."

At great cost to her personal dignity, Ida walked from her house to Joseph's shed house. A little footpath had been worn through the grass, worn by careless feet of carefree children toting plates of ham and cabbage, buttermilk and coffee, collards and shoulder meat, grits and eggs, bringing back dirty dishes, bearing messages and glee for the grandfather. It was a path that she avoided except when plates and glasses were missing from her cupboard. She had a need to talk to the old man, whom she was not in the habit of visiting, in a shed house that she never told him to move into in the first place. She knocked. He opened his door a crack and inhaled.

"Come in."

"No. I can ask you from right here in the doorway." Her thoughts stumbled. She staggered at the notion that her father-in-law lived in a place where, as short in stature as he was, he could not stand up straight. She regained herself to put force in her voice. "Who was at the Smith house with you two?"

"Nobody. Mrs. Smith and us."

"Was you ever separate from Kinchen?"

"Naw. What on your mind, woman?"

"I want to know what happened!"

He took a moment. It was the first time in years that she had stood still in front of him. He thought of the times that he asked her a question and waited. So, he tapped out his pipe. Blew through to clear it. Tapped it against the chair back, careless of the flakes of tobacco that fell to the splintered floor. As he filled tobacco into the bowl, he sighed and said, "Nothin' happened. We fixed the roof. Like you knowed we did."

"Kinchen come home crowin' like a bantam rooster. Tell me what happened! Did he go inside the house?"

He sucked the fire from a jumbo kitchen match, drawing the flame through the hollow of the pipe. "Naw. He work outside." Sucked again. "I went inside. It was me and oh, I forgot. Lela was there. She Mrs. Smith's maid. You know that. She helpin' 'round the house. Why you think somethin' happen?" She was just like Rebecca. "You worried 'bout the white woman?"

Ida had kept up all Rebecca's fears, saved up like a treasure. Rebecca had lived most of the time, as far as white people were concerned, acting like some lone gun-toting woman guarding all the Cobb men from all the white folks in the universe. He tried to gurgle up a chuckle in his throat, but it was air. He sighed. Lela was Colored.

"And what did Lela and Kinchen do?"

"Lela took Kinchen a drink of water several times," he said, thinking, *'she scared 'bout somethin ', sure enough. In her mind, she got Kinchen getting lynched. He scratched his head. But, Lela Colored. She gone to worry that bone some. Even after I tell her, a Colored woman fanning 'round over there got Kinchen excited. I enjoyin' this.'*

"Lela was frisky." He couldn't believe how much he was enjoying this. "She was friskin' round Kinchen. But before God, they didn't do nothin'," thinking again, *'This woman a witch. Mean as the people that whipped Jesus. But she think she know somethin'.'* She might have got his nature up, but ain't nothin' happened. I swear."

"Lela was friskin' 'round Kinchen". What 'bout Mrs. Smith?"

"In the bed, sick. Didn't hardly see her. Neither one of us."

"In the bed drunk, most likely."

But Ida refused to be totally relieved. She shifted from the blinding fear that Kinchen might have looked too long at the white woman and come home whistling because of that, making himself attractive to a rope, and on to the more tolerable fear of a woman like herself. She was happier to have to think about Lela.

She gave it some thought and clapped her hands. "Praise God. I thought he done got worked up over that white woman and was gonna get his self killed. Know what kind of danger that put us in? Had me thinkin' 'bout that hidin' room of Miss Rebecca's inside the house that she had y'all build." She thought for a moment and said, "I ought to slap him again," and left running before Joseph could say anything.

Joseph closed the door of the shed house and thought about white women and education. Either one. Together or separate, so very bad for a Colored man. The two things that made his Rebecca direct the building of the hiding room. Because of white women and education, voting and white people's stuff. Wilmington, North Carolina, a burned black newspaper office, its owner run out of town. For once in his whole life, Joseph agreed with his daughter-in-law, but he had not raised a fool of a son who would try to throw his leg over that Smith woman. He did not even have to think about it anymore. Then, he chuckled about how strange it was for Ida to have to come and knock on his door. He chuckled again at the thought that he almost got her inside.

⁕

The next time Kinchen came home from town, he surprised Ida with a radio, which operated from a car battery and sat on a table. A table model, it called itself on the outside of the box. It was 14 by 18 inches, a cavity for a rechargeable, and RCA Victor one, picturing a little dog leaning toward the front of a funnel.

Ida again and again warned Kinchen about his going to the meetings about the Colored high school for Nova County.

Kinchen said, "You a smart woman. You ought to go with me."

"Kinchen, I is scared. These white people do not want us to have no high school, no ways, no how."

Joseph found himself agreeing with Ida and hoping in his heart that Kinchen would listen. She was scared, Joseph was angry. That childhood friend, Winston Lockheed, they were the ring leaders, meeting with the white people trying to get more schooling in Griffinton, more than the Colored children needed to work on farms.

In February of 1931, Kinchen had come home one evening from a meeting full of laughter. He told how the meeting had lasted until 10 o'clock at night. The lamps had nearly burned out.

"Sloane Smith, he on our side. He made a speech. And you know how much money he got, and his old granddaddy used to be a judge, and his mama's daddy was a colonel in the war. But, get this. His reason, he say, he is sick and tired of dealing with ignorant Negroes. He claim that he tol' Cecil to bury some cans of gasoline in the ground. They poured it into a hole and walked back to him with the empty cans. I didn't have the heart to tell him the Colored men is not as stupid as they pretend, sometime." He shook his head. "Poured it out in the dirt. And handed him empty cans."

Kinchen laughed, holding his middle.

"Is that true?"

"Yeah. They told me 'bout it once. He couldn't a made it up. He told it at a time when old man Woodruff was threatening to turn any sharecropper off his place that had to have a high school education for they children. Sloane told that story and everybody laughed. Anyway, Sloane is givin' the land. Look like the Rosenwald people goin' to put up the building. Either them or the Eastman people from Rochester, New York. Look like it is done. Just got to get the county to pay our teachers."

Ida did not like Sloane's approach to pacifying the other landowners. She knew that her father-in-law paid taxes on his land and that other Colored farmers did the same or contributed out of their hard work for meager compensation. The sharecroppers did not pay taxes, but they poured their sweat into the land, disproportionate to their earnings. It was a shame that there had to be discussion and she had to stay up late every time Kinchen went out to one of the meetings. But, she was relieved that the struggle was nearly over. This one, anyway. Her Robert Earl and Hart Lee, Lenore, and Millie would go to high school! So would the children all around, Doll's boys and Rose.

But in May of that same year, after the plans had been drawn up for the new school, Kinchen discovered that the battle was far from over. He kept to himself the threats and the difficulties and only later told Ida that the Rosenwalds wanted the Negroes to have an industrial high school. He had to convince Sloane Smith to help him convince the county that it was a waste of money to teach people how to sweep and mop. The compromise finally came. The Negro high school could have literary courses and some mathematics and science, only if they took the used books from the white high school. Again, Ida was fearful when Winston told her that he and Kinchen had reminded the white people that the Cobbs and the Amoses were taxpayers, too.

They did not tell Ida that Mr. Woodruff publicly reminded Winston that he lived in town and was meddling. Winston said that he was concerned for his nieces and nephews still in Griffinton and that he had had to leave Griffinton to go to high school.

There was nothing on the radio about the new high school that the Cobb children would attend. Joseph was furious about the new high school keeping children away from the farm work, and he could find no one to listen except those popeyed children who ran and played and gave him no answer when he told them they would get more stupid the more book learning they got.

⌑

On November 4, 1936, Ida heard on the radio that Roosevelt was elected president of the United States by a landslide, defeating Alf Landon. She said to her husband and children, "I'm so happy. If we could vote, that is exactly who we woulda voted for. He got a nice wife. They say the only states that went for Landon was Vermont and Maine. I don't know nobody live there. Maybe that's how come."

Robert Earl asked, "How come Daddy don't vote?"

"Don't be foolish. He don't vote 'cause he a Colored man in North Carolina. They won't let him. I don't vote 'cause I a woman, ain't I?"

⌑

The radio said that an anti-lynching bill failed in Congress in 1935, the commentator jubilant in his report. Ida said she knew all along that it never had a chance, and she thought of Rebecca Brake Cobb and wondered idly where that closet of a hiding room was located.

Ida was listening to the radio when the news came that the Colored Jesse Owens won four gold medals in Berlin that Adolf Hitler refused to salute him for. Kinchen said that the radio news made Ida nervous when she cried over the hanging of Colored Rainey Bethea in front of 20,000 people. By 1937, Kinchen, with his lap full of children, was listening to boxing and cheering Joe Louis, with Joseph sitting in a chair outside under a window, listening and cheering when Louis knocked out James Braddock.

The next thing Doll and Ida knew, the baby girls, Rose and Lenore, were out of their arms, off their laps and walking away by themselves, wandering off. The mothers had to stand up, shade their eyes, and peer into the horizon to find the slips of red, yellow, stripes, polka dots, or gingham carried on little brown pencil legs streaking across the fields. Lenore often tramped across the property line alone to play with Rose, and Rose strode to meet her. The next thing the mothers knew, they were seeing the two little pint-sized girls funneling secrets into each other's ears and getting back giggles.

Doll and Ida, each from her respective porch, watched the two struggle to separate at the day's end. The girls had a way of one walking the other, the old *I'll walk you part the way home, you walk me back*, as they quartered the space, eighthed it, sixteenthed it until finally, pulled away by the mothers' voices, they inched themselves away from each other.

It was just before church. Rose snuck outdoors in her Sunday dress to where Doll later found her tending some things spilling out of her wagon, things that reached eerily into the air. The air was humid and heavy. The morning earth sent up a steam that clouded the vision. But, at the end of the porch, Rose tended three garter snakes, trying against their wills to wrap them in a towel "like babies."

"Oh, my God. Eeeeeeeeeow! Get them things away from here!"

"They won't hurt you, Mama."

"Them things venomous."

"No. Daddy taught me how to tell. He told me ain't but

four venomous snakes in the whole Nunited States Merica. Want me to tell you what they is?"

"No. Missy. I want you to take your hips back inside and wash your nasty hands and get on in this car so we can go."

Rose rushed past her grandmother, who laughed in the doorway. She called to Rose's back, "Put some Vaseline on your little ashy legs, too, little girl."

Daddy sat in the driver's seat waiting to go, with Rose's three brothers in the back seat.

At church, during devotional, Miss Annie Boston stood up and tearfully announced that she had something to tell the whole church. Gripping the back of the bench in front of her, she said:

"Church. I don' 'spect to be here with y'all next year this time. Praise the Lord." She buckled at her knees and then straightened herself. "The Lord is got a place for me up in heaven and I am goin' home to glory. This time next year I will be gone from here. And I will see my mother and my father. Lord de mercy."

She sat down and led a song. *Soona willa be done with the troubles of the world, troubles of the world.* She waved her arms in the air above her head and sat down sobbing as the congregation concluded, troubles of the world, *troubles of the world, troubles of the world.*

Rose Amos rolled her eyes, not at anyone or for anyone to see. A message to herself. Her best friend, Lenore, was at the opposite end of the bench. The schoolteacher, Miss Bright, saw the eye rolling and primped up her mouth in disapproval. It felt good, though, to Rose, to roll her eyes back and tell herself that the grown people were at it again. She was 11 years old, for gracious sakes, but hadn't Miss Annie promised to die last year when Rose was 10? Certainly she had said something about going on her trip to heaven when Rose was nine.

The old women were sobbing in the Amen corner. Again. They were sobbing before Miss Annie got up to testify. Now, Miss Atline stood up from among them. Everybody knew that Miss Atline's husband started drinking every Friday at six o'clock in the evening and drank on and on until that Sunday at four-thirty. That was every week that the Lord sent. Everybody thought that either Miss Atline cried on Sunday at church because he was drunk or she cried about what made him drink, but Rose thought it was because she was old, because Rose's grandmother cried on Sunday in church too.

Rose kept up a wiggling motion even though her mother said every Sunday, "You is gettin' big enough to sit still in church." Rose had to do something other than just sit there and watch Grandmother Tab cry.

She had asked herself many times. "How come? How come you cry in church all the time? And the other old ladies." All she could get was something about God made her so happy. Well, if she was happy, why was she crying?

Miss Atline was telling the church how God was so good. How he brought her so much joy. Rose didn't think God talked to children. But, something he had said caused a joy she did not want to know about.

Rose sat next to her mother, Doll. On the other side was Miss Ida and Lenore. As usual, Lenore and Rose had started out side-by-side, before the missionary part of the service. After a time of whispering behind their hands and snickers spilling over, the two mothers looked at each other and, on cue, stood up and separated the girls. On the same bench were Mrs. Battle and her bad little boys who kept kicking the bench, causing her to swat at their legs with her fan.

Rose's grandmother stood up to testify about how much she loved Jesus, who had thoughtfully and gently roused her from sleep, clothed her right mind, and brought her once more and again to church. Rose smiled, thinking, *it was Daddy who brought us to church, for gracious sakes.* And then she hoped that her grandmama Tab would not promise to die. Suddenly, she itched all over and tried to scratch her own back, causing her mother to take her hand.

When the preacher preached, Rose likely never realized that she did not hear a single word he said from the pulpit. She thought of Lenore's grandfather, Joseph, telling her about the hidden room. A hidey-hole, he called it. Miss Bright had said, for an assignment for overnight, "Draw me anything you want, as long as it is real." Lenore drew a stove and a pot boiling over on it. Rose decided to draw her best friend's house. She had looked at it so much. It reminded her of a lady's head with the windows for eyes: the front door the nose, the front steps the lady's mouth. And then, that one room up top was the lady's hat. She had measured the outside by putting her feet heel to toe and walking it off for no reason. That was what Mr. Joseph caught her doing. Walking it. Then he told her to do the same thing inside the house, making allowances for walls inside. She wasn't careful in her count until he told her there was some hidden space. She said to him, "Come show me."

He was ducking a blow. "Naw. Naw. Naw. Ain't been in that house since before that gal Lenore was a baby. Ain't never goin' to set foot in Miss Boss Lady's house."

It sure was fun finding that room. Lenore didn't know about the room, either, until Rose told her. It was upstairs in the room where Robert Earl and Hart Lee slept. Two narrow heads at one end, each under the eaves. At the other end, in front of a window, an oak table sat on top of a piece of linoleum. Rose and Lenore put their narrow shoulders to the job and pushed together to move the table. They lifted the linoleum. Rose pried up the timber with a screwdriver and, lying on their stomachs, they looked into a perfect closet with no door except from above where they looked down from. They squealed with laughter that day.

Later, Rose asked Mr. Joseph, "What is that room for? The hidden room?"

"It was built to help my wife get over nightmares." He hurried away without looking back.

His wife must be the dead woman, Lenore's dead grandmother. Rose thought about her own dreams. She dreamed of flying through the air like a bird. Sometimes, she dreamed of trains. A few times, the train had gotten too close and had run over her. She awoke with an ache in her legs. She had some bad dreams, but she couldn't remember them. Other than the train coming at her. She wondered how somebody would need a closet that opened at the top, hidden from view, to get over a bad dream. Her own grandmother Tab said that bad dreams were caused by what you ate. These thoughts made the church bench hard against her backside. Rose shifted her weight and sighed, pulling her hand away from her mother.

Everybody was getting up to take their money to the collection table at the front of the church in front of the pulpit. With the sermon over, Lenore slipped past her mother and squeezed in next to Rose. They put their hands to their mouths and did audible shrugs, lost in the song that the congregation sang. "*By and by, when the morning come. All the saints of God are coming home. We will tell the story.*"

Clutching the pennies that came warm from their daddies' hands, the girls stood up, making sure the hems of their dresses were not caught in the splits of their behinds, brushing the backs of the skirts downward. Rose's legs were slippery with Vaseline and felt so good that she walked knock-kneed, feeling the sleekness of herself. They had talked the day before, and both were wearing pink. They walked in the line to the collection table and back to their seats for the benediction.

Outside, the word was passed that next Saturday, all day long or as long as it took, the church people would gather to clean the cemetery. Rose and Lenore looked at each other, visualizing the good outdoor cooked soup and plenty of cakes and pies that would be had.

That Sunday, on the church grounds before going home, the parishioners began a long and tedious argument about a newcomer to Griffinton. Lila Belle Coppage had built a little cinder block house on two acres of land and moved to what was back home for her husband. They had two children, a teenaged boy and a toddler of a girl. She alone worshiped for the first time that day. The argument, begun that day, was about whether or not she was pretty, causing the people to leave the Sunday services in great confusion and agitation.

On the church grounds parking lot, grandmama Tab was shaking hands and laughing. No one would know that she had sobbed minutes before. Rose decided she was going to keep on asking why she and the other old women came to church dressed up in their Sunday clothes, wearing hats, calm as you please, and sat down and wept, knocking their hats off their heads, dropping glasses off their faces and scaring her.

Rose's daddy pinched her at the back of her neck. "Get in the car, Sugar Foot."

They didn't go straight home but stopped at the driveway next to their own, at the Cobb house. Rose and Lenore galloped off into the house, using all the energy that they had been keeping pent up in church. The grown people stayed outside, the men leaning on the gate at the hog pen looking at Mr. Kinchen's hogs, while the women surveyed Miss Ida's vegetable garden.

Lenore and Rose ran on into the front room, and Lenore decided to turn on the radio while in motion. She swung by it two times. On the third turn, she caught the dial, twisting as she swiped but not quite letting the dial go in time. She dragged the radio off the bookshelf, and it crashed to the floor with a clang.

"Oh, my God. Mama goin' to kill me." Lenore looked down at how the dial had stayed in her hand. The battery was out of the cavity, and it looked as though the wires had come loose. "What must we do?"

"My gracious. I don't know. Wait. Wait. Let's try to fix it. Set it up. Okay. Okay. Now push the battery back in. It so big, big as a car battery."

"Rose, it won't go."

"Lenore. Wait a minute. Wait a minute. Your mama got any glue?"

"I don't think so. Do, I don' know where it is. You got any at your house?"

"Naw. What we got to do, we got to get it to stick together just enough so you walk in, it don' look broke. Then your mama turn it on, it fall apart, she think she done it."

Just then, one of Lenore's brothers, Hart Lee, came through. He thumped Lenore on the back of the head, eliciting an "OW!" and passed on through.

It was Lenore who got the idea that she explained: "Open the window, pull the curtain back and make it look like the wind did it and—"

Hart Lee was coming back through and said the words that chilled Rose and Lenore. "What is y'all doin'? You done broke Mama's radio, I'm goin' to tell," and he was gone.

"Rose. Help me. My mama's goin' to kill me. Don't you think? I need to hide."

They looked at each other. Looked at the radio and flew up the stairs. Rose was glad she was strong. Once Lenore got down in that hold, she was going to have to pull the table back over the linoleum by herself.

Ida Cobb knocked on the door. That was not unusual, but what Doll read in her face told her that something was wrong. "What's the matter with you? You look awful."

"Looking for Lenore. Is she here?"

"Naw. I haven't seen her since we left your house. Come to think of it, she didn't come to the car with Rose when we left. Anything the matter?"

"I got some talk for her. She broke my radio and ain't said a word. Hart Lee told me. Right after y'all left. She not in her room." She twirled around and went back out the door without so much as a goodbye nod.

Forty-five minutes later, Ida was back. She looked more worried than before. "We can't find her nowhere."

"Well, what you lookin' at me for? She not here."

"How you know? With that Rose of yours, runnin' 'round like a wild deer."

Doll pointed to the outside. "Rose is sittin' there in the doorway of the barn makin' cat's cradle out of string."

"And don't you think she mighty quiet?"

They looked at each other and flew toward the outside where Rose sat.

Doll got a little irritated with Ida. Ida was her friend, and they had raised their children side-by-side for the past 17, 18 years. Lord knew, Doll's children were not perfect, but neither were those heathens that Ida was raising. Those boys were something else. That Robert Earl. Already there were rumors about him. It seemed as though he was going for an award in seeing how many girls he could get pregnant. She and Ida had talked about it. At least, Doll had listened to Ida talk about how none of the babies were his. As for Hart Lee, everybody knew that he had a temper, as a little fellow was always fighting and crying when he was younger. Now, he walked with a swagger and seemed to want to go for bad. If Ida had not looked so worried, Doll would have suggested that Miss Lenore was playing one of her games and maybe needed a good swat. How many times had Ida said that if Rose were her child, she would skin her alive.

With those thoughts, Doll stepped outside with Ida. She was beginning to feel Ida's concern, whether she wanted to or not. The two mothers hurried together to the corn crib where Rose sat on the step untangling string. "Rose. Is you seen Lenore? Her mama is mighty worried."

Rose put down her string, crossed her fingers behind her and said, "Not since I left your house, Mrs. Ida."

"She didn't sneak home hiding in the car with you?"

"Nome." She picked up her string and wrapped it deftly around her fingers.

Doll looked hard at Rose and stayed staring at her while Ida ran back toward her own house. Then Doll followed. It took a moment to catch up. "Don't worry, Ida, it ain't like we live on a busy street in Rocky Mount 'round a whole passel of bad people. She safe enough."

"Naw. She somewhere hidin'. She will come out sooner or later. But where could she be?"

They searched all the barns, smokehouses, looked under the tractor, under the wagon, in the mule stables and the cow barn, under the house, behind every building, shrub, tree, in the pantry, in the boys' room, under all the beds. Finally, Ida concluded that since both Kinchen and Gass were gone, maybe she had slipped off with them in Kinchen's truck. "Where is the menfolk when you need them?"

Doll went home to wait. She saw Rose take down the dictionary and start looking at pages with unusual interest. She saw that Rose was quiet and not worried. She decided to watch her. "Rose, come in the kitchen with me. Don' go out of my sight."

She put several fists full of corn meal into a bowl, broke open an egg, added milk and stirred.

"Okay. Tell me 'bout venomous snakes. How you tell."

Rose stood in the doorway, watching night come on. Wishing that she could get a glass of water to Lenore, who was probably tired of standing up all this time since she had been hiding since three o'clock, and now it was seven. She couldn't remember what her father had said. But Doll was insisting. "Tell me. Go ahead. About the venomous snakes."

Rose was very preoccupied and disconnected. "Somethin' 'bout, what was it? Red beside yellow, run from the fellow, red beside black, put that fellow in your sack."

"Where is she, Rose?"

"Last time I seen her, she was in they house."

"Is that the truth?"

"Yes, mam." She kept her fingers crossed behind her back.

"Well, she ain't there now. And all afternoon you have not asked to go see her, how come?"

Rose heard her father outside and ran toward him to escape further questions. Her mother was busy getting the bread in the oven. Rose was desperate to get away to try to get back in the Cobb house and up the stairs to check on Lenore and see if she was ready to come out.

Doll watched her circling outside, circling like she had springs inside her.

When darkness came, Ida Cobb sat herself down in her front room in the chair next to the broken radio and cried. Doll sent Rose to the Cobb house with a message: *"Don' worry so much, it not huntin' season."* She hurriedly brushed the tears away when the child Rose came into the room with Doll's message. Ida did not see Rose tiptoe upstairs.

Hart Lee made kissing sounds at Rose on the stairs. "What you doin' goin' upstairs to my room? Where me and Robert Earl sleep? Want me to come wit cha? You want me to put my key in your lock, little 'oman?"

He tried to grab her. She got away. He followed behind, on her heel with her swatting back at him as if she would a fly. She was very determined with what was on her mind. Plus, he was not a grown person, just bigger. It was only the grown people you had to do what they said.

She was in Hart Lee's and Robert Earl's room. He walked slowly toward her with a stupid grin on his face. She knew that boys liked to try to get their fingers under girls' dresses. She stamped her feet. "Stop it, stupid. Help me move this table."

He licked his lips. He looked like a tree all knotted up, those muscles in his arms and back. He had eyes dark and empty like a fish. She pointed to the table. He looked at it in surprise as though he didn't know it was there. Then, he made a big to-do of picking it up. He held it for a second and placed it a few feet back. She fell to her knees and plucked at the corner of the piece of linoleum. It was old and cracked. Pieces fell away. She slid it aside.

"What you doin'?"

"Don' ask. You'll see."

Lenore called, "Hurry up."

Hart Lee jumped. "Where you at?"

Rose had gotten the linoleum up.

"What you doin'?"

Lenore called, "Hurry up."

Rose was prying at the timbers with a screwdriver that she took from her pocket. She and Hart Lee could see the top of Lenore's head.

Hart Lee asked her, "How you know this hole was here? What Lenore doin' in there? What y'all up to? I'm gonna tell."

"That's right. You tell everything you know. Like a crybaby."

Hart Lee frowned, and Rose knew that he would be too proud to tell anything if it made him feel less like a man. She pushed a little more, then said: "You just a big ol' cry baby."

He was not going to bother her. At least, not this day.

Lenore was pulling herself up out of the room. "Help her out, stupid."

"This a hidin' place. How you know it here, you two?"

Your granddaddy show me. He know a lot of things."

"That old man. I never talk to him."

"Don't you like him? I told you, you stupid." Rose stuck out her tongue and turned back to Lenore, who was pulling herself up out of the hole. Crying. Shaking. Lenore's hair was soaking wet. Her clothes hugged damply all over. Then she was out. Rose heard Doll calling her to come home. She clambered down the stairs and ran out of the house and took her shortcut across the field.

When Ida saw Lenore, she allowed herself to believe the ridiculous tale of her having fallen asleep in the barn under a piece of wagon cover. Ida could not remember ever having been so scared for five or six hours, not since she was living with her grandfather. Then, there was the condition that Lenore was in, soaked in her own sweat in her clothes and hair, agitated and unhappy. Ida could not verify that anyone had looked under the wagon covers during the search. She was not thinking about the radio, but instead thinking about how hard it was to be a mother. She forgot herself and later smiled at her father-in-law for no reason.

Doll drove Ida to town to pick up her radio from the repair shop. When she came to the car, Doll asked, "Did you try it out?"

"No. I probably should, but I didn't like bein' in there with him. He say it worked. He guarantee his work."

That was in the morning. Doll was hanging up clothes at the line when she saw Ida getting into the truck with Hart Lee at the wheel. Ida called out to her. "That man ain't fixed my radio. I paid $2.50 and I turned it on. The dial fell off and it don' make a bit more noise than a grain of sand."

Doll agreed and waved her off, but inside she thought, *Ida, be careful.*

But they were gone.

⌒⋆⌒

Ida showed Hart Lee where to turn in. The repairman worked out of the garage of his house. Ida walked up the steps, telling Hart Lee to wait in the car. For some reason, Hart Lee got out and followed his mother, but at some distance behind. Ida never looked back and was not aware of his having followed her. She knocked on the screen and then lifted the outside latch. She held the radio in one hand, her receipt in the other.

"You said you guaranteed your work. This radio don' work. You either fix it or give me my money back."

She had one foot stepping up, the other behind her on the lower level of the outside. The repairman suddenly ran toward her and blocked her way in.

"Git the hell out of my place. I never seen you before in my life."

Ida stumbled back, got her balance, pushed against him, and got herself inside. It was crowded in there, with all the appliances stacked on tables and some hanging on the far wall. She set the radio down on the floor, so she could shake the receipt in the air for him to see. "I was just here this morning. Picked up this radio. This here is my receipt."

The next thing she knew, the repairman had pulled the

receipt out of her hand and was tearing it into bits. Ida sprang for him, a move that got her even farther into the room. The repairman dropped the torn pieces and started to look around as though he were for all the world looking for something to hit Ida with. That was what she later realized, what he had looked like, and what it must have looked like to Hart Lee. Hart Lee, it turned out, was all the way into the room with them. He believed the repairman was about to hit his mother. He looked around in all that junk and saw a two-by-four plank, picked it up and swung it like a baseball bat above the man's head. The man backed away, his arms above his head.

Ida saw that he looked terrified. She grabbed Hart Lee and pushed him out the door. Ran back, picked up her radio. She and Hart Lee, once outside, ran to the truck while she asked, "Boy, what did you think you were doin' in there?"

"What the matter with you? You think I goin' to stand still while a white man hit my mama?"

He accelerated into the street just as the repairman ran out of the garage shop, suddenly having gained courage to shake his fist in the air and calling, "Niggers, you had better run. I will kill you, Nigger bitch, and that boy of yours, too."

⁂

Joseph hitched up one of the mules to the wagon. The wagon was empty except for a hoe, rake, pick, and shovel. He started out of the driveway. Ida called from the house.

"Stop, Mr. Joe. Kinchen say he not goin'. You know, he don't never like to visit Miss Rebecca's grave. I and the girls ride with you in the wagon."

He said, "Yeah," and waited for her to climb in. "It too far to walk the five miles. But wouldn' you rather have Hart Lee drive you in the truck?"

He thought, *She must want to go pretty bad to have to ask me for a ride.*

"Naw. I don' want Hart Lee to take me nowhere."

She arranged herself in the wagon and sat on the horizontal board next to Joseph. Lenore and Millie faced backwards, legs dangling from the back. Joseph clicked his tongue and gently shook the line. The mule ambled good-naturedly along, was turned and headed for the church yard. "What did happen to you and Hart Lee yesterday? I mean to ask."

He was thinking, *You have never tol' me. I would have had to ask Kinchen.*

"I took the radio back and complained, and that mean old white man tried to hit me. Hart Lee taken a two-by-four to the man. I had to pull him out o' there before he hit him and we run for the truck and drove out o' there like there was a fire comin' behind us."

Joseph laughed. He enjoyed thinking how much fun it would have been to see someone, anyone, threaten Miss Boss Lady.·

"It ain't funny. He called me out of my names, and talked all up under my clothes."

Joseph swallowed laughter and admitted to himself that, for this one time, Ida was to be pitied. But, for a moment, he enjoyed Miss Boss Lady getting her due. Then, he thought about the white man. "Ida. Do he know where you live?"

"Who?"

"The radio repairman."

"Naw. I ain't never give him no address or even my name. Why?"

"Jus' wonderin'."

"Naw. He ain't hardly gone be able to come after Hart Lee. Naw, this be the last we hear of that radio repairman."

He started to say, "You don' know white men," but he and his daughter-in-law were not in the habit of having conversations that lasted more than one or two words. Yet, for the only time in his life, he hoped she was right. He slapped the reins on the mule's back and put him into a trot. Light giggles emitted from the girls behind them.

They arrived at the place where many had buried their dead, where the sun fell in long, gentle angles—a scene from the late 1930s, when the town still wispered about old ghosts and newer sins. A dozen or more families in their working clothes, some who had brought small bushes and shrubs, were ready to clear away runaway vines and briars to clean off the graves. Before they began to work, the families formed a circle and allowed Deacon Jones to lead them in prayer. During the prayer, Joseph stood a little apart, straightened himself, and with eyes wide open looked up at the sky; it was his way of letting them know that he was not participating. They had heard him say how he thought that people banding together to question God and beg was unseemly.

Doll Amos was there with Rose. Rose and Lenore skipped to get as far away from grown people as they were allowed.

As they worked, Ida told of her adventure with the radio repairman and how her radio was still needing fixing. That she was out of the money for the bad repair. She ended with, "Now that I look back on it, it is funny. But at the time, it won't."

Doll and the women assured her, "You was right to get out of there. White men is not to be trifled with. God knows."

They pulled up grape vines that were pulling down tombstones, dug up poison ivy and wire grass.

The children gathered a little way off from the graves.

"All men and women do it," said one little girl who lived in a two-room house with flimsy walls.

They formed a circle, arms linked, heads touching in the middle, huddled together, shuffling secrets to pass while the grown people tried to cut back the forest that was encroaching on the dead. The girls conferred together on a great riddle. They were varied ages of 10, 11, and 12-year-olds, and their skin tones ranged from high yellow to deep, dark brown. There were six of them. They were long-haired, short-haired, and one was freckled.

One child said, "All men and womens do it they get by themselves."

Another child said, "The husbands and wives do it, and a lot of times, people do it what ain't married to each other, but not kin people." She shook her head solemnly. "It bad for kin people to do it together."

A child of sharecroppers who lived in a one-room house, the rooms sectioned by burlap curtains, contributed her knowledge. She whispered, "I watch through a crack in the curtain and I seen the insurance man doin' it to Mama. It look like a fight. And it look like the insurance man won. I was cryin'. Thought he was hurtin' my mama."

The girls all had eyes too big for their heads. She reassured them, "No. She wasn't hurt or nothin'. When he was finished, he had his head down for a long time like was sick and weak."

They concluded it had something to do with men pissing inside women, and for some reason, women didn't seem to mind.

The circle broke into smaller cliques. Rose and Lenore walked off and exclaimed together, "I don' believe it. That's too nasty."

"You don' know nothin'."

"You don' know nothin' your own self."

They were annoyed because they had no stories to tell about their mothers and fathers in the roomy houses they lived in compared to the others. They confessed to each other, there was no way their daddies would do anything as nasty as the girl had talked about. Not anymore. But, they were here and were their parents' children. Standing atop some sunken graves, they admitted to each other that their parents, God forbid, must have done it a long time ago. Yeah. Maybe 12 or 13 years ago. But Millie was only seven. Lenore started to laugh.

"What?"

"I was thinkin' bout Granddaddy, Joseph."

"Yeah."

"I can't picture him doin' it."

"Well, how your daddy get here then?"

"You shut up."

"No, you shut up."

In another part of the cemetery, someone picked up the thread of what was becoming a favorite topic and part of a long and tedious argument among Black residents in Griffinton regarding the Coppage family, particularly Mrs. Lila Belle Coppage. At this time, some Griffinton residents had not figured out that she was the area's newest bootlegger. They would all know soon. In the meantime, men and boys mumbled oaths at each other, indicating that she was the prettiest woman they had seen walking.

One elderly man, who had seen her at church on Sunday, having suddenly looked up and seen her standing under a tree, was speechless on the steps leading out of the church and had to be forced by an impatient push on his shoulder to move, to grant space to those behind him. He then had to be helped down the steps by the owner of the hand. One of the deacons this day at the graveyard cleanup said, as though he was making a confession, "Every move she make is pretty," recalling how she had crossed the parking lot after pausing under the tree and fingering a cigarette that she seemed to have decided not to smoke.

The women agreed among themselves that she was "a witchy woman." Several little girls who overheard her name as the topic of grown people's conversation remembered how she had put one hand on one thin hip and swayed slowly, and they thought of the patent leather high heeled shoes, the red silk dress that squeezed the waist, white gloves edged in lace along the wrists, jet black straight hair parted on one side, nearly covering one eye with the swirl of a bang.

A fat man who remembered said, "She can make a man steal."

But it was Ida Cobb who said, "I don' know myself, but she look to me like just a whore, seem like. Or, maybe she look more like a hant."

Doll Amos whispered to Ida, "I looked at her good at church on Sunday. And it look to me like she didn' have on no drawers."

The women spread the food in the bed of someone's wagon at midday. A soup had been cooked in the open, in a huge black pot, containing tomatoes, okra, chicken, beans, peas, macaroni. Good to be soaked up in cornbread. Eaten in bowls. Sweet potato pies, coconut cakes, and someone had brought a tin of tea cake cookies.

The old men started their sentences with, "Remember the time," and told of the things forgotten that the time among tombstones had aroused from memory. There was a deliberate attempt to dredge up bizarre and humorous memories by the dozen. Men and women who stood upon ground that had caught so many sorrowful tears. No one cried this day. They put their shoulders together, tidying up the graves, like a great making up of rumpled beds, communally.

"I remember the time when we was diggin' the grave for old Mrs. Burt, the white lady. In the private family graveyard. Won't but two buried there. Old Lockheed was still livin' then. Old Lockheed got down in that 'ere grave to square it off inside. From outside, couldn' see nothin' but the top of his head. Dunk's ol' dog seen the top of his head and went squirrel huntin'. He he he. That dog took a runnin' jump, fell in the grave with Lockheed."

The men ha-ha-ha'ed together as the womenfolk handed them bowls of soup. They laid aside axes, picks, and blades, and, with their hats under their arms, partook.

"Yeah. I remember. Lockheed come up out o' hat grave

like he didn't have no legs. Bouncin' like a rubber ball."

"Yeah. Dog thought he seen a squirrel. Hair on top of Lockheed's head."

"Yeah. Lockheed had hair then. By the time he died, was baldheaded."

"Was so much noise, like to had to close Griffinton down that day. People was laughin' all over this county."

Mrs. Boston, having been reminded of her own mortality, started a song. *This world is not my home. I'm just a passing through. If heaven's not home, then Lord what will I do.* The small children ran and played. Boys pulled the hair of the girls, popped with sticks, and generally displayed the discomfort that boys feel for the opposite sex as they grow. The girls aired their tongues, threw stones and taunted.

Adults shouted, "Stop runnin'."

"Stop kickin' up that dust."

"Don' run on the graves."

"Show respect for the dead, else tonight they come and get you."

Doll took Rose to plant a berry bush next to the headstone that read: BURL AMOS, BORN ABOUT 1830, DIED 1900. "This is your ancestor. He is the one who walked 140 miles lookin' for freedom and came back here 'cause he said he didn' see anything that looked like it."

Ida beckoned Lenore and Millie to where Joseph had planted a cactus plant and was kneeling, smoothing the dirt. "This grave here, this your grandmother, Rebecca. Born 1880. Died 1922. Wife. Mother."

"This Granddaddy Joseph's wife," Lenore said.

Millie frowned. "That's Daddy mother. Where is yours?"

"My what?"

"Your mother."

"I don' know where my mother is."

"How can you not know?" Lenore asked.

Ida thought for a moment and then demanded, "Shut up, both of you," and walked away.

⌘

Rose said, "Daddy. You don't never take me fishin'. How come I can't go huntin' like my brothers?. I'm tough. I ain't scared of nobody. I can beat Matthew's brains out right now if l wanted to." She caught her breath. "I don' want to learn how to sew. Sewing is for stupid girls." Her father did not answer, so Rose caught Matthew's side with a tobacco stick, then ran. When Matthew chased, Rose called out, "Daddy, help me!"

Gass sat in a ladder-back chair in the doorway of the barn, filing an ax head. "Now, Matthew, I done tol' you boys not to hit your little sister. She a girl and your sister."

Rose had run to the house for cover and peeped out from behind her father's chair at Matthew who complained, "Rose, you is a bully, 11 year old. Daddy, it is not fair. How come you never see her when she hit me? You always look just after when I'm just getting' reach to try to kill her."

"Alright, Rose, stop hittin' the boys." Doll sneezed, nearly losing her balance because she was laughing at the same time. "And don' wipe you nose on your sleeve."

Matthew stood next to his father and mouthed the words, "I'm gonna get you."

Gass said, "You need to act your age, Rose. Boys, go untie the goat and let him chew some of the grass in the front yard."

"Daddy, how come Rose don' have to do no kind of work?"

Rose stuck out her tongue from her place behind her father as a shield.

"You don' never have to wash dishes."

"If I did, wouldn' take all day like you do."

Gass looked toward the sound of Rose's voice. "Rose, where you at? Come sit on my lap."

Rose reappeared from her corner of the house, frowning. "Naw, Daddy, the boys don' sit on your lap." She walked toward him. "Take me squirrel hunting. I'm big enough now. I'm almost 12."

"No. Not a place for a girl." He watched until she got beside him and pulled her to him and tried to hug her. She squirmed and leaned away from him. "What's that? Somethin' wigglin' in your pocket?"

He held her at arms' length, but holding tight so that she could not get away. He thrust his hand into the pocket of her dress and came out with a fidgeting garter snake.

Doll made an involuntary groan. "Now, that's what I mean. Why can't you play with dolls like other girls?"

Doll quickly went into the house. Rose turned to glare at her mother's back, annoyed at her lack of enthusiasm for the little reptile as it got out of Gass' hand and flopped to the ground. It zipped away with Rose chasing after it, running across the yard, into the fields.

An hour later, Doll stood in her yard and shaded her eyes. She searched the horizon for the girl. The child was barefoot, and Doll hoped that she would not step on a rusty nail or cut her foot running over a piece of glass. She spotted Rose and thought of a wild doe, beautiful from a distance. She beckoned Rose home.

When Rose was 12-and-a-half, she woke up one morning in a pool of blood in her bed. She cried out, "Mama, I think I'm dyin'!"

She expected her mother to bring a fear to match her own, but she heard instead a belly laugh. Doll tore up a bed sheet to make napkins and smiled. She said something over and over and each time she said it, she stilled her hands and nailed Rose to the bed with a look.

"You is becomin' a woman now. You have got to stay away from boys from now on. And stop all your runnin' and rippin' around all over creation like a wild deer."

Rose made up her mind then, lying there bloody and shivering from shame and fear, she was not ready to become a woman yet. She would skip alone as before, even if she had to wait three to seven days. She did not trust everything grown people said. All the girls went to each other for truth and wisdom. They had the advantage of pooling all the observations of all the parents and old people and coming up with conclusions. When Lenore showed up, Doll told her that Rose was sleeping. On Monday morning, Lenore slapped Rose when she found out that Rose had gotten her period and said, "I got a better handwritin' than you."

Rose countered, "I knew my fractions and my addition better than you. And I learned my fractions first, too. Plus, you don' have to write pretty to be smart. A whole lot of smart people don' write pretty."

She stuck out her tongue. Lenore turned her head with a snap. They stopped speaking for an entire hour, but walking home together, Lenore took her friend's hand and asked, "Do it hurt?"

CHAPTER SEVEN

On the day that the dentist, Dr. Winston Lockheed, changed his mind about mouth gold, he hastened along a downtown Rocky Mount sidewalk, intent on getting to the liquor store before closing. It was 1934, the first year after Prohibition ended. He passed businesses that were locking up for the day. A throng of farm boys poured in his direction, flowing out of the several tobacco warehouses, gathering and increasing as they came.

What he saw threw him back in his mind to days when he farmed tobacco. He knew it too well—that nasty, attention-grabbing herb. He had planted seeds of tobacco in beds, transplanted the seedlings into fields, cultivated, weeded, fertilized, and cultivated them again. As soon as the stalks grew to be as tall as mannish boys, heavy flowers burst through the tops. The flowers were great clustered blossoms like white rose petals. Winston had topped off the blooms by hand, walking row by row, reaching and sweating, one stalk at a time.

It was tobacco market season. It was a time when crowds took to the streets all day. A market goer brushed Winston's shoulder rushing by. He didn't give it much thought. His mind was far from what took to the pavement around where he stood. He was remembering how the topping off of blooms forced tobacco stalks to send their vitality into the growth of the leaves. He shook his head at the thought. Many a day he had coated his hands in the black bitter gum that accumulated from the plants. Another shoulder brushed him. He realized he had stopped in the way of pedestrians.

Almost all of them were farm youth. Some were boys whose fathers, uncles, or grandfathers had brought flats of cured tobacco leaves to market. The crop was one that they had carried from field to barn for cutting, from barn to warehouse for grading and tying, and finally now to warehouse floors for auction.

Two more boys came toward him and passed by. They wore overalls stained with traces of red mud and black tobacco gum. Winston's grandfather, a former slave, had once showed him a red clay field and said, "When I was a boy, that dirt was black and rich and terraced'ed. You could spit a watermelon seed out your mouth. It grow right up and out the ground. That was b'fore they put tobacco on it. They harried the dirt flat. Tobacco stole the rich outen the land. Between the two thieves, tobacco and the rollin' rain, the land got skint red."

On this tobacco market day, the boys were rumpled and rough dried. He smelled their musk, made heavy in the excitement of being off the farm and in town. A few had probably tried to make themselves smell clean, as he once did every time he came to town from the barn with a crop. He had hurriedly rubbed baking soda under his armpits in between the dirty work, only to ride on the outside of the truck or in a wagon on top of the burlap sheets of the dust-shedding herb, stewing in a leathery sweat the whole way. These boys had finished unloading tobacco onto the warehouse floor and spilled into the street looking for excitement. They were young colts who had wiggled off their lead ropes.

Winston walked toward his destination. The boys twisted in and out of the foot traffic of farmers, businesspeople, and shoppers going toward the place that Winston had left, across the railroad track but beyond. He watched them circling each other, taking up their spaces on the sidewalk, stepping off when their paths coincided with white people. He chuckled at how they pretended nonchalance as they strutted and dipped their heads in time. They hated being more at home walking behind plows on clods of dirt and tree twigs and roots. In the fields, they were probably fleet footed and sure on softer ground. The sidewalk was unfamiliar, and they struggled to hide that unfamiliarity.

Winston arrived at the liquor store and went inside. While he waited his turn, he looked at tributaries of wrinkles that crisscrossed the back of the elderly woman in front of him. She seemed intent upon sucking the life out of her cigarette. He wondered how much she needed to make a purchase. He contented himself with the comfort of one stiff drink a day. Any day that he wanted, he could forego a drink, though today seemed to need more than one.

The woman touched her little finger to a curl when she told the clerk what she wanted to buy. The clerk smiled and bowed to her. When he handed her a bottle, she placed her money in the liquor clerk's hand. When it was Winston's turn at the counter, he named his brand of gin. The liquor clerk handed Winston a bottle from a wall shelf and thumped the counter between them. Winston gritted his teeth and sullenly placed his money on the counter and, instead of thinking of the contempt that they each held for the other's skin color, he thought of how he valued the end of prohibition, which allowed him to seek comfort in the open. He pocketed the small bottle and walked back on the street toward his office, in the direction the boys had gone. He looked up and down the streets, Thomas and Main. He was sure that the boys had gone to the Colored business section. They would not arrive at their destination from a straight line, but from wobbles back and forth toward their alley. They had to walk and talk, call and respond. He heard them calling each other's names and measuring themselves by the comebacks, although he could not hear them clearly.

Winston passed the post office, where two white men stood on the sidewalk moving their lips, slits at the bottoms of their faces. As Winston approached, the slits closed. The two men both turned to stare at Winston, probably at his matched suit of clothes with pressed pants. His white coat hung in his office. Winston squeezed the gin bottle in his pocket and heard the bag crackle. The two men looked at each other, again moved their lips, and seemed to lose sight of him.

The train whistled. He decided not to try to cross before it. As it thundered by, he saw its windows were filled with stone faces. He stood in the pose of a man taking a leak. He thought of the pose because one or two stones strained to get a clearer look at him.

The caboose rumbled past, faster than the previous cars, it seemed. As he crossed the track, Winston crunched cinders under his shoes. He traversed gravel and then pavement in front of the LaNear Beauty and Cosmetology shop for Colored women. It was a place where customers rushed in with dull stiff hair and pranced out again in marcel curls and waves, smelling of Royal Crown and bergamot. He could see women inside, some daydreaming while others handled their hair, pulling hot combs through the strands, one or two talking with their arms. He passed the Booker T. Washington movie theater and dodged a circle of people in front. Winston looked up at a fabulous night sky that the city was making. He knew that the boys loved being under this sky, a sky so different from the big one that hung over the tobacco fields and seemed to send back echoes of the crickets and frogs and night peepers. He heard them again.

"Your Mama."

They were assembling at their place in the alley. Winston stood in front of the building that housed the pool room on the first floor and the Winston Lockheed dental office upstairs. He entered. As he climbed the stairs going past the pool room to the landing, he looked up at the top of the stairs to see the sign: *Winston Lockheed, Dentist.* The letters on the window still sometimes surprised him. Yes, he had remembered to turn the closed sign around. It made no difference. No one had seen it, either the OPEN or CLOSED.

He unlocked the door behind the sign. Just inside, he pulled off his pinstriped jacket and put on white. In the dying of the day, he crossed the room and stood by the window to look down on the noise of the boys.

Three dark figures swaggered into the alley like the first birds to the roost. They looked 12, maybe 14. Carolyn had boys that age.

"Your Mama, she a streetcar. Everybody done ride on her."

He was just in time to see them gather, even though they had started out before he bought his bottle of gin. Without taking his eyes off the back alley down below, he twisted the cap loose. He saw the boys among discarded barrels and crates. They were what he used to be, before high school, before normal school, before dentistry. He turned from the window and walked to his treatment chair, which he dragged noisily across the room. It made a bumping sound on the wood floor, and he expected someone from down below to pound the ceiling with a pool cue. With the chair squarely in front of the window for a spectator seat over the alley below, he settled down.

On the way to sitting down, he plopped a glass from a shelf into his left hand, put the bottle under his arm, and twisted off the cap all the way to pour himself a thimble-sized portion. The chair was too low. He could see the rooftop of the seed store on the next street but not the alley below. He ratchetted the chair up to its ultimate height and tried again. He swirled his drink around in his mouth and winced when he swallowed. Then, he gave the scene below his full attention. They were becoming shadowy in the fading light.

He recognized the dozens. He had played, though not too vigorously. He had lost his mother at the age of seven, and only the cruelest of boys will talk about your dead mama.

It had been a long journey to here. Five years ago, in 1935, he moved his equipment up these stairs and set up shop after passing the state exam. Then he still had enough money. Up til then, he had been lucky, completing college in 1922, and then dental school in 1929 at age 28. He made it through the Depression working at the post office, where the older black men sorted letters and packages for him, telling him how proud they were and giving him time to hide and study. They listened for the supervisors and coughed signals when one of them was walking toward him. He always held a prear-ranged handful of letters and was just standing up from just having picked them up. He closed his eyes and sipped. He rubbed his eyes with the bones of his knuckles, still holding his drink.

With all the encouragement of the patronizing old men, it took a lot of nerve to leave the post office in Washington, D.C., even after he saved the money to buy his equipment, the chair he sat on, the picks, bowls, drills. He decided that the country was in sufficient recovery for him to move back home. He had always been lucky, or maybe smart, until he started turning away his patients who wanted gold teeth as replacements for healthy white ones.

"Your mama so short, she have to stand on a ladder to climb a grain of sand."

"Damn, your mama so old, if they told her to act her age she would die."

His wife and his friends had said that when he counted the money he was losing, he would change his mind. That day, the day that he watched the flocking together of the farm, the boys in the alley, he worried over rumors that a white dentist in town had constructed a rear entrance leading to a small separate "Colored" waiting room for patients who dreamed of flashing gold behind their lips.

"Your mama so po, she was kickin' a can down the street and somebody ask her what was she doin', and she said she was movin."

There came a gray, stooped silhouette of a man. He sucked his gums and chuckled to himself over a secret he carried to share. He walked warily and seemed distrustful of his feet. In what light remained, his tattered shirt and the legs of his pants fluttered like lace.

One boy, who came to the flock when it was becoming hard for the dentist to count, ducked his head and swayed back and forth while the others mocked him for wearing one shoe. "Hey, Lee Roy, you so ugly, you scared off your other shoe." He carried it with the flapping sole under his arm.

The boys greeted one who waddled in among them. "Hey, Bow Willie. Git enough sweet potatoes to eat yet?"

A lean boy wiped his nose with his sleeve. "Hey, keep your boogers to yourself, Jim Robert," they told him.

The dentist had seen several of the faces in better light on the street. He now heard them salute each other, singing out names into the night: Bow Willie, Jim Charles, Lee Roy, Otis Ray, John Rob.

They even called out one who seemed not to be there, Hart Lee. The face most recognizable and of interest was that of John Robert Cobb. The dentist grew up with Kinchen Cobb and had been barely separated from him until seventh grade, which was the highest grade offered in Griffinton in 1913. The dentist, as a boy, moved into a town to attend a high school.

In the mixture of darkness and lantern light, John Robert smiled and joined in.

"Your mama so black, when she blink her eyes, look like two trains comin'."

When the dark covered everything, he could see two lanterns below, and in the lantern light, the alley had filled with men ranging in height from knee high to six feet, shown to the dentist darkened on one side and lit on the other. They drank and slapped each other while opening and closing their legs as they spoke. Lanterns swayed and dipped with laugh punchlines. A few of the voices came huskily from the just-weened, the ones who had just let go their mother's skirts and wanted to find their way under the skirts of women of no kin. Other voices sounded newly changed to low crackling, between boy and manhood. Three of the voices sounded worn, the voices of men whose outlines hunched. They smacked their lips around their words. They tasted memories more absorbing for them than the present. They came hoping for one of the boys to furnish a wrinkled dollar bill for those of legal age to make a purchase from the liquor store, Prohibition having just ended.

In the darkness, all the male children seemed more manly, less consumptive, less fat, less thin, less young. The younger voices came out of straighter, stronger bodies than daylight could ever allow for the dark forms gathered below, beating their sides like wings, stomping their feet, passing bottles hidden in brown paper bags, blowing smoke like little devils; Doin' the Dozens. The dentist told himself that he was neither like the boys nor the old winos. The dentist drank from his clean glass, sitting in his shiny elevated cushioned dental chair, wearing his clean white shirt, crisp black bow tie, creased pants and a white linen coat. His white coat wrinkled in the seat where had sat all day, the same stain-free coat that he had put on 11 hours before.

No one had come into his office all day.

He wondered if the white dentists who did gold used separate equipment for Colored mouths, in keeping with the separate entrance and waiting room. They probably did not sterilize those instruments of the patients who came in by the back door and sat in the special, small waiting room.

The white patients were certainly meant to think so. He looked into his nearly empty gin bottle and it seemed that he had found the answer to his other question. He began to drink the rest. He could change. He would outfit gold teeth wherever they liked, up their asses if they wanted.

Satisfied with his decision, he looked down on the boys, happy that he was not like them anymore. At least he was happy in that one way. He had an occupation. A calling. As soon as he got the word out of his willingness to pull out healthy, solid teeth to replace those teeth with gold teeth, his calling would absorb him again.

The little men down below passed a rumor with a bottle hidden in a brown bag. "Alice Lee, she pregnant."

"Yeah, man. They say it Robert Earl's baby."

"Yeah, man. Robert Earl, how many babies is you done got?"

He shrugged and dragged on a cigarette.

"Robert Earl don' know," someone said and swung closer to slap Robert Earl's back. "Many as Rob can git, dude."

The dentist and Robert Earl Cobb's daddy, Kinchen Cobb, had been the smartest boys in Griffinton township in 1912, though Kinchen was the champion speller. The dentist regretted how old Joseph Cobb had raged at the idea that Kinchen wanted to leave the land to go to town for school.

"Whoo-oo-oo-ee!" from the alley. "Robert Earl done it again. Done knocked up another girl."

"That make it four what say it his'n. Them babies."

"Four babies and he ain't but 18 years old."

"He a reeaall coooool dude. He can pop more cherries than a flying bullet with a bunch of women lined up and shot all in a row."

"A reeaall man."

They circled him, some bowing, as in a highly ritualistic recognition of their nonchalant hero, the honoree. Robert Earl Cobb ducked his head and shuffled his feet in an "Aw shucks twernt nothin','"' attitude that only encouraged them to go on exalting him and, at the same time, fumbling for a crowning title.

"He worst than Moses. He lead the women to the promised land."

"Naw. He the holy ghost. He give them salvation."

"He git more babies than a rabbit."

"THAT'S WHAT HE IS, A RABBIT!"

"He can blow up a woman faster'n a rabbit."

"Yeah. Just like a rabbit."

And then they began to laugh, wonderful belly-cleansing laughs, different from those that had sprinkled their utterances before. "Rabbit!" Every single male allowed the laughter to take hold and rock him, allowing himself to forget and remember everything all at once. "Rabbit!" The dentist laughed too, and absentmindedly he lifted the empty fifth. With his head thrown back, he drained a last drop onto his tongue. His hands were slightly numb, but the feeling would return by the time someone showed up with a toothache. He knew that manhood had been, if not conferred, recognized. He knew also that the boys were rubbing their dicks through their pants down below when they chorused between the laughter, "Rabbit," while the two old men remembered. He strained to see them laughing at each other, pretending not to know that they were laughing at themselves. He thought that they were laughing at what they did not have, maintaining their distance with each other while keeping each other company. They were laughing by proxy.

"Robert is a rabbit. Robert Rabbit. Jack Rabbit. That's what he is, Jack Rabbit."

"Rabbit" smiled to himself. He liked what they had titled him. He smiled and chuckled inside himself, careful not to laugh out loud.

CHAPTER EIGHT

On a July day in the summer of 1939, 14-year-old Rose Amos got tired of picking blackberries in the heat with her mother, Doll Amos, and her grandmother, Tab Amos. Rose threw down her bucket at the edge of the fig grove as the two women strode ahead, talking of recipes for blackberry jam, fundraising for the church home mission, and the yearly collections for Shaw University. They talked of stuffings for bed quilts.

Rose slapped herself and frowned at the chigger bites on her arms and legs. She had not worn a pair of her brother's long pants as Doll had instructed. In the heat, Rose loved the way her gauze dress flew up in the breeze and the way the breeze felt on her thighs. Grandmama Tab called back to her. "You better keep up. Always tryin' to hide from work. You step on a high land Moccasin, he'll bite you for sure. That'll learn you a lesson."

But, didn't she have the right to daydream and walk slowly by herself?

Moving deeper into the fig grove and out of sight, Rose thought about sneaking back home and hiding in her room, but if she tried to get past her daddy, it would prove tedious.

He would send her back to pick the stupid berries. She propped herself against a limb, leaned back and lay on the ground. She made a frame with her hands to look through to the outlines of a feverish light that filled the space just beyond the fig bushes. A butterfly flitted to a place where she framed him, and she followed him with her hands shaped around the sight of him.

A tree branch snapped. A shadow and a heaviness slowly reduced the light in her frame. A pair of legs stood over her. She should have called out for help. She could hear her mother and her grandmother's voices a few hundred yards away, fading. She had enough time to cry out from her hiding place, but she didn't want to hear her Grandma Tab scold, "You shouldn' run away from work, child. Learn a lesson. Learn a lesson."

When she decided that she should cry out, she changed her mind again, because she recognized him just as he slapped his hand over her mouth. Then he pulled her toward him and pressed himself hard on her. She felt a rigid part of him swelling roughly against her gauze dress, which he managed to lift by holding up on one knee.

"I got somethin' good for you," he said and licked her ear. Her face tingled. Goosebumps rose on her arms. But it was only Robert Earl Cobb, the one they nicknamed Rabbit, from next door. What a nuisance. She tried to sit up and got her shoulders off the ground. But when she tried to whack at him, her arms got baled against her, inside his large arms. But, it was only Rabbit, Lenore's brother. He was nobody to be scared of. He was just playing and would soon let her go.

She tried to say, "Ok, that's enough now." But when she shook her head, he held even tighter against her. She tried to bite his hand. She would give him a piece of her mind when he let go of her mouth.

"I got something real good for you." He seemed to believe himself, because he smiled broadly and lowered her head and shoulders back to the ground. Still holding her mouth, he stretched himself full on top of her, down where the roof of the scrubby figs made a shade in a hollowed-out place on the ground where maybe, by the smell of it, dogs had lain, hiding from the same sun that had driven her there. Now, she was steaming, and tears came from her straining against him. But despite the straining, she was unable to move.

He kept his hand over her mouth. "Don' make me hurt you. I tell you, it's gonna be good for you."

He was not able to wonder at her feelings at that moment, absorbed in the press of his own hunger. It had been seren-dipitous, his seeing her from the higher point of his back porch, with the sight of a stalker-ready 19-year-old.

He pulled his hand away and quickly closed his lips over hers. He pried opened her lips with his and slid his tongue along her teeth. She gagged. He loosened a little to let her get her breath and realized that he loved the taste of her. He had to show her how good she felt to him. He thought he was gentle with her, maybe because her softness felt like part of him, but each time she strained against him, he tightened into one great chokehold.

He could not believe that she was not ready. Most girls would be creaming all over by now. Usually, the tongue in the ear did it. When he probed with his fingers, she was dry, a closed and tiny tunnel. He was more than ready and tried to bore his penis into her, and he realized that he had to break through and was amazed.

"This is your first time?" He could not believe his luck. He bore in, breaking and tearing her and drawing blood. And then, he was alone, driving into her, rocking there until the blast and then the quake that caused him to drool in her hair. Her mouth was free, but she now had no sound to make, and he seemed nearly asleep on top of her. But at least he was still. She no longer wanted to move, not right away.

He was burning in the damp places on his skin, his skin nettled from the dirt that they lay in. He noticed that his sweat mixed itchily with hers. He saw that buzzing June bugs were peeping at them, their little engines running as they soared away. The voices of the mother and grandmother had faded completely in the thick air. He let go of Rose and swatted a gnat. His penis softened and shriveled out of her. She dragged herself out from under him.

He wished she were not crying, but it was her first time, after all. He sat up and watched her run from the lair, her two long legs barely touching the ground. The sight of her running was familiar and a solace in his slight discomfort at what he had done. He brushed the thought away from his mind as he swatted at the air, the thought of her having been a virgin. He was sure he had made it good for her, though it was brief. She was really sweet. He buttoned his fly front, brushed the dirt from his denim overalls, and walked out of the grove a few minutes later.

Gass Amos sat on his porch where he feigned wakefulness. It was a day when the fields needed rest to increase, and the kind of day that women needed for nesting, canning, sewing, and making soap. He moved with the shade and napped. Half aroused, he winked and shifted the rocker to tilt it to just the right angle but not rocking. He was about to lose his eyes again but saw his daughter Rose make a dash for the house. He left his rocker to meet his baby girl.

She said it was chigger bites, so he touched her arms and neck, covered with red bumps. She told him that she tore her dress; that was why she was holding it by the hem. She said she was burning like fire. "Ha. I thought you had run up on a copperhead the way your legs was carryin' you over that field. Where you come from? The fig grove? Hidin' from your mama, again? I'll draw you some water for a bath. Stop that cryin' now. Chigger bites can't be all that bad."

She would always remember how he heated the water on the kitchen stove and poured it into the zinc tub that he placed in the middle of the kitchen floor for her.

"Wash with this lye soap, it will take the sting out," he chuckled again, and closed the door behind him as he left her alone to undress. She took off the gauze dress and her soiled bloomers. There was pain there where Rabbit had torn into her. She spread her legs to wash off the smell of him. It was the smell that she had feared for her father to smell. She sobbed. She shouldn't have run away from the berry picking. She had felt his hot germs run into her, so much of it that some had run down her legs and scattered along the way during her run to her house that day. She had tried to hide that dribbling wetness. There was blood, too. And she was sore.

"The reason you always get your plaits pulled, you day-dream all the time. You never look back to see what is comin' at you." Lenore was always telling her that in school. It was her fault for running and hiding from her mother, and since it was all her fault, she could not tell her father or anyone. The grownup people must not know.

⸙

Two months after the berry picking day, Doll saw Rose vomit three mornings in a row. On the third morning, Doll walked out of the house and into her garden. She stopped still among the vines of crowder peas and leaned on the handle of her hoe. She froze in thought and leaned so still as to deceive all the life around her. A snake that wriggled up the pole to stop near her arm, felt the cold air coming from Doll's open mouth. The legless, voiceless creature sizzled back down to the ground and zipped out of sight. Rose watched from an upstairs window. She saw the thing wiggle away and saw that her mother had not seen it. She knew that her mother thought of her and Rose remained determined to guard her growing secret. She tried not to think of how it would distend and announce itself, soon. But she still wasn't going to tell.

Doll stood, chilled at the thought that something had happened in the field that day when she saw the boy from the next farm coming out of the fig grove. That Rabbit, they called him. Doll had left her mother-in-law in mid-sentence, something about the pastor's request for a salary increase, dropped her bucket of berries and ran home thinking of Rose. That child would tie her father's shoelaces together when he napped and wait in hiding for him to stand up. The same child giggled like the sound of water gushing from a hand pump for no reason. But that day, the reason Doll ran across the field, to the path and crossed another field after seeing that boy coming out of the fig grove, was that she had seen Rose begin to harness her giggles in a self-conscious, non-girl way. Rose's eyes were darker and harder to read for the mother. Rose's thoughts were secret. The mother knew that the child believed that the screw turns pulsing in her veins were singular in herself, and something that no other young female on earth had ever known.

That day, Doll had found the fig grove empty and had run homeward, relieved when she got there to find her husband still resting with Rose in her room, freshly bathed and sitting on the side of her bed, rubbing wet chewing tobacco into her chigger bites. Now, leaning on the handle of her hoe, thinking back, Doll Amos was sure that she had missed something that day. Looking back in her mind, while standing in the garden, she smelled the smoke of a wood fire, like that of a burning stove.

A few days later, on a Saturday morning, Gass Amos rolled Rose's clothes into a suitcase as Doll watched from the doorway in silence. He left Doll Amos at home to finish the breakfast dishes that Rose had begun to wash, and drove Rose in his pickup truck, down his long, sandy driveway to the dirt road and into the next driveway to the farm that was separated from his by cotton fields. They arrived at Kinchen Cobb's house with a train of dust racing behind, skidded to a stop in front of the porch where Kinchen Cobb sat. "Alight. Alight. Alight, and come in. Gass, Rose, how y'all do, today?"

"Not so good."

"Gass, I see you got little Rose with you. Lord, she do grow. I've known you all your life, so I have seen you grow. How old is she now?"

"She is 14 years old, and I took her to see Dr. Strong yesterday because of the headaches and vomiting and sickliness. I thought she had consumption or something."

"Do tell. She don' look too bad to me, today."

"Oh, she look fine, today. She just pregnant, tha's all." Gass was choking. "Your boy done it. Jack Rabbit. He ruint her and I tell you what, I'm goin' give her to you."

Kinchen recognized anger in his old friend. Gass could sometimes be hotheaded and raise his voice in church or Sunday school. Everyone always looked to Cobb to calm the man down. They were best friends who visited each other every single day of their lives and farmed their crops together, exchanging labor, borrowing tools, and sharing laughter. This day, Cobb watched his friend and neighbor walk around to open the passenger door of the truck and decided to not put his hand to the man's shoulder. Rose climbed down. Gass handed her the suitcase, slammed the door behind her, and drove back down the hilly drive.

Rose stood, her arms around herself, watching him drive away. That day, just a couple months ago, the same father had touched her neck and arms speckled with chigger bites, at the moment that the sticky stuff was running down her legs. What was it Grandmama Tab was always talking about? Lessons? Maybe there was a lesson. She raised her arms around her head. And, all her energy went into not making a sound, even though Mr. Cobb looked as though he felt sorry for her.

When Ida Cobb, who had been listening from inside the house, walked to the screen door to look out, she sucked a lemon by the pull of her face and stood on the inner door jamb, staring at Rose, whom she had taught in Sunday school.

Rose had known this woman all her life, Mrs. Ida Cobb, the next-door neighbor, the mother of her friend Lenore, and the one who everyone joked about her preoccupation with impending death, a death that had been coming as long as Rose could remember. She looked particularly healthy this day as she frowned toward Rose.

"It ain't his baby," the woman hissed. "I seen you, all your life, runnin' through the woods like a loose squirrel and now you turn out to be just a cheap Wild Thing. Miss Hot Britches. I'd never thought you'd turn out to be a no-count gal. Tha's all, just a no-count gal, after all, cause, it ain't his. If that baby is born without a widow's peak in its head of hair, I'm gone to deal with you myself. I got enough trouble worryin' 'bout my own health, and to say nothin' of my boy Hart Lee. And now, Rabbit. It seem like the whole world is comin' after my boys. Lord. Lord. Lord. Give me strength to live long enough to do them some good."

Later she was heard to say, "I'm so glad I'm sick. I probably won' live to see this baby, of God Know Who, that this child is carryin'," causing the hearers to wonder at the nature of her illness, news of which had been new.

Robert Earl Jack Rabbit Cobb married Rose. Not that day. That day, when he got home from his ramblings with his friends, his father beckoned him out into the middle of a peanut field to talk. No one heard the words that passed between them. To the onlookers—his two sisters, Lenore and Millie, his brother Hart Lee, two cousins, his mother, and Rose—there was no waving of arms and no raised voices. It looked as though the older man chuckled a time or two and maybe Jack Rabbit did an "Aw shucks" kind of shrug. They might have guessed that the elder Cobb said, "A real man can't help himself, sometime. An' she is right cute."

Rose watched a gray sparrow fly over, first near where she sat at one end of the porch, off away from the Cobbs, and then toward the Cobbs, who bunched at the other end of the porch, looking at her as though she were a car wreck. Even the old grandfather, Joseph Cobb, who never went into the house, hovered at the edge of the porch, smacking his lips with both hands cupped over his ears in an attempt to catch one word. The sparrow hovered over the two who convened in the open field, and it flew back to where Rose sat. She watched it fly off into the blue. If she saw it again, she would not recognize it, as it took with it what it had heard.

When the father and son walked back to the house, it was Kinchen Cobb who talked to Rose Amos, not Jack Rabbit. Rabbit looked everywhere except in her eyes that searched for his. She heard the older man say, "Well, you can't go today. It will have to be one day next week after we finish laying the crops by. Plus, we got to fix the loft for you two to have a place to stay."

Rose was put into the bedroom shared by Millie and Lenore, making three on the double bed. Despite the heat of dog days and the closeness in the room, Rose stayed in during the day, hiding from everything outside, staring out of windows. She looked out of the windows trying to see herself . . . maybe skipping over the horizon. She didn't feel like running.

While making sure that Rabbit did not couple with Rose again before the rites, all day long whenever Rabbit was out of her sight, Ida Cobb would call out, "Rose, where you at?" Rose stopped answering the harassing roll call. It became Millie's job, "Millie, go see what done happened to Rose." All day long with Millie's reply, "She in the room by herself lookin' out the window like last time," until Millie got tired and stopped answering.

Rabbit seemed not to notice her at all. She missed seeing her father. She missed her mother's "Go comb your hair," and "Brush your teeth," and "Wash under your arms," and "Wash possible." Rose was sure that her grandmother was sewing and wondered who threaded the old woman's sewing needles.

At night, Rose undressed under covers in bed to avoid wrestling with Millie who tried to see her stomach. On that fourth night, Rose did one more thing to not ingratiate herself to Rabbit's mother. She slapped Millie, who had jumped from under the bed and tried to pull the covers off Rose. Rose did not want to see her own belly, much less show it to a child who stopped playing with a doll to look.

One evening, Ida Cobb sat on the side of the bed talking to her two daughters, one on each side of her. "Don' be like Rose, keep your dresses down. Don' let the boys get under your clothes. Make them respect you."

The youngest, nine-year-old Millie, twirled her finger in a plait of hair and pouted as she asked her mother, "How come she got to sleep with us?"

"'Cause ain't no where else for her to sleep."

"So, how come she here? How come she don' go back home, back 'cross the field where she belong?"

"'Cause she gone marry your brother in a few days, and we got to put her somewhere. Y'all, you and her and Lenore can sleep three to a bed for a while. T'won' be long."

Millie sucked her thumb. Lenore spoke. "Mama, you don' want her here anymore than we do, do you?"

"Naw. I don' want that fast tail thang, half-raised wild deer in my house, but I'm gone keep her where your brothers can't get at her. I'll know when the baby come. If he don't have that widow's peak in his hair like your brothers, I'll put her out of here."

Rose was standing just inside the doorway listening. She was not going to cry. It didn't matter what they said. She would not cry. She was also not going to walk across the way to the house where she grew up, though she missed her mother. Well, it had only been four days.

Rose met her future mother-in-law's eyes as the woman came from the girls' bedroom. When Rose was inside the door, Millie picked up her doll and skipped from the room, bumping Rose as she went. They were alone, Rose and Lenore. Lenore watched her mother leave before turning to smile at Rose. "I really want to know. What do it feel like?"

"What do *what* feel like?"

"You know. A dick. How do it feel?"

The day that Rose and Rabbit were married, the skies poured. Rose sat in the back seat of the car next to Rabbit, feeling damp and limp. She wore blue velvet with lace at the collar, the only nice dress she was able to button over her growing breasts. The dress was like one her grandmother had made for a white woman's child in town, the daughter of the newspaper publisher. Rose had seen it and said, "Make me one like it."

That morning, Lenore had said, "When this gets too tight for you, give it to me, okay?" Rose stuck out her tongue.

Rose had walked across the field to her childhood home to look for something to wear to the courthouse. While there, she threaded several needles for her grandmother and kept looking away from her mother's swollen face. Her father had been away. Her mother cried when Rose walked through the door, and again when she left to cross the field for the Cobb household, the velvet dress under her arm. Doll said, "I won' go to the courthouse tomorrow. I can't bear it."

The grandmother said, "This man that 'bout to be your husband. He will be alright. Just trust in God." She was not crying. It seemed that she only cried in church, looking up at the cross.

Her future mother- and father-in-law rode up front with Kinchen Cobb driving. Rabbit wore a shirt and necktie. At the courthouse, as Rose climbed the 19 concrete steps, she looked at her future husband's father, sparse gray hair sprinkled about his head of soft wool, a head that wrinkled when he grinned. His habit was to grin while he let his wife talk. Rose had found the Cobb house and its mix-matched rooms not like the house where she grew up, in which her mother and father talked back and forth. Mr. Kinchen was solid and quiet while his Ida bossed all day. It was as old Mr. Joseph said. She was Boss Lady.

Rose tripped. Rabbit caught her and as he held her elbow, he whispered mischievously and threateningly, "I can't wait."

Once inside the clerk's office, Rose's father appeared. He had come to sign his name for her condition of "under-aged-ness." His signature seemed to be the cure for the affliction. Finally, the bride and groom stood side by side facing the clerk, who sat behind a desk and kept calling Rose "Liza." For a long moment, while the two of them stood with the desk separating them from the clerk, Rose knew that all the people standing or sitting in the brick courthouse building on all three floors, the court rooms and the deed and tax office, and the ones on the street, even those in their cars outside, waited for her voice. In that long moment, her father, his mother and father, the white man with glassy eyes, waited for her to find it.

Everything that had happened from the day in the fig grove brought her to the moment when she found herself standing next to the person to whom she promised her life, while outside the rain was washing her away. Even though she did not want to, she did not think about not getting married. She never stood this still on rainy days. That was what you did when you got caught pregnant without a husband. Getting married was what covered up something that had happened in the fields, on the backseat of a car, up against a tree in a church yard during revival week. Only very loose women with no pride got knocked-up by someone who did not want to give the baby a name after the belly started to swell. The day before, her mother had said that she was lucky that the Cobb boy accepted her. She found her voice, "I do." Though she had promised herself not to, she cried, but they were back outside so fast that in the rain, the rain and tears mixed and no one seemed to notice.

Her father, the same one who had left her in the Cobb front yard, the one she had not seen for four days, after she found her voice to say, "I do," put his arms around her back out on the courthouse steps in the rain and said, "Everything gonna be alright."

"Do I have to live with them? Can't I come home with you?"

"No, baby. You married now. You not grown, but you married. You got to grow up now. I wished you hadda waited. But, you can come and visit."

In the back seat of the car, Rabbit grinned at her and mouthed, "Can't wait." Rose saw rain on his face. She heard the windshield wipers beating across the front of the car. Mr. Cobb wore his one good suit and carried a Rebeccabrook fountain pen in his lapel pocket. He had told Rose that his grandfather, Joseph Cobb, had given him the pen when he was in the seventh grade and that he stopped using it soon after. He said he did not know if it could be made to write if you put ink in it. She had been in the Cobb house for four days, but she had not seen him write anything.

Now in the car, Mr. Cobb looked up at the rearview mirror at Rose and said, "You a Cobb family member now. Welcome."

He looked expectantly at his wife Ida who looked at the rain.

Finally Ida Cobb spoke. "See my boy. See his hair how it grow on his head? He got the widow's peak in the middle of his head. His daddy got it, his daddy's daddy got it. When your baby come, I'm gone look for that."

As Rabbit helped her from the car at the house, Rose refused his hand. She had been caught off her guard in the fig grove that day three months before. She had been stupid to let him hold her down like that. Before, the boys had only pulled at her plaits. But she had always been able to fight off the boys when she had her mind on them. She had been wrestling with her brothers all her life. She'd have chewed his lips off rather than be stuck in that house with a mother-in-law who went about throwing salt over her shoulders, breaking needles and talking about bad luck everywhere.

What if the baby didn't come? What if she fell down on it and it just wasn't born? Not killed, just not born. What if all that came to pass? Would it hurt her? What if? She leaped from the car, not waiting for the outstretched hands holding cover from the rain, and slipped quietly into the house. Once thing was for sure. He would never touch her again. She felt around in her suitcase and found the hatpin, the only thing she had packed. It had a carved handle of celluloid. She slipped it inside the long sleeve of the velvet dress. Moments later, she was almost relaxed while her mother-in-law listed off her chores, which would begin the next day. She was to gather eggs for the family and carry food to the grandfather, who lived in the little hut on the edge of the yard.

The morning after her wedding night, the Cobbs, everyone but Ida, laughed over breakfast about the bumping sounds coming from the bedroom the night before. Rabbit looked sheepish.

Hart Lee whispered, "Mus' feel real good fuckin' a 'oman what be buckin' and kickin' around like Rose do. We heard you las' night, bro."

Rose paid little attention to the talk. In this house, she was a mute, her voice having been lost in the fig grove.

Rose always felt like the center in the house she grew up in, where they listened to her chatter and watched her circumnavigate. Now, they had warned her not to ride a bicycle. Grandma Tab said, "Maybe it's a boy, to get the land when your daddy die."

What was there for her to say, and who in this house wanted to listen? Their words flew about her, the words about the great lovemaking going on upstairs were like dust that you couldn't see until it settled, and she couldn't see it even then. She could only think about her swelling belly, the one that Millie kept trying to see.

In the coming days, Rabbit did not let them know that every night, he fell back to his side of the bed, away from Rose's hatpin, after wrestling with her with her tiny hands flying about. It was a joke. He could have snatched the hat pin from her anytime during the first few seconds of that first night. She was his wife.

Maybe nothing much changed. He was in his father's house. He had never looked farther ahead than a day. What difference did it all make? He thought that he wanted to fuck his wife in the worst way. But he had made up his mind. He had had her once. He would never touch her again until she was ready. And it was sure making him feel funny that she was taking so long. He wanted her to want him. He shocked himself. He had never wanted many things where there was doubt about getting them. She was like the grapes, and he was the fox. She was so young and so small, but once he was alone with her and she was legally his, he found himself restrained. Each night he gave up struggling against her when she fell back on her side of the bed into a coil, turtle-like, circled into herself as though she went to sleep. But she seemed to always be awake every time he looked. She didn't want any limb stretched out for him to grab hold of. At meals, he looked across the table at her. She was swelling up, even in the face. Cute face, but rounder. Still the high cheek bones. She was not that cute before. She was getting under his skin, the heifer. He could not believe how much he wanted her to want him.

He could not tell his friend, Bow Willie, or his brother, Hart Lee, that he, a newly married man, the champion stud, was not doing it to his wife; that all day long, anytime he saw her, she looked prettier than any gal he had ever seen. It wasn't their business. All he knew was that she was looking better and better to him. After the law gave her to him, she looked even better. Then, 18 days had passed. Still, he had seen nothing of her below the neck or above her calf, yet he could not just run off and fuck any of his old standbys. He was so famished, they would know. Women were witches anyway.

CHAPTER NINE

The newlywed, 14-year-old pregnant Rose Amos Cobb sat in Dr. Strong's crowded waiting room, squeezed between two women her mother's age. The women leaned around Rose talking to each other. One dampened Rose's ear with her words.

"Mr. Dean, funeral tomorrow."

"Joe Dean? The one go to St. Joe's church?"

Rose did not know the man they talked about and tried hard to tune them out.

"Naw, some of his peoples, though. He the one that—"

The pointy-chinned, busy-faced woman searched Rose's face, leaning her head back to focus. Rose knew full well that the two expected her to leap right in and tell them about herself; why she was sitting in the doctor's office waiting room, blown up woman-sized, but she did not.

The other woman held her hands, one in the other and turned her lean frame, making a graceful line, one shoulder curved slightly, causing Rose to look to see if a camera was set up somewhere.

Across the room, an elderly man was sitting in a ladder-back chair. He began to talk to no one in particular.

"What about the war we hearin' 'bout?" He paused and looked about, then asked, "Young folks' business? Them that ain't went in the army, is tryin' to." No one answered. "In the last days, they say, and we livin' in the last days, in the last days they say there be wars and rumors of wars, like in the Bible. Just like now. It's all a secret," he whispered, "but they is in the Pacific, I hear."

Rose would not be persuaded to think about a war somewhere. She was trying hard enough to not think about the life that had stolen itself into her and was now growing under her navel. She unwrapped her arms and crossed them over her belly and shuddered.

The pointed-chinned woman took the old man's lure. "I don' think Negro boys should fight overseas, mean as white folks been to us here. My son, he joined the army. Tried to join the marines. Didn' know no better. Dat's all white."

The preening woman turned her shoulder toward the man and said, "Maybe white people will see that our boys fight good and that will change things here."

"Naw! You crazy or what?" the old man said, and added, "At least, not in my lifetime."

Rose rubbed her fingers along her sides. Her dress was tight about the middle. Her shoes pinched. She could not cross her legs. She turned to relieve the strain in her back and crossed her ankles. She tugged at the hem of her skirt that formed a tent over her knees. She looked around the room and saw sick women, children, and old people. Several of the women were pregnant. A girl child sat on the floor in front of her mother, who sat on a stool. The child drew herself up, gagged and coughed and put out a string of phlegm and blood. The mother held the girl's head as she emptied into a large muslin square and for what seemed a long time. It was like a tiny sock coming out of a wringer. When she finished, the mother, with a sad and quiet face, folded the blood and phlegm out of sight and held a fresh cloth, waiting for the next spasm of coughing. Rose tried not to think about how the mother felt.

Across the room, a well-dressed woman sat apart. Rose thought that she looked as though she wanted to breathe particles of air different from those available to them in that room. She spoke to no one. Maybe she was sick, too, but not like Rose. Rose spoke to no one as well, especially the women who were intent on squeezing her between them. Rose was sick, too. Rose tried not to think of her own illness, brought on by a person who smiled and laughed a lot.

Morning became midmorning. People arranged themselves. Some stood and walked about the room and then sat again. From a corner, a little boy showed Rose his tongue. She refused to look at him again but saw from the corner of an eye that he turned himself inside out trying to regain her attention. Another boy threw a bit of folded paper at her, which landed at the feet of the busy-faced woman. Finally, at a little past noon, just after the morning had died, the receptionist called Rose's name and walked her through into the examining room, where she had never gone without her mother or father. The doctor stood waiting until the receptionist had closed the door from the outside. Rose sat down on the examining table. The doctor stood next to her. They were nearly touching.

"My, my, you are one scared looking thing. Pity you didn't think about that when you were making this baby."

She had not spoken a word since checking in at eight-thirty, except for "umpf," and she said hoarsely, "I . . . was . . . raped."

She felt a door inside her open up, a gateway that had rusted shut, and now as it opened, particles of rust fell away in protest as she felt them settling, maybe, grating her insides so that she couldn't help but think.

She told of that day when she lay on the ground in the

fig grove, daydreaming and looking at butterflies between a frame that she had made with her fingers until her neighbor, someone whom she had known all her life, her best friend's brother, the son of her father's best friend, clapped his hand over her mouth. She described how she felt him flatten himself on top of her, with a part of him swelling to bursting open. As she talked, she heard the creaking door and saw the child's string of phlegm and blood and knew that it had come from some place deep, a secret place from where affliction and breath were hidden. When she finished, she felt weightless in her chest even after the door closed back.

Dr. Strong cleared his throat. "You didn't tell me the day when your daddy brought you here and he was so scared by you being sick."

"When you told him what was wrong with me, he got real upset, remember?"

The doctor nodded, put his hands in his pocket, took them out again. A teen afraid to speak up in front of a parent. He knew what that was. Her daddy had been scared that she had contracted consumption. He said that. He came in thinking his little girl could die. When he found out that she was pregnant and going to live, he felt worse; he was unhinged by the news.

It reminded the doctor. Thinking of the parent's anger and disappointment reminded him. He backed away from the examination table. They were no longer almost touching.

His own father planned with him to get him to college and medical school, something they could not talk about in front of his mother. Dr. Strong's mother fell in love with Jesus while he was growing up and spent her waking days at church, whenever there was a gap in the church door. If there wasn't and the door was locked, then she was thinking and planning for church instead. Her love affair began just as her husband and Dr. Strong's father became followers of Marcus Garvey. The elder Strong took a second job to save money to take his wife and teenage son back to Africa. The doctor, however, had been able to talk his father into lending him the savings for college and medical school, and just when he was finished, a federal court convicted a Jamaican man called Marcus Garvey of mail fraud. The 1929 stock market crash brought down the bank where the older Strong's money would have been, the money that the now Dr. Strong had spent. But the mother, she had been the one they whispered about. He was scared to death to tell her of his dreams. The reason Rose gave for not having mentioned her rape before, it made sense to him.

"Is your father alright now?"

"Yes, he's fine. Except he say for me to not be ashamed. Like it was my fault."

"Doesn't he know you were raped?"

She hesitated. "I didn't tell him until I was too late to tell him. He didn't believe me and then said it don' matter no way. Anyway, it was probably my fault, not paying more attention to myself."

She thought about Lenore teasing and saying, "It don' make no sense how the boys can sneak up on you every day and pull your hair." She clutched a pocketbook with her bit of lunch inside. She folded her arms around herself with the purse hanging on her arm, and again she promised herself that no one would ever come up on her again without her knowing.

"Do you feel ashamed?"

"Yes," she whispered.

He sat down in the only chair in the examination room. He turned to face the window. She cleared her throat a few times. He thanked his God for being a male.

"They always blame the girl, don't they?" he said aloud but to himself. Finally, he spoke to her. "What's done is done. Your father is right. It makes no difference now how it got done.

Well, it does. But, he did marry you. It won't be so bad. A lot of very good marriages started out with a pregnancy. But, he is right that you should not feel ashamed. You are lucky. You'll be fine. Bring your husband next time. I want to talk to him." He saw her frown. "No. No. I'm not going to tell him what you told me unless you want me to. What you told me stays right here. I just want to talk to him about being a father."

The doctor had heard lots of confessions. He had heard women admit they had been beaten, or had struck a child too roughly. That they had picked up an itch of their organs from lying with another man, or that the broken arm was not a farm accident, but from a drunken lover. He knew the risk of doing up the tiny slip that brought retaliation later at home, beyond his help. Her frown must have been that kind of fear. He reassured her with that in mind.

But Rose had not been thinking about him telling Rabbit that she had talked about the rape. She was thinking of the sex. It had been nearly three months of twisting and turning and wrestling in the bed. Rabbit had snatched her hatpin to show her that he could force her. But he didn't. And he didn't give up trying to make her want to. Rabbit said that one day she would be ready to give him his sweets. But she was not going to give in, if she could help it. That was the secret Rose had, not what Dr. Strong thought. Her grandmother had called it a sin for a woman to hold back her sex from her lawful husband. But she wondered, how much longer could she get away with it? She had tried to go home, although the place where she grew up was not her home anymore, it seemed. Her mother told her, "You a married woman now. I am sorry about that, but it's a fact."

That meant that she did not have a home. And lately, they had been saying that she needed to think about being a mother. She thought again of the woman with the bloodied, pus-covered rag. She thought of how the child's shoulders moved, but the mother's face stayed the same. A patient face. She would never be like that.

He was telling her that he was leaving to give her time to undress. Later, when the examination was over, he left the room a second time and came back when she was dressed. "I have one final thing to say. You may be too young to understand this, but I hope you will not be a victim." She frowned. "I know it doesn't make sense what I am saying to you right now, but I hope you won't leave it up to the people who hurt you to decide for you what you are."

Back at the receptionist's desk, Rose unfolded a five-dollar bill and two ones. The receptionist moved her closed lips as she wrote a receipt and when finished, she chewed her gum with lips well apart.

⁘

The next month, Rabbit drove Rose to the doctor in the pickup truck.

"What do the doctor need to talk to me about for you, you think?" He kept the engine running while she climbed down from the truck. "I'll be back to circle every couple hours."

Rose watched the truck roll away, abandoned to sit in the waiting room on her own. She remembered too late that he had the money for the office visit.

That day, it seemed that all the mothers in the world had convened in Dr. Strong's waiting room to warn her that childbirth was for real women, not for girls. And that her real trials were coming. A man in the waiting room was seized with convulsions and blew foamy bubbles out of his mouth and nose while the whole of him shook. Rose couldn't stand to look. Instead, she focused on a woman trying to hold three small children, who all tumbled on and off her lap like oranges on a moving tray. As usual, so much of the time now, she tried not to think of actually being a mother. With almost four months to go, there was plenty of time to not think about it yet.

Every day, from early morning until sometime after three o'clock, she thought about school: blackboards, chalk, papers, dusty hallways, desks, boys trying to look up girls' dresses and being so stupid when called on. This day, she did not want to be sitting in the doctor's office, waiting to have him feel up inside her. She missed world history and geography, recess and lunchtime with Lenore, and Alice, and Kate. Now that she lived in the same house as Lenore, they did not seem to like each other as much as before. It was probably because Rose had trouble looking at Lenore, and because Lenore seemed to always be looking straight at her.

Four hours later, the doctor saw Rose, after she changed positions many times in her chair. Dr. Strong did not seem to remember that he had said he wanted to see Rabbit. He was no different from all the other grown people who blew hard and then faded out. When her examination was done, the receptionist stared at her.

"My husband will be back in a little while with the money." Rose heard herself say the word "husband" and tried not to think about that, too. She went outside to wait for him.

Rabbit had said he would circle back every couple hours. Outside, Rose turned herself toward the direction she expected to see him coming from. She took a hunk of hoop cheese from her pocketbook and ate, standing almost at attention until her knees locked. She was hungry all the time. She walked back and forth, noticing how swollen her feet were. After 45 minutes passed and she could no longer stand, she spread a handkerchief upon the grass and sat. Another hour went by.

The doctor sped past her twice, probably rushing to a house call, leaving his waiting room full, but Rose saw no sign of her father-in-law's truck. She walked to the corner, almost to the funeral home, and sat on a bench. As she faced the beauty parlor, with her back to the dentist's office and the pool room, a familiar figure appeared and came toward her. It was Miss Bright. Rose stood up.

The tall schoolteacher, rushing toward the beauty parlor, stopped. She and looked down to where Rose's waist should have narrowed, were she not pregnant.

"I'm sorry you were not able to come back to school, Rose," Miss Bright said. "I was so sure you would be one of the ones to go to college."

Then she looked off, similar to the way the doctor had stared out the window that previous visit. When she spoke, it was almost to herself:

"Too many changes going on right now. There is talk of the boys going off to war, and the white people want to keep them out." Miss Bright blinked and turned her attention to Rose. She came back to herself, "Well, you are going to be alright. You are smart. And your baby will have a name."

Rose felt ashamed. Sweat trickled from under her arms. Every strand of hair on her head was tender. This was not like the little twinges of embarrassment that one felt over a too-long slip peeking out from under a skirtdress, or even the telltale spot of blood on the back of the dress just at your seat. No, this was shame at its purest. This was the kind of shame that made you look down at the ground to see if it had split wide enough for you to squeeze between. Rose dropped her head.

"Yes, mam. I'm married now."

Miss Bright was not married. Maybe nobody had asked her, or nobody had ever raped her. She was very old to not be married, at least over 25 years old. She probably slept by herself on a cot. Most people who slept by themselves slept on a cot. Maybe she had a big bed just for herself, like Rose's grandmother. Maybe she lived with her people.

"Oh, I know. I heard all about you getting married. I'm still sorry." Miss Bright looked at Rose then with such sadness that it settled into Rose, joining the pain in her ankles and feet and the hunger that tore at her middle. It sat there along with the shame. Miss Bright turned away. "Well,' I'm late for my appointment." And she rushed off.

Rose sat back down, still looking at the earth and wishing it would swallow her up. She reached into her pocketbook again, then took out a ham biscuit that her mother-in-law had given her.

"A pregnant woman hungry is the hungriest thing in the world," the older woman had said.

As Rose chewed, she wondered what the class operetta would be this year, witches and goblins or fairies and princesses. Last year, she had starred as Princess Maea. The thought was too painful; she tried to push it away.

When Rabbit finally pulled up in the truck, Rose climbed in and rubbed her ankles. Rabbit grinned at her and puckered his lips, making smacking noises. He handed her a barbecue sandwich and a paper cup of tea. The tea was lukewarm and there was no sugar, but still, she was amazed. She had planned to lash him with her words but, instead, she ate and drank.

When finished, she said, "That was nice of you," she said when she finished. "Where did you get the food?"

"Lila Belle said you would be hungry."

"The bootlegger woman?"

"You sound surprised. She is a person, too."

Rose shrugged. "I saw Miss Bright."

Rabbit kept his eyes ahead and said nothing. Rose looked at him.

"Rabbit, why did you quit school?" she asked. "Didn't you like it?"

"Sometimes I did. Sometimes I didn't," he said, his smile different from any Rose had seen before. "I was real good in math. I could figure in my head. Still can. 'Cause numbers, they make sense. They fit together. And they do things together. But I couldn't spell. I knowed that letters fit together but they don't make sense like numbers. They don' have no value. All letters the same. No big ones and little ones. Just stupid letters that if you put together wrong, you can't spell. And the teacher worried me to death, she thinkin' if I could do long division in my head, why couldn't I spell? Wouldn' let me be. Gone make me do it. Was gone to make me miss time with my boys. What was they gonna think? I told my mama—"

He laughed. "And you know Ida. She let me quit 'cause nobody mess with her children. I was 15. Now, I know I was wrong. But it was my fault, not mama's. Several of my boys quit with me. I was 15. One year older than you now. And look at you. Gettin' ready to have my baby."

He leaned over and kissed her on the place just below her lips, a teasing kiss that was meant to make her want more. Rose didn't move, but she felt the thrill run through her.

"What you talkin' about?" Rose said. "You got vowels and consonants. And when you put them together, they make up sounds."

The truck was speeding a little too fast out of town, and when he turned onto the county road, she fell against him and smelled liquor. He had been at the bootlegger's all day!

"Where is the money your daddy gave you for me to pay the doctor?" Rose asked. Rabbit pulled three dollars out of his pocket and handed it to her. Rose frowned. "Where is the rest?"

Rabbit didn't answer, and he didn't have to. Rose knew he was drunk. God. He was drunk. She stuffed it into her sock and sat the rest of the way with her lips pinched.

When Rose was in her sixth month, her father died. Gass Amos passed away, sitting peacefully in a rocking chair on

162

his porch, watching a sunset. Rose was devastated and let her husband hold her hand and comfort her at the funeral. She was more devastated when Doll Amos packed her mobile things and moved back to South Carolina, saying that Griffinton had never been her home anyway.

CHAPTER TEN

The radio repairman did not recognize Hart Lee on the street. It had been a year. All Negroes looked the same to him, except the women. The boys were stringy, with bullet hair and thick lips. He would not have noticed any difference between the mocha-colored Hart Lee and the dark chocolate-colored Rabbit if they all there were in the same room. If Hart Lee hadn't called attention to himself, the repairman wouldn't have connected the young man to the incident in the repair shop a year before.

But Hart Lee did call attention to himself. Their paths crossed in front of a warehouse, going in opposite directions. Hart Lee did not step off the sidewalk to let the man pass. Instead, he let out a sarcastic, "Howdy."

The repairman did not respond.

Hart Lee stared at the man and said in his voice that had only months before stopped cracking and now only cracked some of the time:

"White man, I better not catch you out in the dark." The man was alone. Hart Lee wanted to test a theory. He had heard that white men were not so tough alone, without other white men around. Hart Lee wanted to know, and he said it with his teenage blood rising. He said it as a lark.

Everybody said he wasn't much fun. He did not have the same easy air as Robert Earl; he could not get girls, though he had picked up some leftovers, as well as a few girls who would not have noticed him if he wasn't Robert Earl's younger brother. He didn't deliberately try not to be fun for others. He hated being teased, but he put all his energy into not letting anyone know. Everybody got teased. Boys teased each other, all the time in the doubles or just pure daily derision, slapping the backs of each other's heads, tripping each other. Hart Lee was always the first to get upset and got called a "crybaby" for it by the other boys.

"That ain't fair," he'd say, provoking the other boys to giggle and say, "Cry baby." He wished they could see him picking at this white man. Nobody could tell him then that he wasn't fun. No one would fail to see how brave he was. This *was* fun.

The repairman walked away without a word, but his white skin had gone ruddy red.

Hart Lee chuckled and skipped to his father's truck to wait for Kinchen.

He did see the man glance back over his shoulder, marking the truck in his mind. He did not know that the man immediately went to get help. Hart Lee changed his mind and, instead of waiting for his father, he took to walking along the street. Because of this, he did not see the repairman and his three white friends return and approach the car with baseball bats and a gun.

The men discussed smashing the windows of the truck, but they were afraid that it might be the property of a white man, being driven by that man's Negro worker. The truck would be easy enough to describe to the sheriff, who was familiar with most of the vehicles in the area. As the darkness that Hart Lee alluded to fell, the man went in search of the sheriff to tell him of Hart Lee's felonious assault.

Sometime later, Kinchen got into that truck and drove home alone.

Later that night, it was that same night, just before midnight, when the sheriff knocked on the door of the Cobb house, waking the house and getting Kinchen out of bed. The sheriff would not say why he wanted to see Hart Lee. When he left, Kinchen Cobb dressed himself. He took his shotgun down from the wall shelf, loaded it, and went outside into the night. He fired a shot up at the stars.

"For good measure," he told Ida. An answering shot came, probably from his friend, Gass Amos' house. Other shots could be heard. No, it was not Christmas Eve or New Years, and not the Fourth of July. But, like on the holidays, the Colored men were letting the white people know that they had guns. In the morning, Kinchen would tell the shooters that one of his boys might be in trouble.

Kinchen spent the night on the porch, calm as he pleased and unaware that white men wanted to talk to him. He still sat on the porch, awake, when Hart Lee came running along the path home, announcing himself with whistling—not an easy-going breezy whistling, but a breathy monotone percussive whistling, pushed out of his lungs as he ran. Breathless with the walking and puffing, he greeted his father.

"What you doin', Daddy?" Kinchen saw the boy's eyebrows arched, probably at the sight of the gun lying on the porch behind. "Hawks after a chicken or what?"

Hart Lee slowed to a trot as he got closer. He moved like he was backing up while gaining ground. His father realized that he was swinging wide, giving them space, coming in sideways, coming home after being missing all night.

"Naw. Ain't waitin' for no hawks." Kinchen put his hands on his knees to hold on and waited, very still.

"Goin' huntin', Daddy?" Hart was rising up on his feet and flattening down again, as though he had springs inside.

"Naw, ain't goin' huntin'. It ain't huntin' season." Kinchen paused, and the boy watched him expectantly.

At the edge of the porch, off to the side, Hart Lee slowed down and stood, as if he had a motor running inside, vibrating him.

"Tell me, Hart Lee. What would the sheriff want with you?"

Kinchen was motionless except for his eyes that searched Hart Lee, just as Hart Lee spotted his mother standing in the doorway behind the screen door.

"Don' know, Daddy." Hart Lee scratched the back of his head and swatted behind himself.

Ida Cobb spoke from the doorway just as Hart Lee saw the red in both his parents' eyes.

"Full moon last night," Ida Cobb said from the doorway. "Lordy mercy, you gone to have to leave here and go up North."

"Wait a minute, Ida," Kinchen said before addressing his son. "Don' you know the sheriff was looking for you, Boy? Said he just wanted to talk. What he want to talk to you 'bout, you think?"

"Told ya, don' know, Daddy." Hart Lee stood frozen and frowning. Kinchen pressed on.

"Where you been?"

"I was—well, see, I . . . what I done . . . I—," he looked at his mother, who seemed coiled, ready to leap to help him with his answer.

"Tell me the truth, Boy," Kinchen demanded. "Tell me the truth."

"I was with a girl. That's the truth, Daddy. I went by the liquor house, but I didn' do—nothin', I—real bad—I—."

"Well, did you see anything that the sheriff might want to know 'bout?"

Hart Lee only shrugged, looking anywhere but his father.

Kinchen hated that his son's eyes were dull and darting.

Then, he saw recognition come into those eyes. He saw his memory stirring there like something new creeping through a crowded place.

Hart Lee slapped himself hard on the front of his face with the open heel of his hand. "Damn!"

"Watch your mouth, Boy, in front of your mama," Kinchen warned, but he gave him a moment to think on his next words. A moment passed while Kinchen gave him time to think, still measuring him by the sight of him.

Then, in a soft, cracking voice, his motor still running, Hart Lee said, drooped a little. "I forgot, I seen that old radio repairman."

Kinchen leaned forward and Ida went rigid. "What you say to 'im?"

Hart Lee avoided their searching eyes. "I just . . . told him to be careful. It was getting dark. That's the truth."

His parents exchanged a glance. They looked at him and at each other; Ida made a sign of disbelief that Kinchen read and nodded to. They looked back at him, open-mouthed.

Kitchen said slowly, "Is that all you said?"

Hart Lee shrugged. "I said, 'Howdy'."

Both Ida and Kinchen knew that something had been left out. They knew that this was the child they could trust only so far. They knew there was no point in pressing further. He repeated himself for emphasis: "I said, I said, 'Howdy'."

Ida and Kinchen Cobb looked at Hart Lee and asked in unison, "Why?"

Hart Lee didn't answer. Time seemed to stop.

Just then, the stillness was interrupted by the rumble of an engine and the crunch of wheels coming up the driveway. The sheriff pulled to a stop and got out of the car.

They formed a tableau, the mother who came from behind the screen door, the daddy, who had stood up and put his gun on his shoulder.

"I'm gone have to take him with me," the sheriff announced. "I'll bring him back. Kinchen, I've knowed you a long time. I won't let nothin' happen to him."

Kinchen took a step forward. "What is this about?"

"Tell the truth, just somebody lookin' for trouble."

Hart Lee frowned. Slapped his thigh, shook his head and got into the back seat of the sheriff's car. They drove off.

Kinchen was the next to move. He bolted to Joseph's shed, came back to the porch, and went into the house to search for the keys to the truck. A few minutes later, he left with Joseph beside him, the Joseph who never went inside the house that Kinchen lived in, never went to church except to the graveyard once in a while, never visited anybody, much less went into town.

Hart Lee spent the night in jail. He was released the next day, after Kinchen and Joseph bailed him out. Joseph signed his name on the lawyer's papers, once the lawyer had seen to things. Ida had gone weak and sick with worry; she threatened her other children with the consequences of what would happen to them if they were sent to jail, but they didn't need to be told. They were scared, too.

When Kinchen, Joseph, and Hart Lee came home, Ida was clutching a stick for support. After that, her children would see her leaning on the stick while cooking in the kitchen or while wringing a chicken's neck with one hand in the backyard. The Cobb house, once neat and always arranged, became the kind of house where people had trouble finding a pair of scissors or a piece of store-bought soap. Things just got misplaced from then on.

The next night, in the dark, in bed after Hart Lee's night in jail, Kinchen lay next to Ida and explained to her that he and Joseph had trouble getting Hart Lee to understand the meaning of the word *bond.*

"First he say he understand about a bond, but then he say he don' understand," Kinchen said, heartache in his voice. "What he mean is, he don' *agree.* He don' care. He don' want nobody tellin' him what to do. But, it don' matter. He ain't got nowhere to go."

Although she heard the heartbreak in his voice, Ida spoke of her own concerns: "I don' want him to have to understand about no bond," Ida said. "I just don' want him to see the inside of a jail ever again."

Kinchen was quiet.

"The trial will be in two months and then it all be over," he said after a moment.

Ida said, "I don' want him to know. I don' want him to have to understand."

Just before he fell asleep, Kinchen thought of a house with windows at each end, with the wind blowing in from both sides, and the strong cross-currents in the middle tearing everything apart.

⁘

Rabbit jumped down off the wagon. He dropped the team's lines on the ground and proceeded to toss sacks of potash into the wagon bed. He circled the wagon and, just then, turned around once or twice and caught his foot in the reins. The mules felt the small jerk to their lines and began to walk. Rabbit fell to the ground with a yell, and the mules went faster. They dragged him along by his foot as they sped up into a run.

Kinchen looked up at the sound of his son's shout and sprinted towards the moving wagon. He caught up and stopped the runaway mules. Ida hurried out of the house and managed to catch up and stop the runaways. Rose had been coming from the hens' nests and came running, screaming as she held her belly in front of her. She discovered that she did not want Rabbit hurt, even though their marriage had not gotten beyond him wrestling with her every night.

When she saw Kinchen and Ida put Rabbit into the truck, she cried out in horror. Rabbit held his leg with the bone exposed. His clothes were torn, and he was covered in a mixture of blood and dirt.

"We got to clean him up," Kinchen said.

"There's no time!" Ida pushed Rose into the back of the truck and sat beside her.

The truck sped into town with Kinchen at the wheel with Rabbit beside him, shaking all over in silence.

Kinchen put his head out the window, flying down the road and said to the womenfolk in the back, "I would have drove the car if I had a knowed that all of Griffinton had to come."

Ida said, "Shut up." Rose whimpered. Ida, bumping along, sitting in the truck bed next to her pregnant daughter-in-law, added, "You shut up, too. I didn't have any idea you cared so much about him."

"I didn't either," Rose whispered and tried to get control of her sobs. Her hands stayed closed in fists that she held for all the 15 miles into town, as the truck bumped along, swallowing the dust on the dirt road until they got to the pavement of the big highway.

Outside the doctor's office, Kinchen half lifted, half dragged Rabbit to the door. Rabbit hadn't said anything the whole ride. His parents and wife knew that meant he was in extreme pain.

"I think it is mainly his ribs and his leg, look like," Kinchen said as they hurried through the waiting room.

The doctor bandaged Rabbit's face and chest, and after the doctor had set Rabbit's leg, he pulled up a chair up beside him and rested an arm alongside where Rabbit lay on a table, bandages about his face and chest, a cast on his leg. His good arm was tucked up behind his head, his elbows pointing to the ceiling.

"I was hoping to speak with you the last time your little wife was here," the doctor said. "I wanted to talk to you about her pregnancy, since this is your first—well, the first of your marriage. I sent you word to come, but you didn't. Well, finally maybe I went 'bout it the wrong way. All it took was you go picking a fight with some mules and here you come today."

"Didn' pick no fight. Just wasn't payin' no attention. Must have fell asleep."

"Humph. The way you smell, you were drinking. No? This early in the morning?"

"Not today. Yesterday."

"And how much you drink?" the doctor asked. "Enough for it to be seepin' out your pores a day later."

Rabbit pressed his lips together and didn't say anything.

The doctor sighed and let it go. "Alright, fine, you wasn't payin' attention and them mules ran away with you and dragged you by that leg," he continued. "That was the reason you had the accident. Now, what was the reason you didn't let me see you before today?"

"I was drinkin' that day. That is what I do now when I'm not workin'!"

"And real serious, too, it seems. Why is that?"

"'Cause I like to get 'bout drunk. No other reason to drink, is it?"

Dr. Strong was thinking how Rabbit did not look like any a rapist Dr. Strong had ever seen, and he had seen a number of them over the years. Boys he delivered who grew up to be evil. Those boys were tough on the outside, but this young man seemed gentle and unconcerned. Where other boys were desperate, he had the smile and swagger of a boy who had genuine charm; he was attractive enough to not have trouble talking a girl into yielding. But, just now, something was eating at him, other than that he had just been dragged by a mule. Dr. Strong saw it in Rabbit's refusal to look at him. Patients rarely did that under these circumstances.

"And why is that?"

"Sir?"

"Why you like to get drunk like that?" Dr. Strong asked.

"Nothin' special," Rabbit answered with a shrug. "I don' worry a whole lot about anything. I just drink to feel the floaty feeling. No other reason."

But he didn't tell the doctor about the things he didn't worry about when he was drunk. There was plenty he didn't want to deal with that this rich man would never understand. Someone once said, maybe one of his teachers, that people like Strong planned everything in their lives, and that that was how they got through school to be wearing white coats, and driving shiny cars, and putting soft hands on farm people like himself.

He looked at the doctor's fingers. His beige hands were hairy on the knuckles with snow-white, evenly cut fingernails. When he touched Rabbit, his hands felt like the hands of a woman, like how Rose's fingers had been when she first came to live with him five months ago. Now, her hands had become rough from the chores his mother assigned, and he had still had not consummated the union.

Rabbit swallowed. "I hadn' planned on bein' married. My daddy he tol' me to do my duty. He say my duty to marry Rose. My mama said wait an' see is the baby mines."

"She doesn't seem to me the kind of girl who has had sex with a whole lot of men," the doctor told him. "She is a child. You knew damn well that the child was yours."

"I know. It's not that I don' think it's my duty," Rabbit hesitated before making his confession. "It's that I don' want this duty. I ain't goin' nowhere. I know it's wrong to say. I hadn' planned on it."

"What had you planned on?"

"Nothin'."

"Beg your pardon?"

"I said nothin'."

"Kinda too late to decide that now, isn't it?"

They looked at each other for a moment. Rabbit didn't answer. Dr. Strong took a pipe from his pocket, shaking his head slowly, and packed tobacco into the bowl. Finally, the doctor seemed to realize that Rabbit wasn't going to answer.

"I am not a stranger," he said. "I know every room in the houses of your people and your neighbors. I know which houses have indoor plumbing, which ones have chamber pots and outdoor toilets, and I know which people go to the bathroom in the woods. What children I didn't deliver, Miss Sophie and Miss Mack midwifed."

Rabbit watched the doctor strike a match and hold it to the bowl of tobacco, puffing in and out to get it smoking. Dr. Strong lowered his voice to a whisper: "I have heard your name in the birthing rooms. And I've heard that you don't want obligation," Dr. Strong continued. He pushed a hand in a pocket and drew out a wooden matchstick. "This child is carrying your baby. She was minding her own business, looking at insects and blades of grass the day you gave her that baby. From what she told me, she is more than a burden to you. You have loaded her up like she was some goddamned pack mule at the tender age of 14." He leaned back and thumped the tobacco in the pipe bowl.

Rabbit looked away, only gave the doctor half his ear. Then he looked back, and he noticed how slight the man was. Like a child. It made Rabbit feel better that he was taller, more muscular. More manly.

The doctor stood up. He lifted a shoe behind his back and struck a match on the sole, balancing himself perfectly. Rabbit was surprised and a little annoyed at his agility. The doctor sucked the light into the pipe.

"Did you see how worried she was about you?" Dr. Strong stood. "Today, I mean."

"Worried?" Rabbit repeated. "Damn. She don' even want me to—"

He stopped himself; he was too much a man to reveal the truth, that his wife wouldn't have him. Dr. Strong lifted a knowing brow and Rabbit felt a prickle of irritation.

"What I mean is, she don' want me to do it certain times, I mean, well, she funny."

The doctor leaned forward.

"I know," he whispered with a hint of mockery. "I have examined her."

Rabbit's jaw clenched, throat tight with embarrassment. Dr. Strong took a deep pull from his pipe and exhaled the smoke.

"I know. She is tight. Don't worry. The way she teared up over your little fight with the mules, she will come around." The doctor paused, then added seriously, "But, Rabbit, be good to her."

Rabbit jerked his shoulders and tried to look incredulous.

"What? I don' do nothin' to her. She hardly let me touch her."

"You blame her for that? You think you deserve to?" Dr. Strong's voice was calm enough, but the hardness behind it was like steel. He spat a piece of tobacco. "You ain't planned for nothin', right? Well, well. You deserve it. She is all out of shape now. But, make a place for her in your unplanned life."

"We added another chair at the supper table," Rabbit said. Dr. Strong couldn't tell if he was trying to be funny or not.

"Is that enough, you think? Women and children have a way of making themselves their own place at tables."

He tried to read Rabbit and was disappointed in what he thought he saw. But then, Rabbit seemed gentle enough. But the doctor had seen plenty enough young marriages where the woman became the scratching stake for the not-ready husband to sharpen his claws against. This particular girl, Rose, inspired a protective feeling in him. Probably because he had seen her likes before. She was like one who had been here before, on this earth, and had learned with each return. Bright girls full of life who usually took about three to five years, slumped into a beast of burden with little similarity to her younger self. A person could only see so many of these souls before each weighed heavily on their own.

Dr. Strong shook himself. He reminded himself that he had others in the waiting room. He set aside his pipe and picked up Rabbit's chart, turning and scratching notes on it.

"That leg will heal, but there'll be scarring," he said. "You'll need to stretch it gently, gradually. Do that and the limp won't be as bad."

"Limp?" Rabbit's eyes widened and he looked more like a child in that moment than he had in the entire visit.

"You young," the doctor assured him. "Easier for things like this to heal when a person's your age. If you take care to be gentle."

The two men stared at each other, and Rabbit knew that Dr. Strong was talking about more than the leg. Rabbit gave a small nod, and the doctor released him.

A place at the table. Yes, she had weaseled her way to a place inside him even though he had not planned for her. He had planned on just being like he always was. That had been on his mind for the last few days. He had been thinking about how he had not had plans before Rose, and how much he had not wanted any change in the way he going before she lay sprawled in his path with her pretty legs and hips and eyes, sliding through his world pretending she didn't want him to suck all the sweetness out of her. He would rather have tasted her and moved on to the next. But her swelling belly stayed in his life, and she was a nagging, an irritation, a pebble in his shoe. He had fucked her only that one time. All too hurriedly on the ground in the fig grove and not in the slow-moving way that he liked.

The doctor had said that he would heal, but that there would be scar tissue, and he needed to move and stretch that new tissue gently and gradually. That if he moved correctly, the limp might not be too bad. He was young. The lessons would keep coming. This would not be the only scar tissue. What did he know? He was a doctor. Just because he knew babies didn't mean that he knew people.

On his way out of the office, his mother clucked like a setting hen, Rose whined like a bird, his father pushed him to take it like a man, and Rabbit looked up at a picture on the wall. He remembered that someone once told him that pictures and art were not the same. He looked down and saw a crust of manure in the fold of his pants and wondered if he could still draw pictures, and he thought about being able to draw a picture so that one could see that a mule was standing just on the outside. There was more in life that a picture could remind you of. He was not sure of what. He was not sure he wanted to be reminded of everything.

Rabbit recuperated in the loft of his parents' house, with his seven-months pregnant wife carting food, water, and lemonade up the stairs to him. In the daytime, Rabbit sat with his leg outstretched and drew pictures. Mostly pictures of Rose, sketched as he watched her tend to him or lay out to rest on the bed. She caught him watching her several times and stopped looking away when their eyes met. Then one day, in the daytime, she reached out her arms for him and placed his bare hands on her belly. The movement was tender and gentle, and Rose slowly guided his hands up and down her body, her eyes intent upon his, letting him know that he could give himself to her.

Ruby was born in March of 1940. By June of that year, Rose's breast milk dried up, only to return two months later in August, when she began vomiting again when waking in the morning. That baby, Sarah, came in April of 1941, and then they were four breathing human beings, living in the one room of the loft, the hat atop the lady's face.

Kinchen probed patiently as he bent his head next to his son's while they mended a tire together. He pointed which way to swing the harrow after loosening it from a mule hitch. Through a combination of his father's subtle nudging and his own weariness at the lack of space, the idea took hold in Rabbit's mind that he was a man with a family and needed to strike out on his own. With Ruby learning to throw things, and Sarah trying to suck her toes, both babies were in diapers. On rainy days, Rose cleaned the soiled diapers and draped them to dry on every surface of that upstairs room, herself in a crouched position in the draping.

Down the stairs and out the door, news of the war was growing, but the natural world around them was unconcerned. Dogwood blossoms unfurled, giving way to green leaves. The strawberries appeared outside the kitchen door. Early one morning, Rabbit borrowed his father's cart and drove to his friend Bow Willie's house. Bow Willie was the one who had sense enough to not knock up a girl that he would have to marry. He and Bow Willie drove into town.

Bow Willie slumped in the passenger seat, chewed a wooden matchstick and asked, "So, man. What you goin' to do, huh?"

Rabbit took a breath and spoke the words aloud for the first time. "I'm gonna enlist."

"Right now?" Bow Willie yelped.

"Right now?" Rabbit repeated mockingly, gripping the wheel. "Yeah, right now."

"You want to go to war?" Bow Willie was hesitant. The

thought of enlisting pulled at his insides. He did not have a wife and two babies like Rabbit. "You want to fight? You want to die?"

"Die?" Rabbit repeated as if he had never considered the possibility. "Naw. I need me a job. It's about a job."

"Rabbit, you ain't got to go to war for no job. You could go up North. You could sharecrop right here. You farmin' with your daddy."

Rabbit shook his head. "He ain't got enough land allotment for a family of mines and he ain't got no control. If they tell him he got to grow only three acres of tobacco for his land, he can't go add on another three to support for me and my family. They make him plow it up."

"Yeah, man, but you always been lucky," Bow Willie said. "You had to marry a girl, but she was a good girl. Not no whore. You know, can't love no whore. And you know, me and you, we made plenty whores. And you got your daddy, besides."

"You call that luck?" Rabbit scoffed. He lifted his palms. "Well, 'scccuusse me, Mr. Know-Everything-About-Me. What do you think you are, the expert know about love and whores and who's lucky and who ain't? Either one?"

Bow Willie was quiet for a moment.

"Don' you care nothin' 'bout her, man?" he asked finally.

Rabbit glanced at him sharply. "Now, that is none of your business."

But Bow Willie's smile was knowing and he nodded. "Oh, yeah. She got that collar round your neck for sure. And you tryin' to leave her 'cause you scared, that's what."

They located the war office by the life-sized Uncle Sam, his white face glowering with his finger pointing out as he demanded, "I want you!" Rabbit and Bow Willie went inside. A few minutes later, they came back out again, Rabbit and Bow Willie, each with hands shoved deep in their pockets, saying nothing to each other. They drove home in silence. The man had taken one look at them and said:

"Boys, ain't no need for you to fill out no papers even if you can read, which I doubt. You with that gimp leg, and you, boy, too fat. Probably got blood pressure."

When Rose found out Rabbit had tried to enlist, she erupted, throwing things in her whirlwind until Kinchen came up the stairs and said, "Daughter, quiet down and go to sleep."

Relatives came to visit from up North. They were Vate's and Florence's daughters, Delia and Alice, along with their husbands. They were in the habit of visiting each summer, spending one week in Rocky Mount and one week with Kinchen and Ida in Griffinton. They brought much gaiety and bright colors, in their cheap and hastily-gathered-for-the-trip shiny clothes with the price tags still on.

One night after supper, Delia, Alice, and Kinchen sat on the porch visiting with Joseph. Joseph had placed a chair in the yard and sat facing the porch.

Joseph asked, "Well, is the North got streets paved with gold?"

"Naw," Delia chuckled. "But we don' got to work in the hot sun."

"Reckon not," Joe shrugged. He looked out at the surrounding land. "So, you own your own place up there in New York, or you rentin' in a building with strangers, smelling the garlic and not even got a thick enough wall or a yard between you? Piled up on top of each other like rats?"

"Aw, Uncle Joe."

The two women both made slapping gestures and lit cigarettes. None of the women in Griffinton smoked except the Coppage woman, her sisters, and the women who frequented the bootlegger's.

"Who you workin' for, people who don' know your name?" Joe went on. Alice narrowed her eyes and puffed on her cigarette.

"Why you talkin' 'bout the North?" she asked. "What 'bout they puttin' your grandson's child in jail for sayin' 'Howdy' to a white man?"

Kinchen's shoulders slumped, but Joe waved it away.

"Oh, he be alright. I got him a lawyer and we got him out on bond."

"On bond?" Delia repeated.

"Yeah," Kinchen sighed. "Daddy wouldn' borrow money to send nobody to school, but he put his land on the lineup for Hart Lee's foolishness."

"On bond?" Delia said again, tapping ash off her cigarette. "Sittin' here waitin' for a trial that ain't gonna be fair? What, what, Uncle Joe, you *want* Hart Lee to go to prison, or the road, or what? Kinchen, what about you?"

"Naw. I don' want my boy in jail," Kinchen leaned back into his chair. "I know that whatever he done, it didn' call for all this. He probably didn' do nothin' and it ain't fair, none of it. But when this world give a damn about fair?"

No one said anything after that. The ladies smoked, and Kinchen drank with their quiet husbands, who hid the liquor from the women in paper bags.

During their visit, Rabbit paid the relatives little mind, except the compliments of the women, who admonished, "Pity you is kin. Pity you is married. Pity you is younger," in exchange for Rabbit's disarming smile. They played with his two babies and smiled at his little wife. Offered her cigarettes that she refused. The women said to each other, "She a busy little thing, ain't she? Rabbit, you ought to bring your family up to the North and get a job." Rabbit shrugged and went to the fields.

Hart Lee listened and asked questions about the city. Tall buildings? How tall? Taller than Planters Bank? Is it a place where there are so many people that you could walk around and not worry about somebody saying they saw you do something or go somewhere? A place that don't have porches where people sit looking out at cars that go by and guess where they are going? A place where maybe rumors don't circulate like the air itself? Where women wear short dresses and smoke cigarettes walking down the street?

In the days before they left, before their annual vacation was up, with all her smiling that hurt her face as smiles do when they come from outside, it was not hard for Ida to convince the women to take Hart Lee away with them. Everybody sat around the dinner table, when the conversation eventually got around to Hart Lee and his being out on bail and awaiting trial. What was to become of him? What usually happened when a white man got up in court and pointed a finger at a Colored?

Only Joseph seemed to have faith that everything would turn out. Joseph believed that because he was in the owner-ship class, his land protected him and his own from ordinary troubles.

But Ida was not so sure. She saw the trouble in Kinchen's eyes and knew that he felt the same way. But she also knew that Kinchen would never agree to Hart Lee running away. Menfolk had a thing about what it was to be a man, and running away was not a part of it. They wavered when white men pointed the finger, but still, there was the matter of the land. It was the source of all that had made their lives bearable. It kept them from poverty. It wasn't so bad working in gummy tobacco when it was for yourself.

Even so, Ida did not care one ounce for the land when

she thought of her son wearing prison stripes and chains on his ankles. All prison was for Black people was a place to grind and grub their lives away. Besides, she would not have minded leaving the land and going to the city, where she would not have to throw her dishwater out the kitchen door. It did not seem to her a bad thing to live way up high in a building, looking out at the lights of other people's homes. She had lived in a city once, but she barely remembered it. Now, all she could easily see was the sun that beat down in the summer, berating the workers of the land, and the moon that hung like a picture at night, determining when they planted or harvested, changing as it hung.

None of it was worth risking the life and freedom of her son.

Luckily, the visiting husbands were tumbledown drunks and had not even bothered to try to pack the car themselves, but sat by while their wives did the work for the trip. The day they left, the men couldn't stand up straight enough to place a car boot. Ida had seen to that. She'd done something the day before that she never thought she would do. With her egg money, she bought a gallon of whiskey from the Coppage woman, the bootlegger, telling her that it was for colds and flu, just in case. And just after breakfast, she gave it to the husbands to share. They were like babies, as if they had never been weaned from the breast. Always drinking and sucking a bottle or a tit, like the only time they could feel anything good was when something wet and strong ran down their throats.

Then, as the women packed the car, Ida made her final move to appeal for Hart Lee. If he stayed, he was almost guaranteed to see time on a chain gang. Ida couldn't let that happen. She would take on the whole world for him and make a pact with the devil to save him from that. All that week she had kept her lips peeled from her teeth as a show of warmth to hide what she was planning to do.

"Dis don' make no kinda sense. What is all y'all got in the trunk of this car that you got the seats piled up like it is?"

Everybody was there to see them off. Rose stood on the porch holding her children, the oldest clutching a doll with no head that the Smith woman had given. Rabbit smiled and bent to kiss his cousins' cheeks. Kinchen winked at the men. Joseph teased them about leaving civilization to go back to the cold-hearted northerners. Lenore and Millie stood by, smiling and waving. Only Hart Lee was missing, and when Kinchen noticed this, Ida claimed he was still in bed.

Ida waved goodbye to the visitors as the Dodge automobile rolled out of the Cobb backyard, pointed toward New York. She leaned on the porch rail, sweat pooling at her armpits and sliding off her nose and upper lip. She had been stooped and curled in on herself, bent over since the night Hart Lee spent in jail. Now she bit her lip to hide her relief, trying not to let Kinchen see her happiness. He would think that she was glad to be rid of the sisters instead of guessing the secret in the trunk.

They came every year at the same time and brought their complaints with them.

"I can't get used to being so far from a store." Alice would sigh.

"And all these flies. How do you deal with the flies?" Delia once said, nose pinched between her index finger and thumb. "And all the dirt. All this dirt."

Every morning, she would ask Alice, "Did you hear the rooster crow? Seem like I was sleepin' so good. I'm not gonna miss that one bit."

But at the dinner table, they moaned with pleasure and confessed that they loved country food: the fresh vegetables, the plentiful hog meat, the cured-almost-rancid salt hams, and Ida's wonderful red-eye gravy.

There on the porch, when the car had driven away, Ida placed her hand under her breasts after she rolled it into a fist and held it there where she felt a hollow. The boy in the trunk of the car was her flesh and had once filled that hollow place. She had not carried him there only to have him molder in a prison or toil away on a chain gang. The car shrank in the distance, and Ida had the terrible feeling that she would never see him again. But that could not be. He was her flesh. He could not be separated from her.

CHAPTER ELEVEN

Lenore wrote to Rose from Saint Augustine College in Raleigh, North Carolina.

October 23, 1943

Dear Rose,

> *I'm writin' cause I want you to write me so I will have mail like the other girls. And I don't think Mama will write. We are learning so much, not just in books but how to be ladylike. I guess you won't understand.*

love,
Lenore.

When Rose read the letter, she had just finished wiping Ruby's behind. She did not write back. Lenore did not give up right away.

November 20, 1943

Dear Rose,

> *Are you mad at me cause I am in school and you not? Not my fault. I have not had any mail*

since I got here and everybody gets letters from home but me. I know you busy with two babies. But you not too busy to write.

Love,
Lenore Cobb

Rose said to everyone who would listen, "I don' have time to write to Lenore. Somebody write her and tell her that for me, please."

So, Kinchen responded,

Nov. 27, 1943

Dear Lenore,

They tell me you want some mail. I will write you.

How come you didn' tell ME? You know I loved school myself and want to hear about everything. I am so proud of you. We fixing a fence around the new ground. I remember when you were a baby, we blasted the stumps.

Your daddy,
Kinchen.

Dec. 6, 1943

Dear Daddy,

I like getting letters from you. Now I can walk from the mailbox reading and pretend I have a boyfriend somewhere. Smiles. I forgot to ask, how come you didn't finish school?

Your daughter,
Lee

Dec. 19, 1943

Dear Lenore,

I finished school. In my day Griffinton had nothing but a school from first grade to seventh.

I finished that. Not only that, ask your Granddaddy.

I won the spelling contest in 1910! The best speller in the whole school. I spelled the word constitutionality and was the only one still standing up when I finish.

What do you know!? I even helped get the high school that you went to. They did not want the Colored to have a high school. We had the help of the Colored Baptist Church first. Then, by the time you got there, the county had took over.

Your daddy,
Kinchen Cobb

January 8, 1944

Dear Daddy,

How come mom doesn't write me?

January 20, 1944

Dear Lenore Baby,

Your mama is busy running this house. And she worry about Hart Lee, not knowing where he is. I don't think she written a letter since before I married her.

Then she didn't have much to say. We cleared off the corn fields and switch it so we put cotton there next year and corn fields where the cotton used to be.

You know bout how cotton is a thief . . . It robs the ground so it not a good idea to plant it in the same place more than two years in a row. Bet they don't teach you that in that school.

Be sweet.

your daddy,
Kinchen Cobb

January 27, 1944

Dear Daddy,

Naw! We don't study bout crazy stuff like that where to put corn or cotton. We learn about history and ancient Greeks and the Romans.

I don't like the math, but I try hard. Don't like Biology either.

Lee

February 15, 1944

Dear Lenore,

When did you get to be Lee? Was that what I name you? You learn about the Romans and Greeks in church and Sunday School. It put you way ahead. Do they teach bout the Romans killing the Christians?

Your brother and Rose is had another pretty baby girl.

Be sweet.

your daddy,
Kinchen

February 23, 1944

Dear Daddy,

I told you we learn real stuff here! Not that stuff you think. In a hurry, got to go.

Lee

March 1, 1944

Dear Daddy,

I am so happy. I am now an Episcopalian. The Episcopalians don't make all that noise like the Baptists. I have memorized all my prayers.

Love,
Lee

March 17, 1944

Dear Lenore,

First of all your name not no lee, you Lenore and how dares you leave the Christian Church?

your mama, Ida

The last letter that Lenore wrote home from college was in the year of her graduation, 1948.

May 1, 1948

Dear Daddy,

there is no need for you to come to my graduation or mama or anybody. I will find a way home. Don't come.

Lee

It was after Hart Lee left, breaking his bond, that Kinchen sat down to talk with Rabbit about his and Rose's future.

"Someday, they will take this land away from us. Your brother and his mother have seen to that. Sloane Smith spoke to me, askin' if you want a job drivin' tractor for him. Used to be that white boy, Thomas, but he got in some trouble and ran. Sloane have a house you can move into. Go talk to him." Kinchen paused, glancing back at the house. "Be good for you to get away from here. I don' think Rose and your mama will ever be the best of friends. He have a house you can move into."

CHAPTER TWELVE

Rabbit finished plowing for the day. He eased up on the brake and drove along the edge of the field and then turned onto the road. The tractor sounded a deep *put-put-put* sound. Rabbit lit a cigarette and tossed the empty pack onto the side of the road. He drove onto the pavement and followed the road until he reached the turnoff for his house, but then he passed it to continue to Dozier's store a quarter of a mile away. He drove into the parking lot, a bald spread of packed ground covered with discarded soft drink caps that had been driven into the dirt by car tracks. He stopped the tractor next to the Royal Crown Cola sign with the smiling woman offering the world a bottle. The tractor rocked anxiously beneath him a second or two after he had turned off the engine.

It was Friday afternoon. The sun had dropped low over the freshly plowed fields. If it had been a mule, the tractor would have rolled over, while the mule kicked up its heels on the dirt and got back up on its feet to stand hangdog, pointing toward the stable.

Rose did not like for him to go inside Dozier's store. Rose said that Dozier was a Ku Klux Klan member. Rose worried a lot, both about things she could point to specifically and also about things that just felt funny to her.

Four years after their marriage, it seemed she was always warning him and reacting and full of feelings. She missed her mother and saw signs everywhere. She had feelings that bad things were going to happen and didn't know why.

She had claimed bad feelings back before Peggy's baby was killed too. Peggy was a Griffinton who had gone to school with Rose. Rose was pregnant before Peggy, but poor Peggy did not marry and was spurned and described by the putative father as being as common as pig's tracks, his reason for not marrying her. The baby died a bloody death. All that time, when she had the bad feelings, Rose had kept her own children under close watch, saying that she felt something coming, something bad, something with wings that made a whooshing sound as it swooped down. Later, she said that the dogs had probably gone right past the house the day that they broke out after the storm.

But during that time, Rabbit had paid little attention to Rose's ramblings, because she was always reacting, always guarded. There was that time when Mrs. Smith stopped by the house with boxes of hand-me-downs for Rose and the children. It seemed that one of her relatives in Rocky Mount had given them to her, or so she said. Rose had a fit over a headless doll in one of the boxes.

"Is that white woman crazy? What she think my children can do with this?"

While she was hollering at Rabbit about the doll, Ruby picked it up and began to cuddle it against to her neck. Eventually Rose made a head for the doll, but Rabbit was not able to get Rose to choose more carefully the things she reacted to.

"Don' worry about everything," he kept telling her, but Rose kept on. That didn't mean that Rabbit had to go along with it, though.

Rabbit stepped down from the tractor and walked across the gravel to the front door. He heard the crunch of footsteps behind him, following him inside. The door closed and Rabbit approached the counter. Someone came onto the grounds just as he went in and closed the door behind him from inside. Before him, Dozier sat behind the counter in a rocking chair on the opposite side. Dozier held a flyswatter taut in one hand, and ready to strike at some tiny, unseen gnat.

He wasn't like Sloane Smith who, nearly each time Rabbit called, had to put down a book and reach for a discarded envelope to fold or tear a corner of a newspaper to mark his place. Dozier never looked like a man who was thinking, more like something that was empty.

"I'd like a pack of Camels," Rabbit said.

Dozier glanced at him, then over his shoulder.

"Wait, boy," Dozier said without looking at Rabbit. Rabbit turned to see that Dozier's brother-in-law, a man called Loving and a newcomer to Griffinton, stood behind him. The space between his shoulder blades tightened involuntarily, and he made a small movement away. Loving eyed Rabbit. Dozier continued, answering Loving's unasked question. "This here boy is one of Sloane Smith's nigras."

Loving kept his narrowed eyes on Rabbit a moment longer.

"Now, Smith," Loving said, repeating the name to Dozier. "He seem a lil different from everybody else 'round here. Is he from somewhere else?"

"Naw," Dozier shook his head. "He been off from here, to Yale University and back. But, he one of us. Don' act like it, but he is. That's why ain't nobody runned him off yet, even if he do act like some ol' carpetbagger."

Rabbit fumbled in his pocket for something to do, to appear occupied, and came out with a dollar bill. Not that he had a five dollar bill, but if he had one, he would never trust Dozier to give him the correct change. The two men continued talking as if Rabbit wasn't there, like they had all day to themselves.

"Don' nobody bother to try to talk no sense to Sloane Smith," Dozier continued, shaking his head. Loving tucked his hands into his pockets, listening closely. "We leave him alone cause he is one of us even if he do act like some ol' carpetbagger."

Loving nodded congenially, hanging on every word Dozier spoke. "We understand him and so far, he ain't done nobody no real harm. We keep a eye on 'im, but he is one of us. Trouble is, he ain't never had to scratch like the rest of us."

The two men acted as though not another human being was in the room, waiting between them to buy some smokes. Rabbit stood patiently. Dozier's voice hummed on. "His grand-daddy, during the Civil War, hid a whole bunch of cotton in the middle of the creek—some say right near one hundred bales of it—on some cypress stumps built like platforms and covered with branches and brushtrees and limbs. When the Yankees come through here, they rattled everything around but that stockpile stayed hid off out there, looking like for all the world like a burly snake-infested island."

"I heard about something about that," Loving said, nodding with interest.

"What nobody can't figure out is why not one of them damn slaves told it to a soul. The hidin' place." Dozier shook his head, puzzled, and looked at Rabbit as if he might have the answer or else stunned by the thought of loyal dark-skinned people.

Rabbit lowered his eyes as Dozier looked toward him in puzzlement, but only for a second before the jolt was gone. Dozier continued, "When the Civil War was over, my granddaddy, your wife's granddaddy, and all the rest of the men didn't have nothing but Confederate money and ruined crops. Sloane Smith's granddaddy turnt his cotton over for pure United States currency. Some say he got pretty near to $80,000 cash in 1866. So afterwards, my granddaddy, hell, and all the white men around here, had to give old man Smith mortgages. Some paid out of debt, some didn'. That's how Sloane and his brother—now his brother is more like us—made it. And he went to Chapel Hill, but he didn't do nothin' while he was there and after a couple three years, he come back home. They got these farms that passed on from their granddaddy and from their daddy."

Dozier cleared his throat and packed a lug of chewing tobacco into the hollow of his left fist. He absently tapped at the chunk of tobacco before placing it inside his jaw. "They sent Sloane off to Yale University. I didn' think he'd come back here, but he did. Then, he went away again, off to fight the Great War in Europe the first time in 1918, and then he come back again. And he don' care nothin' about a Colored boy goin' up and down the road drivin' his tractor and he nowhere lookin' after him."

Rabbit shuffled a little to unlock his knees. Dozier cleared his throat and finally directly addresed the young man in front of him.

"Yeah, Rabbit, what you want?" he asked. Then, as if he'd absentmindedly forgotten what Rabbit had asked for instead of disregarding him completely, asked, "Oh. A pack of Camels? You got cash for a *whole* pack, or you want two or three?"

"The whole pack."

Dozier snorted, and Tas he handed the unopened pack to Rabbit, he said to Loving, "And another thing about Sloane Smith. He pay his nigras cash money."

Dozier held the dollar bill that Rabbit handed him up to the light. He took it and gave Rabbit the unopened pack of cigarettes and his change. Rabbit took the cigarettes, closed his fist over his change, and walked to the tractor he had parked beside the store. Just as he hoisted himself up onto the tractor seat, he opened his fist and counted a whole dollar in change. He blinked, looking from the money in his hand and back to the store, unsure of what to do. Dozier would be furious to have his mistake pointed out by a Negro, even if it meant he owed more money. Even so, he had had to listen to the usual Dozier talk. Maybe Rose was right.

It wasn't true what Dozier said about Sloane Smith not keeping close enough' check on his workers. Smith's red Chevrolet pickup truck rolled up and down, back and forth, on weekdays through the 200-year-old settlement of Griffinton: around past tenant houses, over crossroads, past Griffinton's store and churches, past the hall and parlor farm houses, the clipped gable bungalows. It made its rounds by the log tobacco barns, snake fences, and the many triple-A cottages and the fields. In that way, making his rounds, Sloane Hogan Smith managed various income-producing enterprises. He had inherited most of the farms from his father, but one or two came from his wife's late parents. He had inherited a mill, the Hogan textile mill, from his mother's family, and Sloane managed it for himself and his three maiden aunts, all of whom were in their eighties.

Sloane Smith routinely stopped in at the mill in the city. He strode in and out of the seed, feed, and hardware store that had belonged to his grandfather and his father and now belonged to him and his brother, Nathan. Everyone knew his routine as he drove that red pickup up and down and all around Griffinton making his rounds.

Things still looked peaceful and harmonious in 1949 that first Monday, all day, when Sloane Smith's red pickup truck stayed parked in the backyard under the wisteria tree in the spot where he had put it sometime Saturday. Because he was not a church-going man, it was not unusual for it to stay all day Sunday.

In the fields and at the mill, the workers slowed their movements, peeked over their shoulders, and awaited Sloane Smith's appearance. They thought they saw him just coming or just leaving, always just out of the corners of their eyes. On Tuesday, he still did not appear. Those first two days, he was the ghost in their minds, only just a hair out of sight, floating on the edges of what they did. On Wednesday afternoon, the third day of Sloane's absence, the mill supervisor left the mill for the Smith residence, where he knocked on the door.

He was let inside by Sloane's wife. The mill supervisor followed her to a sitting room, walking behind her as she cantered down a dark hallway. She plucked frantically at worrisome areas of her scalp. The mill supervisor came away from the Smith house minutes later, shaking his head. He had a choice, to tell or be silent and alone in his sadness. He chose the sadness, and no amount of questioning could cause him to say what he had seen. His silence fueled the workers' longing to know.

The field workers left the fields furtively. The men lounged about on their porches and drove slowly up and down past Sloane's house. The women whispered as they went about, gathering a vast lack of news but eavesdropping for material to tell. On the fifth day, one field worker, a hardy, white-haired Black man who had worked for Sloane's father, walked stiffly up Sloane Smith's driveway. On the porch, he respectfully removed his hat before knocking on the door. Mrs. Smith invited him in with an impatient wave of the hand. The worker turned his hat in his hands, carrying it like a pie plate as he followed her into the same sitting room that the mill supervisor had invaded a few days before. The worker hooded his eyes when he looked at Sloane, who sat with a gun resting on his knees. Sloane's arms were folded across his belly.

Sloane, who was past 60, with white hair and blue eyes, seemed calm enough. The worker had seen him like that before, sitting in the same chair, his gun nearby. Everyone knew that Sloane loved to shoot almost as much as he loved his dogs. But this day, Sloane simply stared at the wall. The worker felt a familiarity with seeing Sloan sitting there with his gun. But something was a little different. After a moment, the worker said:

"Is you think it gon' rain anytime soon? If do, blue mold'll get the 'bacca, sure."

Sloane gave no answer to the man, whom he had known all his life. He didn't look up or ask about the man's rheumatism, or the latest count of great- grandchildren, for the man to describe the number marching around thirteen. The man waited only a moment and then, without waiting for Mrs. Smith to show him out, walked backwards from the room and into the hallway before he broke into a trot out the door, down the hallway, relieved to reach the daylight.

One or two others followed the old worker who, unlike the mill supervisor, chose to talk and report to all what he had seen. His wife Mrs. Smith opened the door to them and alternately wrung her hands and scratched her head, always looking as though she had tried to dry her face. The workers came equipped with questions the way a doctor might come with stethoscopes and thermometers. It was their way of letting Sloane know what they were doing, their way of trying to bring him back.

"Should we plant corn now or you want to wait?"

"What 'bout the ditches, you want 'em dug?"

"What 'bout the new ground stumps? You have to get the dynamite to blast."

They were not afraid watching him, even when he unfolded his arms and laced his fingers around the barrel of the shotgun that lay across his knees. What they knew about him was that Sloane was not a killer. He was not capable of killing anything, unless the prospective target had hurt a baby.

By the following Monday, Mrs. Smith no longer let them into the sitting room. By the next weekend, they spied on him through the window near the front porch while they waited for his wife to carry questions and messages to him. From the porch through the window, they could see her ask him something, and they could see him not answer.

Rabbit was Sloane's tractor driver. He went to the Smith house to talk to Sloane Smith about a punctured tractor tire, and to say that he needed to attempt a repair, but that he couldn't get the three-foot rim off by himself and couldn't get anyone to help unless Sloane told someone to. The wife brought back the non-answer with a shake of her head and worried eyes. Rabbit walked away feeling tenderness for Sloane Smith and disappointment for himself. His job was at stake, a good, wage-paying job. A job with regular wages that few Black man had. He could not help but think of his future and wonder what would happen to him if Sloane Smith did not get up out of that chair, put the gun away, and make his rounds again, like before?

During the second week of his absence, Sloane Smith tried to kill the glare on the inside of his wife's china cabinet and on the whatnot shelves by shooting up all the carnival glass. He reloaded and then put the gun to his head, but the gun misfired. He had gone on living when he died. Those who saw him had to take his pulse to know that he lived, and, when they did, they found a slow but strong, deliberate beating pulse.

When the doctor left the house, stating that Sloane was in some kind of shock that he could probably come out of when he wished, Sloane Smith's brother, Nathan Smith, apprehended Mrs. Smith as she sat in a straight-back chair, sobbing and scratching her scalp. Nathan handed her a glass of water and a BC powder that he had had the prescience to bring for her from the store. While she held her head back, letting the powder drop on her tongue, before drinking from the glass in his hand, her brother-in-law talked. He saw her thinning hair, and when he touched her cheek with his palm, he felt her yielding, leaning toward him.

"Trust me," he said. "I'll pick you up and bring you back all the times we have to go to the courthouse to file the papers and talk to the clerk and petition to ask for the powers—" his voice trailed off and he finished the sentence with his hands as Mrs. Smith whimpered into her water glass.

"Trust me," he said.

His sister-in-law didn't see she had many other options.

Thus, Nathan Smith and Maggie Smith began the legal circuit to declaring Sloane Smith incompetent to handle his businesses.

The hearing was scheduled a week after the papers were filed, a month and a half after Sloane stopped making rounds. Those that were at the courthouse that day, the ones who saw the notice in the newspaper, said that several of Sloane's neighbors, the white people, among them Dozier and Loving, testified.

The testimony characterized Sloane Smith as a madman. The witnesses cited a number of specific grounds: the fact that he preferred solitude to society, that he loved hunting dogs but refused to kill squirrels or deer or raccoons. They pointed to his talking out loud and reading poetry to his dogs, and his recent shooting up of his wife's carnival glass in their home. They cited his extreme carelessness in giving cash to his Black workers, in a community where the planters preferred that their workers use script in the boss men's stores. They accused him of giving more money than was needed, one witness testifying that when the price of cotton dropped from twenty cents to ten cents per pound, "He still paid his nigras cash, opening up a whole quagmire of complaints coming at us from all the sharecroppers to fret and worry us to death. They nearabout stopped working for meanness."

The dramatic testimony was that Sloane's mental condition had intensified after he decided and carried out the killing of his own prize bulldogs, that before then, Sloane Smith could not be expected to do anything other than shoot tin cans and cardboards tacked to cedar posts.

Sloane's wife was radiant, perhaps due to the restfulness of driving once or twice a week to the state hospital to visit her husband, rather than dodging flying food and empty whiskey glasses. She was radiant on the day she told how, after the great seven-day rainstorm, his dogs had escaped from the electric pen and wandered the countryside of Griffinton. They had come upon a Colored baby lying on a pallet in a patch of sunlight, left sunning on the grounds outside a house.

The mother, Peggy Miller, had placed the baby there to soak up the sun that, after the rain, was new and strange and rare. Sloane Smith's two dogs wandered into the yard, ambled up to the baby lying on its back and clapping at sunbeams. She thought that perhaps they had stopped to sniff the bubblers in the baby's mouth that smelled of its mother's milk. It was her guess that when they finished shaking and chewing the baby, they stood over the bloody remains for a moment before moving on. She had seen them do it to a rat. To a dog, there was probably little difference between the two.

Everyone was sorry, Clara Smith said. The Colored people and the whites always showed each other sympathy and respect when somebody died or got sick, during hurricane cleanups, and after house fires. People of Griffinton loved to take food to the front doors of new and temporary victims of tragedies. Clara herself said that even she even took a whole baked chicken to the family. To her, that was enough. She knew that nobody liked or wanted to see babies suffer, even Colored babies. She could not understand, however, why her husband had gone to such extremes as to giving the mother money for the burial and more besides. And then slumped into a mental state. She had told him just to put the dogs back in their pen. Everyone would soon forget.

When Sloane trained his gun upon the dogs, they had each fidgeted and thumped their feet lovingly on the gravel. He looked each in the eye when he pulled the trigger. She had watched from the kitchen window. It was a silly thing to do. Everyone knew. That was proof he was not a sane white man.

⁕

Rabbit was in Jack John's store when he first heard that the court had ruled on of Sloane's lack of sanity. He considered going home to talk to Rose, but even after four years, he didn't often discuss serious issues with her. She was too easily upset. She often worried about how they would get along. Now that there were three children, she was the great protector who often reminded him of a setting hen.

That day, when he got home, Rose was plodding through the two-room house, straightening, dusting, cleaning. Rabbit began to feel crazy himself. He grumbled at having to shift the position of his legs when she brushed a broom across the floor near him where he sat in a rocking chair; it was too much trouble for him to shift the position of his legs.

It was 1945 and there were five of them now. They, who had begun as two in a fig grove on a hot sticky day, were Rose, Rabbit, Ruby, Sarah, and the baby Nora. Rose was not a girl anymore. At 19, she seemed a decade away from the beginning.

Ruby took the broom from her mother and dragged it across the floor the way she'd watched her mother do it. Nora lay sleeping in a bed roll in the corner. Sarah held onto Rose's leg with one hand while sucking the thumb of the other. Rose walked gently, dragging the laughing Sarah through the room. Rabbit stood up, almost decisively, then hesitated as he looked through the open door to the next room at Rose and Sarah. He watched Rose walk slowly, gently dragging the attached Sarah with her into the kitchen. The little girl giggled. Rabbit sat back down and decided to say nothing about Sloane Smith. For a while, at least.

As soon as he sat down, Ruby came up behind him and draped one arm around his neck, holding the broom with the other. Rabbit tilted his face to press a kiss to the girl's head. Sarah suddenly detached from her mother and ran at her father, throwing herself into his lap. Rose put plates on the table, scraping noisily in the kitchen, and called Rabbit to eat. He stood up, placing the girls in front of him, giving them each a gentle nudge forward. They ran to the table, Ruby dragging the broom along behind her. From the doorway, Rabbit gazed at the greens Rose had set out. There was no sign of any fat meat in the meal. He could tell by the dull smell.

He had nearly reached the table when a noise outside stopped him. He went to the window to look out, squinting through the dust on the glass. The dog, who had been dozing on the porch, had leapt to his feet, and he then rolled himself over the edge of the porch and under the house. The chickens fluttered and clucked, marching briskly into the henhouse in broad daylight. Rabbit frowned, unable to see the disturbance, but something had clearly approached the house. He turned to face his wife and daughters, all seated at the table with wide eyes and raised brows. He heard and felt the dog's bony shoulders touching beneath the floor as he slid into hiding.

Then, suddenly, behind him, the front room door crashed open behind him. Nathan Smith, Sloane's brother and Rabbit's new boss, walked right into the house and came briskly to the kitchen. Rabbit instinctively jolted forward to stand in front of his family. Sloane, the legally insane of the two brothers, would never have put his hand to the doorknob of Rabbit and Rose's house without knocking and waiting to be invited in. But Nathan Smith, evidently, was not the waiting type.

"You Nigras is probably the cause of my brother going crazy," he announced without preamble. "But, I'm in charge now."

Rabbit stood still in front of his wife and children. Ruby dropped the broom and ran around the table to her mother, Rose, who had reached an arm out to her. Rose folded her daughters into the fabric of her dress, nearly placing them under her skirt for protection. They poked and jabbed little hands around her thighs to hold on. From the front room, the baby squalled. Rose twitched toward her, but a tiny twitch of Rabbit's outstretched hand stopped her. Nathan took a step forward and the rest of them took a step back. Rose kept lifting her leg and swatting down at them. They all—Rabbit, Rose, the two children, and the visitor—circled and swayed in that tiny kitchen.

"I don' need you to drive the tractor no more," Nathan continued. "I got me somebody else to do it. If you want to stay here, you welcome to, but you be a sharecropper just like all the other nigras."

Rose walked, dragging the hanging children to the table to put it between her and the man. Rabbit stood in front of the table, fixed to his spot.

Nathan continued. "Monday morning, I want you to tear down your henhouse and get rid of the chickens. I'm going to want to grow crops right up to your front and back doors. And, won't be no garden this year. I know my brother let you do anything you wanted to, but things have changed. From now on, you get your food on credit out of the store. We settle up at the end of the year."

Rabbit saw Rose look expectantly at him, waiting for him to find his voice. He even thought that surely he was going to say something. But he could not lift the weight of his tongue.

The girls grabbed at her, afraid, but she just swat their hands down, preoccupied. Rabbit stared at Nathan, this man who was in their house like he owned it, reminding them that it was his house or his brother's house and, in either case, he did own it.

Rabbit didn't say anything, just standing there rigid and still.

Rose stood up a little straighter.

"Why you takin' away everything we have to feed ourselves?" Rose asked. "We don' have no money."

"Like I said, you don't have to stay here, Rabbit," Nathan said, addressing the man in front of him even though it was Rose who had spoken.

"Can't you keep your woman quiet?"

Then, Nathan Smith looked at Rose the way that Rabbit felt a man should not look at someone else's wife. His eyes rolled up and down her physique. He laughed. "You is busy. I believe she is gone drop you another baby."

Rabbit blinked, then glanced at his wife. Until then, he had not looked at her closely enough and had not known, but now, as he took her in, it was clear.

She's a witch, he thought. They are all witches. All the women she-devils taking his juices and making babies, hungry squealing mouths and bare feet, bare backs and runny noses and question-askers. He thought, as simple as a woman is, *how can she keep going through labor without breaking open?*

Rabbit stared at Rose. She held one hand up as though to reach out to him, one crusted rough hand that probably scratched his children's faces when she touched them. Meanwhile, Nathan Smith left, slipping out the door and chuckling as he went and drove away. Rabbit had momentarily almost forgotten about him. For here was Rose, eyes a mixture of hope and fear and accusation, looking back at him. He who had to let someone walk into his house and tell him what to do, and Rose had seen him unable to talk. All that while, she had stood here with another child hidden in that pouch.

After an indecipherable amount of time, the tense air between them shattered. Rabbit followed Nathan Smith's trajectory and left the house and headed for the bootlegger's, with Rose flinging words at his back. She grew louder and louder as he went further and further away, yelling something about rancid meat and vegetable gardens. He looked back at her on the porch, crying children clinging to her skirts, and he felt a momentary pang. And she cried to him in fury and desperation.

"Don' raise your voice at me!" was all Rabbit said, even though he knew it was Smith she was angry at.

CHAPTER THIRTEEN

In the years after it happened, Joseph would remember the incidents in a back and forth way, as though the present and past got themselves mixed up. First, he would recall having seen Rose's mother on Rose's wedding day. The others had gone to the courthouse for the marriage ceremony. Doll was sitting on her porch. She was rocking back and forth. She said that she kept smelling the wood smoke of a house fire. It wasn't too long after that, a few months, that Rose's father, Gass, died.

The boys had moved on, and Doll moved back to South Carolina to be with her people. The second-to-oldest boy moved back home and took the farm. Rose's other two brothers stayed on up North, both having gone to college, and they were reported to have gone into the mortuary business. The day of the wedding, Doll sat there, her eyes running water because she smelled smoke. But that was before and behind all that happened.

When had it begun? Maybe it started because he kept trying to remember stories to tell the children. He thought about his father's stories. They were either about ghosts or about something true and, therefore, even more frightening.

His father, Nick Cobb, said that childhood was the time to learn all the things you needed to know to stay safe and out of trouble. He told a story over and over, about going North to Virginia to sell a wagonload of watermelons. He arrived in a town and asked the white people at a service station, "Where can I find the Negroes?" only to be told, "Come back here after dark."

He sold his melons at the edge of town. Fifty cents each. Two for seventy-five cents. At the end of the day, he got back to the filling station where the owner was just locking up. "Unscheduled closing," he chuckled and the next thing Nick knew, he was being pushed into the back of a flatbed truck, handed a sheet, and told to put it over his head. He was not alone in the back of the truck. There must have been ten or fifteen men, smelling of liquor, passing a bottle and laughing heartily. They all talked at once, their talk peppered with "coons" and "Niggers." Nick and them men were standing up, holding the sides of the truck while it sped off with its sheeted passengers.

They arrived at a wooded area where Nick, having been mistaken for a white man, watched a Negro man being burned alive. Joseph could not tell that story to little girls, though Nick had told it to him over and over.

So it was because of that that Rabbit and Rose had to work in the fields, someone said—maybe it was Ida who said it, after Rose said that she would not take her children to Ida and leave them every day and have to pick them up each night—"Old man Joseph, he ain't doin' nothin'. I know he is only a man, but at least he could sit down and watch three little girls." Someone else said, "When you get home, baby's diaper will probably be caked and rank, but he can keep them from fallin' down a well."

Joseph had realized that no one talked or listened to him anymore. Kinchen was quietly drinking alone and bothered no one, except to drive Ida to her farm women's clubs and church home missions, or to town and walk behind the mules, stepping like one himself. So, every morning Joseph got himself up and, unmindful of his aching knees, walked the mile or so to Rabbit's and Rose's to sit with their children. And, to pass time, he made up stories that he thought up the night before, as he fell asleep.

After a month, Joseph had snakes talking and fish walking, causing five-year-old Ruby and three-year-old Sarah to jump up and down at the sight of him, with the eight-month-old baby gurgling to their giggles, all of them eager for the next story. He brought them their first knowledge of the boogie man, who jumped out from behind something or rose up from under something, or fell out of trees above, always shocking his victims.

In that back and forth remembering, in the years after it happened, he saw charred bodies being brought out of a house. But that was the end, not the middle. The middle was the day Rose said, early in the morning on her way to the field, "Grandpapa, stop telling the children things to scare them. They don' need no violence. I don' want them to know 'bout no boogie man. Nor no mules that steal children and sell them. Do you hear me?"

Well, he paid her no mind. When he was little, his daddy told stories of the Ku Klux Klan. Plus, he was the elder. She had three children, but at 19, she was not a woman to him. She weighed a little over a hundred pounds soaking wet. That day, he went back to the walking fishes, who even walked the water with Jesus. When Jesus wasn't there walking the water, sometimes he was putting children to sleep. Then, the fishes raced each other. The best of them all were the catfishes who used their whiskers like stingers and walked a kind of upside-down walk and could beat the eels in the fishes' races, and the eels were really fish, even.

That night on her porch, Rose soaked her hands in cold water and then rubbed them together in the water with lye soap.

"Mama! Mama! Catfishes can walk. Did you know that?"

"No, baby," Rose exhaled deeply. "They can't walk. They swim."

Rose bent at the waist, although pains traveled back and forth along her back. She rubbed her hands vigorously and then tried to slow herself. She was rough on herself, she knew. But rubbing hard and walking fast were ways that she kept herself alert. She bit her lower lip, bearing down against the fertilizer burned in places on her hands where the skin was broken. She stretched her neck trying to shake out a ridge of pain that ran the length of her back. Ruby skipped back a step and jumped up and down.

"But Grandpapa Joseph, he say catfishes can walk. He say so. Yes, he do, too."

"I said no. And don' bump me again. You make me spill the water all over everything."

Ruby continued her skipping on the lower steps, only half-obeying her mother, but she wasn't finished with enlightening Rose to her new learned ways of nature. She clutched her doll to her chest. "And Mama. Did I tell you? If a turtle bite you, he don' turn you loose til after it thunder?"

The child held her doll with its homemade head.

"No. Not true." Rose reached for the towel that draped from a nail by the door.

"It's true! Yes! Mama! Grandpapa Joseph said it," Ruby insisted. She paused on the step, clutching her doll to her chest. "An' another thing, he say you must stop killing crickets in the house. He say it bring us bad luck."

Rose frowned at her. "Who said I was killing crickets?"

"I did," Ruby answered simply. "I showed him one and ask him if he want to stomp it or if he kill it for me, like you."

"Hush, child. Give me some peace." Rose rubbed at the aching spots in her back, closing her eyes.

"And Grandpapa Joseph say," Ruby trilled on, "when it thundering and lightening, God speaking and we 'sposed to go somewhere and sit down be quiet."

"Ruby! Go somewhere *now* and sit down and be quiet."

"But Grandpapa Joseph said—" Ruby began to dance up and down, squeezing her knees together and trying to walk at the same time. She followed Rose inside the house. Ruby put her arms around her mother's thighs and was dragged into the kitchen from the porch. Suddenly, she let go, tensed and relaxed. A shiver took the child, moving from her face and down to her feet. She turned apologetic eyes up at Rose. Shame crossed the little face as a puddle formed and spread beneath Ruby's feet. She wet her shoes, socks and the floor.

Rose exploded. She reached out for something, anything hard. A gourd on the walk fell into her hands and became a paddle with which she flailed Ruby's shoulders until she saw herself, and dropped the gourd to the floor. "I'm sorry, baby" she said quietly, before she backed away.

Ruby had been trying to get her breath, and when it came, she screamed and then sobbed.

Rose wanted to hug her little one, but hugged herself instead, out of fear, out of a desperate need to stop her cruel hands by putting them alternately under her armpits.

Ruby walked, trembling with every step, toward the corner of the room. She dropped onto the bench behind the cook stove underneath where the stove pipe connected to the wall for smoke to escape to the outside. Her sobs quieted. The fire warmed her as unmeasurable minutes went by, and she didn't move, sitting in her urine-soaked underwear and shoes and socks. She silently watched Rose cut up pieces of ham to fry. Before long, from the warming of the fire, Rose smelled Ruby. At first it was soft and suffocating, vaguely like cloves, then it became the smell of onions mixed with old men winos as the fire dried her.

At supper, Ruby, finally changed and cleaned up thanks to help from her daddy, sat sniffling into her plate. She looked like someone who was recovering from a fever. Three-year-old Sarah sat opposite Ruby. She picked up her milk glass, put it to her lips and bit down, breaking the glass, nicking the inside of her lower lip. It bled into her milk, turning the cream-colored liquid pinkish. Rabbit picked her up.

"Don't worry about it," he told his daughter, standing to take her out of the room. He glanced back at Rose. "She too young to drink from a glass. You act like you don' want these children to be children." He picked Sarah up and took her from the room.

Rose balked, because it could not have been her fault that she had whipped one child and frightened the other. And Rabbit was no help, as far as she was concerned, because as soon as they were all in bed, he was rolling over on top of her when another baby was the last thing she wanted.

The next morning, Rose kept her children away from their great grandfather. She stood on the porch in front of a locked door and told Joseph that he was barred. Then, she switched her dress tail off, a hoe balanced across her shoulder, and headed for the field.

Joseph looked through the window that morning and saw the three little ones, the skirts of their dresses each under a foot of the bed, holding them held in place. What Joseph did not know was that, on the previous day, Rose had talked to herself in the field, making herself a promise and a vow. It wasn't the first time, but that day, she was looking at herself when she vowed, deep into her own soul, squeezing the hands that held the hoe, fighting weeds, pulling them on the plant bed. She saw herself in the school yard getting her braids pulled by cowardly boys while Lenore laughed at how

Rose never sensed anybody creeping up on her.

The cockleburs were hard to pull up, and she pretended that they were short, little old brown-legged men in need of strangling. Her vow was that she would raise little girls who would fear nothing and who would have none of the foolishness of the world that she had. Her girls would be able to get out of the hell of hard work and marriage to a devil-may-care man whose theme song was "Don' worry."

In the fields, Rabbit often worked beside her. Sometimes, he whistled. From time to time, he laughed. He even seemed to ignore the eye-stinging sweat. He was a lusty and strong 25-year-old. Sometimes he told her that she was too serious and poured water on her head, letting it run down her shoulders and drenching her clothes, despite her slapping and punching him.

"Don' worry. It will cool you and you will dry off in a minute."

He was right. Before she left the field, she would be completely dry and hot all over again. That day, when it happened, he kept looking at her and saying, "Stop frownin'. You too pretty to ball up your forehead like that. Stop worryin' so much."

This was a spring day when the sun was kinder, but the work was hard nevertheless. They finished picking the plant bed and left for the outer fields, where they cut open twenty-pound burlap bags of guano, filled five-gallon buckets, and strode the plowed rows, spreading the guano and swinging their hands while they moved along.

⁓✦⁓

The sun on the fields was pale, shedding cool light. It was a high-up sun, searching for the place to return and push the crops to harvest, familiarizing itself with the poor buggers who had to work.

Suddenly, something stabbed the air around Rose. The familiar monotony of work and the ambience of the field was broken. It was a motion without a sound. It feathered along Rose Amos Cobb's ear and caused her to glance over her shoulder. She resumed her work and then looked back again after a pull, and she saw a billow of smoke noiselessly puffing, blowing itself up bigger, rising and falling, blackening the sky with each puff bigger still. It inched higher while in her deepest ear she heard her babies cry from a mile away.

Rose flew across the fields and thickets, her feet barely touching down on the dead briars of last year's blackberry vines. These disinterested vines tore through her heavy stockings at legs that were too busy to bleed as she ran toward her house, which emerged as a tremendous ball of flames. She had thought that she heard her children's cries, but what she heard was an echo in her heart.

⚶

Ida saw the smoke. It was coming from the general direction of Rabbit's and Rose's house. The smoke was black. The blackest smoke she had ever seen. Ida called to Joseph because Kinchen was gone.

"See the smoke? It is comin' from over there near Rabbit and Rose's house. Let's go see." They hurriedly hitched up a mule to the wagon and rode in that direction. One the way she asked, "Why you not there? Did Rose stay home today?"

Joseph kept hitting the mule, keeping it moving up to speed.

From all over Griffinton they came, Colored and white people, young and old, enough of them with their many arms to hold Rose back from throwing herself into that square of flames. The roof of the house wearily squatted into the crumble and hiss of cross winds, just after Rose and Rabbit got there. Later, Rose wanted to see the bodies, but the old women told her that if she was pregnant, it was bad to look at dead bodies and would mark her unborn. She didn't think much about it; she was too paralyzed to think. But, she was always pregnant, wasn't she?

In all the things that she would never forget, of the many things she was too numb to notice, it did not escape that the old grandfather never said, "I could have told you," or "You shouldn't have locked the door on me." He acted as though he had no memory of the affront. He moved into the grief with the rest of the family. He looked her straight in the eye. He joined in her pain when others asked, "Why wasn't the old man sitting with those babies?" He said, "I should have been." But he didn't say, "It is her fault."

Her mother-in-law acted as though there had never been a harsh word ever exchanged in their history. Rose once heard her say, "An' my daughter-in-law is a hard-workin' mother," as though Rose had always been the picture-perfect mother in Ida's eyes, and as though Ida herself had picked Rose as Rabbit's wife.

CHAPTER FOURTEEN

The women cared for her and comforted her—the old women, some strange women, many familiar women. Her mother came from South Carolina and stayed one month. But there came a time when she was alone with only what she had lost to keep her company. The women had gone to their own homes to answer the calls of their own households, leaving behind their best intentions. Rose was 20 years old and about to have her fourth baby. She longed to wash dirt balls out of the little girls' hair. She wanted to drag back all the words she had fussed out while leaning over those tiny heads.

One November day, a cloudy day with the trees dropping brown leaves all around and a chill wind in the air, Rose looked at Rabbit and wondered. She decided that he was cold in his reaction to losing the girls. That he had no feelings. They had buried their three girls in the church yard near their great-grandmother, and then come home to go on with some kind of crippled life with the field work to keep their hands moving.

In all of that, all the times at the tobacco bench and later in the pack house grading and drying and tying off, she had never seen Rabbit shed a tear. Men had cried for the girls. Joseph had wept openly along with Kinchen. As Joseph had sobbed, Kinchen had stood still and let his eyes water and overflow. Rabbit just sat around the house drawing pictures. He had taken every scrap of cardboard or piece of paper and drawn pictures. When she looked over his shoulder, she saw houses with chimneys. When he finished, he pushed the drawings aside, to fall on the floor or blow in the wind, for all he seemed to care. When she mentioned it to him, nearly every day, he asked, "What you want me to do?"

She had no answer. It had been six months and she still shed tears into her cooking, onto the clothes that she washed and ironed. Tears fell onto her shoes when she was putting them on. Tears wet her face when she was waking up. There was something hard inside, just under her breasts, some organ that she had never been conscious of before the fire. It hurt. It choked. It squeezed.

Rabbit thought it was better, at least, that Rose had stopped crying all day long now. Now, she was dry-eyed and angry. She looked at him as though she was trying to remember something until one morning, she woke up, looked at him and said, "I never saw you shed one tear for our babies."

How would she know? For a full month, she had been completely fenced in by the women. At the funeral, when she choked on her breath, women rushed to her from all sides. She did not have to walk; they practically carried her in their haste to try. They tried to walk for her, holding her hand, wiping her face, fanning her, poking smelling salts under her nose.

Rabbit had walked alone, some forgotten person there. His friends who came, the boys and the men, made eye contact and quickly looked away. Although his father had wept openly, all he had said to Rabbit was that he did not know what to say. His grandfather talked about the apocalypse or some such. No one touched Rabbit. His mother had been in grief herself, surrounded by her women.

Rabbit had felt a scalding sensation in his chest. He had coughed a lot. There were moments when it hurt to breathe. He realized that maybe even during the pain, he looked the same to the ones who looked at him. They must have seen that his eyes were old. They felt old. He wanted to close them and rest them and never see what he had seen. He had seen enough. But if anyone had seen that his eyes burned, no hand reached out to steady or embrace him. Although, to be fair, a couple of strong hands hit him hard on his shoulder, almost too hard and too quickly. Men never held each other up unless they were drunk. Maybe it was because he tried so hard not to stumble or let the quiver inside him show in his walk. He did carry a tiny bottle in his pocket and put it to his lips to stop the coughing.

His lap was empty all the time. Little girls had rolled across his lap and bounced on his knee. He kept thinking about them, wishing Nora was standing there for him to say, "Take your hand out of your mouth," or that he could tell Sarah, "Don't pull the dog's tail, he got feelings, too." He did not know what to say about them to Rose, so he didn't say anything. She kept saying the same thing, as though she thought that he had not heard her the first time:

"I have not seen you shed one tear."

Was that all she needed? For him to shed one tear, not two or three? He was relieved that she didn't seem to remember about the crack in the chimney that he had not fixed.

Then, Joseph told him, "Go stir the ashes, son. The ashes always hold somethin' back."

The next thing he knew, he was there, at the burn site where the house had stood. He pushed a stick into the pile, looking for something of the girls, and pushed aside a piece of chain, his shore crunched upon some bits of crockery. The stick broke. He sifted with his fingers, sitting among the ashes, his legs out in front of him on the ground where his house had stood.

He was amazed at the number of things that had not burned completely and were still intact amid the blackened particles. Pieces of a Bible contained visible words on pages that turned to ashes when he stirred. He plucked up a spinning top that the baby Nora had spun endlessly. It was charred, but whole. Then he saw the body of Sarah's and Ruby's headless doll, the one that Mrs. Smith had given them. Rose had made a cloth head with yarn hair to fit the rubber body. The cloth head and hair had been consumed in the fire. The doll's pink body was burned black, but was still a doll's body. Rabbit walked away from the ashes, absently carrying the doll, clutching it in his left fist and swinging his arm as he strode.

He walked the short distance to the house he and Rose had moved into, a hay house in which hay had been stored before them. He walked the mile and a half to the hay house.

The porch was piled high with the boxes of debris of charity that people had given after the fire. Neighbors had cleaned out their houses to give them something with which to start over. He sat down on the porch step next to the boxes. Something was nagging away at him in his mind. One of the boxes. He remembered now. That woman. She must be evil. She couldn't be that hateful. But, maybe she just wasn't thinking. Maybe she didn't look.

She sent a box with night gowns for Rose, dresses with all the buttons cut off and the old Army jacket that Rabbit wore now. Maybe she thought the new baby would need a toy. Sticking out of one of the boxes of rags was the doll head just like he remembered, and he knew it would fit before he stuck the head on, screwing it down, the pink head with the marble glass eyes of blue and the charred black body of the doll. He put the two together and laid the finished doll on the box.

Rose remembered how hard it had been to have those children tangled about her legs all the time, and to have the little arms forever pulling on her. Now, she fumbled around her own flanks, feeling for them unconsciously. She tried to forget the spankings she had given. She tried to forget going to the field and leaving them behind. She wondered what Rabbit thought about. He looked like a fever.

On one Sunday morning, she could tell that her time had come. She got out of bed sluggishly and decided she did not have an appetite. Rabbit was sitting inside at the table drawing pictures. He asked how she felt. She shrugged an answer, rubbing her enormous belly, and reached for the screen door. She walked out onto the front porch and lowered herself to the front door step, feeling the morning air on her face. She dangled her bare feet on the ground. She looked up and saw Miss Mariah, her nearest neighbor across the road, walk to her mailbox. Rose called out, "The mail don' run on Sunday morning."

Miss Mariah ducked her head and smiled sadly. She looked in her dusty mailbox daily, hoping to hear from a son who had gone North, but had not returned to visit in 11 years and rarely wrote.

Miss Mariah reminded Rose of a tiny sparrow, moving her weightless hands the way a sparrow moved its feet. She joined Rose and sat next to her on the step. She patted Rose's shoulder, her fingers dancing as soon as they came down.

"I felt a pain a little while ago. I thought it might be time, but maybe not," Rose told her. Miss Mariah took her hand away and began to shiver despite the heat. Rose felt the older woman's excitement and wanted to distract her. All the women had been so good to her. "I wish I could have gone to church. My feet were too swollen to put on shoes. My body is holdin' all the water in the world for this greedy baby I'm carryin'."

Then, almost immediately, she felt guilty for criticizing this baby that wasn't even born yet. The other children had been taken. "Well, I don' mean greedy." She could see Miss Mariah watching her.

Rose started to hiccup just as a pain ran through her. Miss Mariah saw it, and when it had passed, she reached down to pull Rose up. Her hands were steady. When she got Rose to her feet, they watched a lizard who, for a moment, blocked the way back into the house and then disappeared. Rose looked up to where she was going and saw Rabbit inside standing by the window. Instead of coming to help, he eased back away from the window and out of sight.

⚜

Rabbit had been watching them two women, Rose and that nosey old woman who lived by herself across the road. He thought about how women tell each other everything and how a real man would never sit around whining to another man about how he was feeling inside, especially since everybody knew that everybody had his own suffering to do. Men like to play cards together or drink together, even tell jokes to each other.

He saw them get up. He didn't want them to see him. He stepped back. He had been thinking, why had he let himself be forced to marry her in the first place? He hadn't even hesitated, even when his mother protested. She had been an impulse one July day when the June bugs were buzzing. She had been so young. He sometimes thought that he might have ruined her life. Maybe he had raped her. But she sure had made him wait after the marriage. Now, all the years later—what was it? Five?—he no longer hungered for her.

He couldn't stop thinking about the cracked chimney that he should have fixed, and he was not going to mention the little dresses pinned under the foot of the bed at the time of the fire. Maybe if he could tell her how he felt about the cracked chimney, she might realize that he hurt, too.

He watched Miss Mariah touching Rose and thought how no man would rub another man like that. Then, Miss Mariah called out to him. When he got to the screen door, he saw the deep frown on Rose's face. He ran to them and carried Rose into the house. He said, "You stay with her, Miss Mariah. I will try to hitch a ride and go for the midwife."

Rose cried out.

He was picked up right away. As he rode along, he thought of Nathan Smith's conversation on Friday.

A storm had come up that day. Rabbit had pulled the mule under the shelter to wait. Smith had been in a talking mood. He talked about how he loved the smell of freshly plowed land during a rainstorm. Rabbit did not say anything at first. Smith asked, "Don't you love it, too?"

Rabbit finally said, "I ain't crazy about it at all. Freshly plowed land just mean that I got a back sore from fixin' it that way."

Smith angrily got into his car and drove away, giving Rabbit the quiet he loved.

Now his fourth baby was on the way. If what some women said was true, it was really his tenth child. He had made no progress in his life, and soon it would be settling up time with bossman Nathan Smith, and he would have to find out how much debt he owed. There was no money for the midwife. He was going to have to lie to her to get her to come.

❧

Kenneth Lee Cobb was born that day, November, 1948.

December, 1948

On his way to the annual settling up, Rabbit had to walk past the bootlegger woman's house. Now, the Coppage house looked innocent despite the network of car tracks in its yard, along with all the debris that suggested what had happened there the night before; all the people who had twisted and dragged about there, brawling and laughing. The house squatted, seeming to slumber really hard. Nothing about it moved. The sight of this day pleased Rabbit.

Lila Belle was a pretty woman who sometimes gave him back rubs, standing behind his chair while he drank because he never came onto her, like the others who, in the end, often did not want to pay for pussy. This day, Lila Belle snuggled up in his mind, so he made himself a solemn promise as he walked down the road, pushing himself past. He vowed that on his way back, with his earnings for the year, he would not stop.

After he passed the house, he thought of what he would do with his earnings. He thought that because it was his first settling up time, and because they had been so careful not to accumulate a lot of debt, that there would be some money. Definitely he would buy the baby something from Santa Claus and then go home to Rose and watch her as she twisted back and forth beneath him. He counted on it.

He passed the cemetery where his girls lay. He quickened his steps coming to the crossroad, and he crossed over to the paved road that led to the store that Sloane Smith had operated until his illness, now in the charge of Nathan Smith. He approached the plank building with his gas tank, the gold liquid visible through the glass. He reached for the door covered with signs for Camels and Lucky Strike cigarettes, Royal Crown Cola and Fletcher's Castoria.

When he got inside, he realized that he was cold, and he walked to the middle of the room and held his hands out to the stove. Then he stepped up to the counter and stood waiting. Nathan Smith usually sat dozing in his rocking chair with his back to the door. In the summertime, the white man would sit there with a fly swatter on his lap, so that if a fly woke him up, he killed it.

This day, Nathan Smith was in his spot, slumped so that Rabbit saw the top of his hat and the shoulder of his lumber jacket. Sometimes, he would be out of the chair with his hat left perched on the chair corner, so that you would have to get really close to notice that he wasn't there behind the counter. Rabbit walked back to the door, opened it, and let it fall shut, making a slamming noise. The rocking chair turned slowly.

"Mornin', Mr. Nathan."

Dead flies littered the windowsill behind the slowly turning chair. Rose would have cleaned them off one by one every day that God sent. On the counter, just in front of him, Rabbit looked at a jar of pigs' feet, tins of sardines stacked beside cans of pork and beans. The salty things were stacked together, all the things that men craved when coming off a drunk. He wasn't going to need any of them.

Nathan Smith rose up. "Come on in here, Jack Rabbit. We got to settle up for the year, ain't we?"

Rabbit looked longingly at the hoop cheese and thought Rose might like a little treat for Christmas.

"Now. Before we git to the crops we sold, you owes the store four-hundred dollars for rations." Smith took a pencil and a clean sheet of paper from a Smith Douglass Fertilizer pad and began to write.

Rabbit sucked in his breath. Was it that much for a little lard and dried beans? Rose had tried really hard to keep the charges down by getting food from his parents after she couldn't have a garden.

"After that, there is them two criminal court fines for public drunkenness that I paid for you at ten dollars apiece, plus court costs."

Rabbit's breath caught again. He had forgotten all about those. Nathan did not bother to say what the costs of the court were, but he wrote something down. The paper was turned so that Rabbit could not see.

"Now. The cotton dropped this year. Didn't bet but nine cents a pound for it." Smith looked at his paper now that he had filled it up with figures, figures that Rabbit could easily add in his head quickly if he could see them. "OH! Forgot about the children. The money for the coffins for them. Sad, wasn't it?"

Rabbit stood still. Smith allowed for a moment of charitable pause before returning to his figures. The pencil scratched along the paper, the sound of the graphite the only thing filling the silence between them. Finally, Smith lifted the pencil and sighed. He mumbled, "nine plus nine, carry the one . . . " as he borrowed, carried, crossed out figures while in between, scratching at his behind with the eraser part of the pencil. Then he said:

"Well, it's like this: with all and all, with everything, you owe me six-hundred and ninety-eight dollars and seventy-three cents for this date of December 24th, 1948. That wipes out what you made. But, out of the goodness of my heart, I'm going to advance you twenty-five dollars and add that to your debt that is left over. You carry forward a debt of seven-hundred and twenty-three dollars, seventy-three cents, starting off the new year to come. While I'm thinkin' of it, I want you and Kelly around New Year's to broadcast manure on the new ground so it be ready for peanuts next."

Rabbit felt the bills being passed into his hand. His throat suddenly filled with phlegm just when he thought to open his mouth to speak a question, and he choked and did not speak. Nathan wasn't finished, anyway.

"Oh. I got a bag o' apples and oranges. My Christmas present. Merry Christmas. Give these to your little wife."

Rabbit cleared his throat. His voice was softer than he wanted it to be. "Beg your pardon, sir. I thought we had a crop. No drought. No hail or boll weevils. Wonder what I woulda made in a bad year?"

He held the neck of the twiny bag of apples under his arm, so that he could reach for the door when he got there. On the way, he turned his cap around in his hand.

"You talkin" to me, boy? Well? Speak up."

He knew that Smith had heard every word. He left there and started back down the road the way he had come, past the church and the cemetery. Then, he tried to pass Lila Belle Coppage's house. Cars had started coming and were filling the yard now as people got ready to be happy for Christmas, most of them sharecroppers like himself, most having received a pittance out of the charity of their landlords. He was unable to keep his vow, and Lila Belle was happy to receive the fruit bag and said that she was happy to see him, as she stroked his back.

⁕

It never occurred to Rose that Rabbit had stirred up the doll torso from the ashes because he never told her that he had revisited the burn site, even when she accused him of having forgotten his dead children. But when she saw the white doll head attached to the charred body, she thought of its remote origin, its past.

While she scrubbed and washed and swept and folded and ironed and tried to cut, all paused. But there were times that she had to slow down to get a drink of water or to touch her finger to the iron, before laying it upon a shirt front, and then again on the top of the wood burning stove. She saw a face, sometimes clear, other times dimmed. She had once seen it straight on, that time when a woman knocked on the door at her in-laws' house, asked for Rose and offered her a job, looking up the ladder stairs with Ida Cobb behind, frowning and shaking her head. "No."

The woman, amazed at the Negro house, had said, "So nice and clean in here. Not like mine. Dust and cobwebs everywhere."

Rabbit and Rose had been married just 13 months, she a 15-year-old with a 21-year-old husband, the first baby in her arms, and the second stretching its embryonic growth. Clara Smith had come to the house and asked Rose to come and clean her house, to wash, to iron her clothes. She had no children. Probably never worked in a field. Never even stood in for her husband in his store. Rose wondered, then, what the woman had planned to do while Rose left her baby and hauled herself, loaded down with the coming baby in her womb, to do Smith's housework. It had truly not mattered to Rose, and she had gone on counting Ruby's tiny toes and fingers, watching her chest move up and down, as she awaited the birth of Sarah. Rose said no to the woman's offer of two dollars a day for two or three days a week.

It was the two-toned survivor who stayed on Rose's mind, nestled so fiercely there that she could not satisfy herself kissing Kenny's belly button, counting his toes and watching him breathe in and out, yielding to his demands. She stood over him, dressing him and talking, not realizing that her deliberations had turned into a shout until Kenny cried. He had come into the world months after his sisters had gone, he a colicky baby who fretted in an arrogant unawareness of the absent sisters, who had twirled themselves about his mother's skirts and tweaked her legs and thighs, sisters last seen with their dress tails tucked under the feet of a bed. But that day, she had to remove something from her life, because it was taking up her space with this baby.

So, Kenny was snuggled on her hip as she walked out the path to the dirt road, holding a black and white doll in her other hand. The pavement began at the crossroads. She stayed on the grassy side of the road and held her anger in the same hand as the doll. She refused all offers of rides, all of them from people who knew her, the poor thing who had lost all her children. She said she needed to walk off some heat. She and Kenny passed the white house with the Grecian columns that they said the white Dr. Walter Cobb had been living in when he committed suicide.

What was wrong with that white woman to give a poor couple like them a doll with no head and later give them the head? Who could be that evil to attach the doll head to the charred body? At the house, she stood in the same worn spot on the front porch where Black workers had strode after coming to ask which fields to plow first, to rehearse how to ask for money for a doctor, or for cash to buy gas to put into a sputtering old car. Later it became the spot for pacing and spying in a window to see the crazy man staring at walls, or his wife wringing her hands and scratching her scalp. Rabbit had told her that. He had not told her that he had connected the doll parts.

The woman looked out from inside, peering at Rose through the window. She ran jerkily for the front door, as if one no one had spoken to her in so long that she feared if she did not hurry to open, this one might depart without a word, a desperately needed word. Rose did not see her coming but saw the door come open, as though on its own. Rose now thought, *Miss Ida would say that a door that opened by itself to a visitor was a sign of bad luck.* But Rose already had bad luck, of that there was no doubt. A thin white arm jutted out through the opened door and pulled Rose in.

The woman's beginning was abrupt with no greeting or a may-I-ask-what-you-could-possibly-want? She began about something old. In the middle of that, "My husband shouldn't have had to have dogs for his best friends. And it wasn't the dogs alone or their lips dripping blood that made him go mad like I told them at the courthouse. I hate that I did that. He is not one of them like they claim."

They were in the hallway. There wasn't anywhere to sit. The only chair in sight, a pretty thing, was no chair for anyone to sit down on. It was so full of months of issues of the *Griffin County Graphic* that the stack leaned heavily to the side.

Rose held up the doll and waited. Mrs. Smith gave it the quickest glance and looked away, as though back to her own program.

"That doll," she said. "I started talking to that doll. I wanted Sloane to feel sorry for me. Since he didn't seem able to love me anymore. I wanted him to hear me talking to the doll and he would change."

"Why in the world would a grown woman do that? What did you tell the doll?"

"I was trying to break through to him. I wasn't crazy. He might have thought so. I'd tell the doll what I wanted him to know."

Rose set the blackened doll with the bright white face on a table in front of them. The doll leaned limply, striking a dejected pose, supported by a tarnished silver bowl with words on the side: "Debating Award, 1927." Rose looked at the doll for a moment and tried to figure out what to say. She wasn't so sure anymore when she realized the weight of the responsibility that had been put on the doll. She looked around. She looked back at Clara Smith's face, straight on, and clamped her fist closed, keeping back her rage. She closed her fists over it. No point in giving it to this woman.

If Clara Smith would just look at the doll, maybe Rose could say what she needed to say, though now she wasn't as sure as to what that would be. Blessing the woman out no longer made sense. There didn't seem to be any need to say anything. She shouldn't have come. Clearly this silly woman was capable of tearing a head off a doll and then giving it as a gift. Clara Smith's hand shook, a shaking like an uncontrolled tremor from being deprived. Rose looked at the front door and nestled Kenny down on the floor a moment to rest from the walk.

As she straightened, she saw how the room that she stood in was intended as a connecting room, a hallway that was cluttered with a broom, a canister full of trash, unread newspapers, and a confusion of unopened letters. Kenny tried to stand, pulled an unopened brown envelope from somewhere and put it directly to his mouth. Clara Smith leaned down, a smile cracking her face. She lifted Kenny up. Rose expected him to cry out. He didn't.

"Who tore the head off the doll?" Rose asked.

"Sloane did it. Because I was laughing and singing to it. He did it."

"Well, you wanted him to pay some attention."

"I didn't know what he had done with it. It was in his box where he kept his ammunition for his guns. I found it after they took him away." A gurgle came from Kenny in her arms. Kenny went on happily biting into the mail. Clara Smith seemed unconcerned for the importance of it. She lowered him to the floor and got down on her knees, eye to eye with him, and laughed with him.

Rose thought she heard something uncontrolled in the woman's laughter and made a sudden move toward Kenny.

"I won't hurt your baby."

Kenny blew bubbles at her and reached for Clara Smith's glasses with a fat little hand. She pushed them to the top of her head. Rose had begun to sweep debris on the floor, thinking, *No man goes crazy just because his wife is acting doofus.* The doll was in the middle of her growing pile of trash with Rose thinking they must have been missing the physical part of that marriage. She couldn't imagine. Only a selfish mis-raised woman would let that happen to herself. But then, she had been that kind of woman the first months of her marriage to Rabbit. But also, this Clara Smith had some secrets that she didn't want to be confused by. Mail confused people, ones who had secrets. People from the outside confused them, too. So, having come in from outside, Rose wasn't going to say anything much else. Just get out as soon as possible after she swept herself a path and Kenny got tired and screamed in the woman's ear.

"Would you make me a cup of coffee?"

It was the woman's own house and she asked Rose like Rose was at home. They walked toward the kitchen, the two women, Kenny being carried by the white one, the other following.

"Where in this kitchen is there room to make somebody a cup of coffee?" Rose asked. "I'll try to as soon as I clear off a place."

Later, she took her baby out of the woman's arms and watched the woman turn the spoon in the coffee, looking deep into it. "Make yourself a cup, too, if you want to."

"No, thanks. I don' drink coffee."

"You were mad at me when you come here, weren't you?"

"I wanted to cut your throat."

"Why?"

"Don' seem so important now."

"What was it you wanted to ask me? About the doll head?"

"Never mind."

Kenny was always sucking bubbles, jumping about and turning the milk in his tummy to clabber. Very little held his attention. With a mind unclouded by ideas or opinions, he looked at the Smith woman. She felt nice when she put her face to his, and the feeling of her ribs and drooped breasts did not bother him. She was not scaring him as she might have if she had been wearing a hat with feathers that tickled when she leaned down, forgetting him for a moment. He had once screamed in the arms of a woman whose feathers pierced him after she lifted him up in the air away from his mother and brought him to her face too quickly. Sometimes he reached out to see if other things were that feather thing, waiting to hurt him.

Rose put him down and began to gather up soiled plates on the side table. She made clacking sounds that he liked and had heard many times. The woman twirled her spoon and looked at him. She saw fuzzy, nearly new hair, soft-looking hair, soft and wild. She wanted to touch it, thinking Negros had beautiful hair, like a sheep, or more like the buffalo. Pity that they didn't seem to know it. She reached down and picked him up from the floor, bringing him to her own face so evenly that he thought he had gone himself instead of being taken there.

Rose had planned to give Clara Smith a piece of her mind, as quiet as it was kept. But, when she saw her colicky baby so still and not squirming in this woman's arms, she waited. And then, Rose thought, it didn't seem fair to pounce on her. Maybe she could say something about the mess that the woman lived in, there all alone, her husband off in the insane asylum. It wouldn't do any good to ask about things the woman had done. What she had done was maybe lie about a signifying action that she had not meant to do. Or maybe it was just that her life had spilled over into theirs as though the two families had overlapping pains. She could see it, a husband in a fit of temper after having walked circles around something for so long.

She didn't know why she swept the woman's floor while the woman held the baby who didn't make a sound. When she finished the kitchen, Rose held out her hands for Kenny who came and was propped on her hip, her hand empty of the doll and the anger, and she could wrap him close to her. Back on the road she sang:

Somebody want you for her little one
But you is mine's
Someone want you to put you in a pretty bed,
I'd raise you on a bed of straw
If I had to
Some wish she could have you
But you is what I got.

She cried for her dead little girls and realized that she couldn't mourn them by using blame, but she would have to do it from inside, one day at a time, every day from then on.

On the walk back, Kenny was tired, hungry, and wet, and he cried the whole way. She gave him a bath, fed him at her breast and put him down to sleep. Strangely, she thought, she remembered sitting in a rocking chair that someone had given. She remembered a day when the grown people pulled up vines and beat back the woods at the graveyard and the little girls puzzled over how men and women could do nasty things with each other.

CHAPTER FIFTEEN

On the day that Rabbit left for good, Rose interrupted a poisonous snake edging its silent way along outside her kitchen door, and though it pointed away from her house, she killed it by bruising its head with a field hoe and then chopped it to bits.

Rabbit was trying to talk to her just as she spotted it. She was coming from the clothesline with a full basket of wet clothes. Rabbit was in the middle of saying something about being "sick and tired." Rose decided the snake was aiming itself toward a hiding place to come from later. She pictured it squeezing itself between the floor timbers and inching into the room where Kenny had learned to walk or crawling across him in the boy's sleep. She crept toward it with the hoe above her head. It felt her coming because by the time the hoe came down, it was coiled. When she got started beating it into the ground, she thought of creeping fire. The picture did not fit with the leathery pieces on the ground, but she had been mixing up pictures for a while.

It was later that she realized Rabbit had said, "I'm glad I'm not that snake." And then, "I'm goin' to go on up the road." He did not say, "Don' worry." She wondered later, had he been leaving for good then, or did he decide later not to return?

She carried the broken pieces of snake on a shovel and dropped the pieces on the burning pile just beyond the kitchen door. She never answered Rabbit. Then, she began to hang her washing, piece by piece, carefully shaking each piece so that wrinkles would be few. She realized later that she had never looked up at him when he, looking at the back of her, said, "I love your ass. Don' change it."

If she had thought about him going, she would have thought he would have left after the fire, especially when she was so unfair in nagging him about not crying. She would have understood then. On the Christmas Eve after the settling up last December, she would not have been surprised if he had not come home at all. As it was, it took him three days to get home that day. She had found him on December 27, lying on the ground outside, his teeth chattering, with an empty bottle nearby and smelling of whiskey. He had lain talking to the moon, threatening it while she turned out his empty pockets, looking for the money from their 12 months of hard work. She found a single five dollar bill. That was the only time that he had stayed away from home. Rose had guessed where he was. She had told Ida, who had asked, "What did you do to him?"

The time he left for good, Rose assumed that he was in the same place, mingling at Lila Belle Coppage's.

That warm spring day, when Rabbit came out of the house by the kitchen door, he saw Rose in the yard with the basket of clothes. He decided to start an argument. That way, he could storm away and make it seem like her fault. He walked toward her. As he got closer, she turned her back, put down the clothes basket and grabbed a hoe. He could see that she was gathered up tight. He came up behind her, trying to tell her that he was sick and tired of the dirt, the sun, the mules, the debts. All of a sudden, she began to beat the earth. He hadn't seen the snake until then. It took him a moment to realize what she was doing.

He had turned and headed for the path out to the road. As he walked, he avoided looking at the fields all around. It was springtime. He did not want to plant any more seeds of any kind. He was weary of growth. He did not want to start again anymore, as he was forced to do every spring. Something about the bare fields waiting for him to plow into them made him sick. He wasn't sure that he could explain anything except that he was sick and tired and could no longer say, "Don' worry."

Days before, Rose had tried to tell him that Sloane Smith was back from the insane asylum. He was sure she had the impression that she had not gotten through to him, but he had heard every word she said. She had told how Mrs. Clara Smith said that he was going to take back his farms. But Rabbit could not see how he could get around all that debt to Nathan Smith. Something was terribly wrong, because he was getting into debt, deeper and deeper, by working hard. Maybe Sloane Smith could help. It seemed really bad to give up just as the night might be over, but he was just sick and tired.

After Rabbit had been missing for four days, Rose asked Mr. Kinchen to go to the Coppage place and tell him to come home and that she wasn't angry or anything. She knew that money problems worried him. She, whenever she felt the urge, went to Clara Smith's and cleaned as much or as little as she wanted, and Clara gave her two or three dollars at a time —and not even for a full day —and played with Kenny while she worked. She kept her money hidden, because she did not want to work and have Lila Belle Coppage take it.

Kenny was trying to put syllables together into the word he thought he heard. Rose thought that Rabbit might enjoy hearing Kenny try to talk. Mr. Kinchen came straight back to say that not only was Rabbit not there, but he had not been seen that week by any of the regulars at Lila Belle's. Rose felt a shiver all over her body that went into her chest and stayed.

1954

There was certainly nothing illegal about walking along the road in broad open daylight carrying a gun, resting safely on a shoulder. Kinchen was in no hurry after he stepped off the path that bordered the field and walked beside the road, holding a shotgun with its barrel pointing up. He had nothing to hide. And even when he heard the ticking of an engine behind him, he did not flinch while it came alongside, and he saw it was Sheriff Grumble in the official car. The lawman turned off the engine and sat with his arms around the steering wheel. Kinchen saw him move his fat fingers back and forth, back and forth, as though to polish a keepsake. Coarse black hairs bristled on the man's knuckles. His eyebrows were thick and unruly, more like a pair of moustaches than eyebrows.

"Kinchen, boy."

"Afternoon, Sheriff Grumble, sir." Kinchen Cobb considered with some annoyance how easily the front of his name rolled from the man's tongue.

"I got my eye on you. I been watching you ever since you and that nigger dentist worked to git the first high school for the young'uns in the 1930's. And later on, there was the business with your boy, Hart Lee, when I had to arrest him and he runned away. To be truthful, I believe ya when ya say ya don' know where that boy of yours done run off to. And, I know niggars."

"Yes, sir." He had read what Grumble said in the *Nashville Graphic*, that they all lie, cheat and steal. Maybe that was why the sheriff sometimes urinated on the pant legs of prisoners.

He had tiny eyes in his oversized head, and now he blinked those tiny eyes like the headlights of a wreck. He talked gleefully, "Now, boy. You know it ain't huntin' season and you out here totin' your piece." He rubbed his hands together.

"Ain't huntin'. Just out shootin' some rats. I put a passel of dead ones at the woods edge where the buzzards could find them." Kinchen pointed with his head.

"Do. What?" Grumble massaged the steering wheel with both hands.

It didn't matter whether Grumble believed him or not. Maybe Grumble needed a minor arrest this day. Kinchen was certainly never going to be caught brawling, stealing, or causing any commotion of any sort, or whatever Sheriff Grumble was looking for.

But when Sheriff Grumble came onto the stagecoach road and saw Kinchen, his Black hands shouldering a shotgun that was probably loaded and it not yet hunting season for squirrels, rabbit, or deer, he turned out to be exactly what the lawman was looking for.

Kinchen struggled in his mind. Couldn't the man see? He carried no dead rabbits or squirrels, curled in any gunny sack hanging from his shoulders. No little dog trotted along the road beside him yapping and switching. "I can take you to the edge of the woods and show you a pile of dead rats I just put there in the last hour."

"Git in the car. I'm gone have to take you in."

Kinchen took stock of where he was—standing beside the road with a loaded gun and having just been told to get into the car with a man who urinated on prisoners for the hell of it and had been known to take people whom he had just arrested into the undertakers as shortcut justice. Grumble's hands no longer caressed the steering wheel.

Kinchen's heart was a fist knocking a passage through his chest as he tried to think about how to stay alive long enough to put the hand that was on his gun to the door latch of the county car. He did not have all the time in the world. He inhaled and slowly raised the hand with the gun, bringing up the empty hand at the same speed. He looked into the gaze of Sheriff Grumble. When the arms and gun were high above his head, an instant of hatred, a wedge of ice stabbed through the hole his heart had made. And it was then that the heartbeat slowed, the moment that he submitted his ego to the moment.

He got into the car after handing the butt end of the gun through the window to Grumble and after having seen the man's hands rise up from the butt of the official pistol strapped to his side. The sheriff put Kinchen's gun on the front seat next to himself. Kinchen knew not to ask to take a moment to tell Ida where he was going. He sat back against the seat and realized the back doors had no knobs.

Kinchen saw people walking about on the street. He felt conspicuous ambling in front of Grumble. He could have been grateful not to be handcuffed. Once inside the sheriff's office, Grumble licked the tip of a lead pencil and read aloud each couple of words as he wrote. "Kinchen Cobb . . . tenant farmer . . . Negro of Route 1, Box 187, Griffinton, North Carolina . . . found on Stagecoach County road, an extension of Rural State Road #43 . . . armed with a Remington 12-gauge pump shotgun and engaged in the sport of squirrel hunting out of season and without the benefit of hunting license."

"I'm not no tenant farmer, you know that."

"You tend a farm, ain't ya?"

"Yes, but tendin' farm and tenant don' mean..." What was the use? The sheriff knew that he was not a sharecropper. Grumble handed him a paper showing the date of his court appearance and turned his back.

A week later, Kinchen stood in a courtroom and defended himself before a judge who looked down at the paper on which he wrote.

"I took my gun and went out to the corn crib to shoot some rats. I killed a dozen or so. They is got so brazen comin' out on the tin roof at night to the cool, and lappin' up rain in the day. And, they is eatin' up my corn for my livestock feed. I taken 'em and dumped 'em by the edge of the woods where buzzards could find them. That is some distance from my house. Instead of goin' straight home, I walked on from there to the old walnut tree. There is this tree behind the corn crib in the opposite direction of my house that some say is over a hundred years old. There is this one low-hangin' limb that is dead. I think one of these storms will bring it down. I went to look to see is it necessary to go 'head on and cut it down. Then I circled on back the long way home when I seen Mr. Sheriff Grumble."

He took a deep breath and decided to say it all. "All I could think was how to not get myself killed and shot down like a dog beside the road with that gun in my hand." There.

The judge shot him a hate-filled glance. Kinchen swallowed all the things he knew not to say, but he would not be made to lower his eyes. Most of the time. Not this day. The judge looked away first and drawled, "Guilty. Sixty dollars plus costs of the court."

Kinchen walked out of the courtroom, down the hall to the outside. He crossed the street to the sheriff's office. Just beyond the door sat a gum-chewing woman with yellow hair. She was behind a metal table. Kinchen walked up to it, with it between him and the woman. To get her out of her daydream, he leaned across and handed her several wrinkled bills and the paper that the district attorney had given him after his guilty verdict.

She counted them while flexing her jaw. She stuck her tongue out, stretching her chewing gum, and then wadded it with her fingers while he waited. She stretched her neck and twirled a piece of hair between her fingers. Then, for no reason that he could tell, she wiggled her tongue in the air, while he waited. He reminded himself that he was not a man in this place and looked down at his hat in his hand and tried not to move.

"Aw right, *smack, smack, smack*," she said as she put the bills inside an envelope that she kept on the table.

Kinchen waited. She examined her nails.

He cleared his throat. "My case is over, Mam. I need to see 'bout gettin' my gun back."

Behind the desk and the jawing woman, a uniform turned to face him. "Kinchen. Now, Boy, what gun is you talkin' 'bout?"

⌒✦⌒

Kinchen drove from the courthouse back home to Griffinton, along tobacco roads past stands of cotton and peanuts. He braked for a sow leading her piglets across the road right after he passed the white people's cemetery. He did not turn around and seek out the farmer who must not have known they were free running. He did not drive straight home, though. He made one stop. He needed a drink before facing Ida. It was not that he wanted one, he needed one.

With a pint bottle in his hip pocket, he reached home. Ida raised a window and shouted out to him as he got out of the truck, how he should have taken Sloane Smith for a character reference. Sloane was recovered enough to talk, most days. One white man of influence against the others was fundamental when a Colored man stood before the law. It was after she told him what he should have done that she asked how he had fared. Kinchen was tired. Tired as much of her mouth as anything.

By the time he was ready to open his bottle, he was thinking about a letter he had received 17 years ago. "Dear Daddy . . . don't come . . . " But that was seventeen years ago.

His second girl had finished college now. He went to that graduation. Why couldn't he forget? He took the bottle from his pocket and emptied a couple of inches down his throat. He cleared his throat, shook his head, and dragged down another two inches, standing beside the car facing the house.

The bad thing about drinking was being only at the beginning of getting drunk, and he was only halfway there. In that first stage, he dipped into memories that maddened him. This day, he remembered having taken Ida into town when she was pregnant with Rabbit. That was before they bought the first car. He had driven the buggy with Lula balking all the way. Ida got out and walked to the seed store to buy some thread. He joined her just as she was handing the clerk her money. Kinchen saw the owner look at Ida's belly. He saw a look that said, "Oh, another one," and felt as though his unborn child had been bullied for no reason.

This day, as he remembered, he walked into the house and to the kitchen. In the kitchen, he picked up a bowl from the table and smashed it to the floor and then wondered why he had done it—to an innocent bowl that had never done anything to him. It had not chewed gum while he waited to retrieve his gun. It had not taken him into the county jail on a trumped-up charge.

Ida came running in and wept as she swept the pieces of pottery onto some cardboard, but on her way out the door she bumped him with her elbow, dropped more pieces of the bowl, and bent down to pick them up. He wished that he could comfort her, but he could not. He would only make it worse. She was not quite as innocent as the bowl, but she meant well. That was all that mattered. That the other person meant well. Kinchen headed out the door for the walnut tree.

The good thing about the drinking was that the bad thoughts disappeared when you were half done with the pint. By then, things got terribly funny. This day, when he had drowned the image of his pregnant wife being ogled by savages, and when letters from strange schoolgirl daughters were gone, he moved on to stage two. In stage two, he chuckled at how ravishing Ida was whenever she was pregnant. He loved watching her hold her back with her hands to sit, how she opened her legs and let him in when they could barely fit. In the third stage, when the bottom of the bottle was gone, he could not talk or think. He was a quiet drunk, the kind who, after he had gotten beyond the early silliness, was quite pleasant.

He found himself sitting astraddle the largest low-hanging limb of the walnut tree. From there he saw Ida come flying out of the house, aiming herself across the field and in the direction of where he sat. Her head was lowered, her skirt flew. She seemed to be fussing to herself. He put his hand on the nearest over-hanging limb and chinned himself up. He threw a leg over and sat, higher this time. He saw her coming, but with her head still down, and the tree surrounded him with its great arms.

In his mind, he rehearsed what she would say. But when she got there, she never looked up. Kinchen decided that the walnut tree would make an excellent hiding place. He was not at all sure why he was hiding from Ida. Maybe it was not Ida that he was hiding from. He was enjoying his drink. The tree was a perfect place to drink, and it obscured him from view. When he approached it, he could not see himself in it. That's how he knew he was safe.

Eventually Ida looked up and saw him there. She tried to talk him down, alternating between yelling and pleading. Finally in tears, she left him there. Thereafter, during the day, she went to the tree to converse with Kinchen, but never looked up. She knew that drivers and passengers in cars on the stagecoach road could see the tree. So once she was there, she pretended to just be standing under a tree, and with her face turned away from him, she talked. It was the first time he was clear about what was on her mind.

She was motherless. Having given life was not enough. She was haunted by the thought that her mother had fallen off the face of the earth without giving her a thought. She was ashamed of her thoughts because she was past 40 years old.

Everyone knew that she went to the walnut tree to talk to her husband. She believed that no one knew. When cars slowed on the road, she pretended to be pulling at the dead branch. She was scared. That was why she fussed. She regretted the cow incident with Joseph. Well, cows had to die sometime. She stood beneath the walnut tree, day after day, and tried to map out a way to get him down. Most days, he simply came down at night. But, before long, he sometimes spent the night and came down to go to the bootlegger's. Ida forgot and put aside her walking cane because she became so agitated about Kinchen. She sometimes stood under the tree, apologizing over and over. Finally, Ida had to ask Joseph to feed the beasts. Planting season came. The walnut tree was still bare from winter. No one pretended anymore. People in cars slowed to see her, with her head thrown back, talking to her husband in the tree.

"Is it there? Up there with you? Can you pass it down?" She asked for her dishes back.

Before he died in 1956, Kinchen became known as the drunk who spent his time in the walnut tree. He climbed the tree and drank. His obit in the Colored weekly newspaper out of Raleigh said that he had started the high school for Negros in Griffinton.

CHAPTER SIXTEEN

1960

Everyone was well aware that after Kinchen's burial, Ida took Millie to Chicago to live with Lenore. That left Joseph alone, still living in the shed. Ida sold the beasts, placed half the money beneath a rock on the step to Joseph's shed and told him to move into the house. Well, she told him in that way that Ida had. Not face to face and as though she meant it. She hollered it back at him as she booted herself up backwards and climbed into the front seat of Lenore's shiny Oldsmobile. Millie sat on the back seat beside some potted purple and pink coleus and fresh collards in a dishpan that Lenore said she was ashamed to transport. Likely as not, the plants died by the time they made it to the Tennessee border and certainly before they got to Chicago. The collards probably survived the trip.

*

They were all gone away. The tobacco, the cotton, and the peanut fields lay fallow. Weeds camouflaged any impression of cultivation. In the absence of Kinchen and his children, rats played in the vicinity of the corn crib and proliferated on the corn and rye that were no longer fed to farm animals. Grasses and young stubby pine grew where the tractor had tilled.

Joseph went into town once and climbed the stairs to an office in the Planters Bank, and he stood with his hat in his hand to ask permission to rent the tilling land to a tenant. He remembered that he had been permitted to sit down the last time he had come. His request was refused. Some said he should have just gone ahead and rented the land without asking, since he still possessed it. Everyone agreed that the bankers acted out of pure meanness. And yet, they did not seem to be in any hurry to take over. It seemed a shame for all that rich soil to remain dormant. Joseph suspected that all the necessary changes about the land had been made on paper, when one November, the tax bill did not come. Once he became determined to not have his mail read to him, and once he faced the fact that there was no way under the sun that he could come up with a certain amount of money, he was left waiting.

There were times when he could feel the interest on his debt in the chatter of his teeth and pulsing through the stiffness of his joints, palpitating away inside, then beside him, and finally overtaking and running off. Those were times he was grateful to be alone. Being alone made waiting bearable.

Everyone was well aware and concerned that Joseph lived alone in a tiny not-quite room of a shelter. Neighbors sometimes turned their cars into the driveway, rolled past the ancestral house and stopped near the shed. They often remained in their cars, brown arms dangling from an open car window, pausing to see if there was anything simple and easy they could do for old Joseph. Conversation was spun out of cores of concern and curiosity. They did not feel the threat of being drawn too far in. They were protected by being not family. The process of the sharing of news and points of view could drag one of the visits on until a weary child escaped the back seat to circle a tree, getting tree bark on a nice dress, or until an anxious wife would open the passenger door and head for the outhouse, reaching beneath her clothes, then change her mind at the sight of ardent reaching briars and overgrown vines covering the doorway, hurrying back to arouse a languid husband sitting behind the steering wheel.

The Watkins man came once a month with his store of linaments and salves, cake flavorings and cooking pots. He sometimes spent the entire day talking and listening to Joseph. Joseph rarely bought anything. The Watkins man told Joseph he was a Jew. Joseph wondered if he loved Jesus, but never asked. They talked of weather and wars. The man said he had secretly given money to the NAACP and seemed to think that Joseph could help him feel better about his secrecy. Joseph told him that very educated Negros seemed to believe in group work, but that he had always had to depend on himself.

On one visit, the Watkins man lit Camel cigarettes and wanted to know why Joseph did not smoke. Joseph shrugged and said, "When I sold tobacco, they never give me no cigarettes. That's strange. They was tobacco companies. At the warehouse. Never give me no cigarettes." The two men laughed for five minutes at the thought.

In his heart, all Joseph wanted to know was how the man could not love Jesus. Rebecca reminded him of some things that night when it was time for bed. He argued with her, saying, "Can't nobody say I don' love Jesus. I jus' don' go to church."

A number of Griffinton's widows began a campaign of toting cakes, pies, messes of salad seasoned with pork, and pots of vegetable soup to Joseph. He did not appreciate their gifts of food. He cooked for himself. He grilled his meats on a rack out of doors and boiled vegetables in a tin pot on the tiny pot-bellied stove in the shed. It took a full year before he had wrung the last neck of the chicken that pecked around his door. Joseph had more than enough pork in the smokehouse and grew his own vegetables. Whenever a widow approached with a smoking dish beneath a tea towel, Joseph spoke as though Rebecca had just rounded the corner, walking away. He succeeded in driving the ladies off by saying things such as, "That's a mighty pretty hat you got on. I was telling Rebecca this morning, it's been mighty long time since I seen her in a new hat."

About a year after Kinchen had been put in the ground, Joseph's well went dry, causing him to walk once a day to the Amos farm where Rose had grown up. He took his two empty buckets to the well, filled them and made his way back home, balancing himself on each side, two gallons in each hand—water to make coffee, wash himself and his few dishes. By the time Rose came to visit him, her first time since Kinchen's funeral, neighbors had combined their efforts in the way of farm people and cleaned Joseph's well. He no longer carried water by hand, getting home with buckets containing whatever dust passing cars had blown.

Still. Although he did not attend church and had few places to go, he would once in a while flag down a ride to get to the store for sugar, lard, dried beans, and coffee. And, once in a great while, he would walk to somebody's house just to say "howdy" and stand at the corner of a porch grinning, watching someone else's grandchildren running and playing. In those times, he thought of how he had always felt better off than sharecroppers and now and then visited one to hear a human voice.

❧

1953

On a cool October day, Rose drove her 1949 two-toned Ford coupe into the Cobb driveway. Her car brushed its undersides on the tall grasses grown up in the old tire tracks of the driveway where, years before, children and traffic had kept them bald. It was a good day to visit, the time of year when the flies had disappeared because of the cold nights. It was harvest season, and dog days were past. Joseph was gathering his popcorn harvest that day and saw Rose with the child who reminded him of Rabbit, with a widow's peak in his hairline and a crooked smile in the corners of his lips, even when he wasn't thinking.

"I'm sooo glad you came. Nobody here now but me and Rebecca. I told her dis mornin', I say, 'my left-hand itchin', maybe Duke comin' by to bring some catfishes to fry. But seein' you and my great-grandson, that's better than barbecue." He laughed and tried to straighten himself, finally gave up, and put his hands on his back.

Kenny stared at the old man. "You are my great-granddaddy?"

"Yes. Don't you 'member me? I haven't seen you since I buried my son, your granddaddy, Kinchen Cobb. You was there."

"Dat's my last name, Cobb."

Rose and Joseph laughed. Kenny shook Rose's hand off his shoulder.

Joseph looked at Rose. "I was mighty glad you came to the funeral and brought him. The Cobbs was not always nice to you."

Kenny backed up beside her; the two of them stood in front of the car facing Joseph. Kenny fidgeted. Rose reached out a hand to steady him. "You remember Great-Grandpapa Joseph? Now that you see him?"

"Naw." He took his mother's hand, swinging it, faster and faster, up and down, pumping it between them. He dropped her hand and sighed, looking around. Joseph's face was marked with disappointment. "Well, Mama say I wasn't but five then. That's a loooooong time ago." Joseph and Rose laughed. They walked to the edge of the big house that stood empty, the house that Rose had once lived in as a bride and as a mother.

Kenny wrinkled his nose and sniffed. "What a ugly house."

"It was a nice-looking house once upon a time," Rose told him.

"Yes, my father started it with one room. When my wife was living, I added on some rooms. My papa and me, we built the wraparound porch for my mama before she died."

Rose suddenly looked at Kenny, who had stopped listening.

Joseph said, "Guess what? That house has a secret."

"What kind of secret?"

"Well, son. It was like this. My wife come here to this place all the way from Wilmington by train. The year was 1898. You know Wilmington?"

"Down by the beach?"

"It was a big city back then. Not so big now. When my wife left Wilmington, it was burning and toiling with a race riot."

"What's a race riot?"

"Well, that one come about when the white folks decide to scare every Negro man to keep him from voting."

"How they do that?"

"Lot of ways. For one, put up signs telling 'em to keep away from the polls. After election day, they turned the streets into madness."

"Like for a big parade?"

"No, boy. Some folks got killed. What it was, was a big mess, people fighting in the street. Houses burning. Started when they burned down the Colored newspaper. What is a race riot? A mighty dangerous thing to be near. A whole heap of Negroes left that city in November, 1898."

"Um. That does sound bad. Why they want to kill some-body over it?"

"They did it for meanness, mostly. I suppose. Anyway, we had to build a secret room 'cause my wife was afraid that if anybody ever came to get me or my daddy, or my son, she was gone hide us."

"Why she think they coming for the men?"

Joseph looked at Rose. "Oh, Lord. You raising this boy by yourself. He will have to learn what it mean to be a Black man." He continued. "Now, we never would have let her stick us up in some secret room. I never give it much credit. I built it when I figured out she was not gone to rest until I did." He laughed. "Ha ha, he he he. Your mama put Lenore down in it. Hid her from Miss Boss Lady to keep her from getting' a whippin'. Had Miss Boss Lady lookin' all over the farm for her. 'Member that?"

"Who is Lenore? And Miss Boss Lady?"

"Lenore is your aunt. My sister-in-law—"

"Can I see the room?"

"Yeah. Go see can you find it."

"Watch out for rats. Your great-grandpapa may not be scared. I am."

"I ain't scared, neither." Kenny broke into a trot.

Rose faced Joseph. "Somebody came to my shop recently," she said. "From down there. Told me that you was gone crazy, talking to Rebecca. Scarin' people and all. I'm glad to see that you know that she is dead."

"Course I know her dead. Still, don' keep me from talkin' to her."

"Okay. Okay. But, I'm glad to see you're not crazy."

"Yes I is. I is as crazy as I want to be. Not one bit more."

"Yes. Yes. Yes."

She fell into step with him when he picked up his basket. He held the barbed wire for her to climb over and into his garden. The vegetables had gone to seed for the fall. Two rows of popcorn had hardened on the stalks. While he plucked ears, Rose collected a couple to take home and pop for herself and Kenny. While they walked and picked, she told of having gone to Beauty School in Durham to learn how to use a straightening comb and hot curlers, how she had ended up owning a beauty shop and the building, with five beauticians who rented chairs. She said that a lawyer rented the upstairs for his office, but that he was not nearly as busy as they were with shampoo and irons.

She smiled like the young girl Joseph used to see romp across the fields and disappear into the woods. She told him how Kenny could out-spell even the girls in his class. A teacher had given him an old mathematics book with the cover torn off, and the boy did drills in it every single day.

"Ever hear from Rabbit?" she asked.

"Naw. But somebody say he was working at the medical school in Hamilton as a janitor. You ever hear from him?"

"Naw. When neither one of them, he nor Hart Lee, come to the funeral, I said, 'Wonder was they dead?' I know one thing. If he have to clean up behind people and slide up and down halls, he probably not happy one bit."

"I thought that, too. But what else can he do? You and his daddy never had no dream for him 'cept right here on the farm."

Joseph did not take that lure. He would not go back over what he might have done to save the men after him. He was not going to spend the balance of his days trying to remember what he should or should not have said. That would be like trying to get axle grease back in the tube. Oh, but they had crashed on him. Kinchen with alcohol. Hart Lee running away from the law. Rabbit running away from his wife and child and his debts. All three chose things that put them beyond his reach. And this woman, herself condemned to raise her son alone. Kenny came up to Joseph's shoulder, and he still did not know that Black men were all fugitives in America. No, living out here alone, some days no human voice to listen to, he was not going to think about or talk about what he might have done wrong.

The moment Rose referred to that part of the past that had to do with dreams and lights, she became contrite. She knew that her father-in-law had wanted an education, that Joseph had watched idly while Rabbit struggled as a share-cropper after Hart Lee had run away. But it was done now and well beyond repair. It had never been in her control. Not one ounce of it.

She did wonder, though, what was happening to the farm. Had somebody somewhere forgotten all the signed papers? Not likely. But Joseph was still here. She knew one thing. She was not going to ask. She picked at a row of dried beans that rattled in the pods. A car drove past and gave a quick blast of its horn. Joseph threw up his hand in greeting without looking toward the road. He picked up his basket with the small hard ears of popcorn, red kernels peeking through the beige husks. He had collected a dozen or so.

Kenny walked dejectedly toward them. "Ain't no secret room in that house. I looked. It's nasty. And need paint. And windows in places. And sweepin' up. That's what it need. Cleanin' up!"

"Cleanin' up?! Kenny think something need cleanin' up?!"

"You know what I mean, Mama." He looked at Joseph. "You live in that house look like that?"

"Naw." Joseph pointed to the shed, which looked on the outside like any old smokehouse or tool room.

"It's small. Why don't you live in that bigger empty house?"

Rose laughed. "He had a fallin' out with your grand-mother. When Lenore and I was babies, I heard. Remember, I told you, you have a grandmother name Ida."

"Miss Boss Lady," Joseph said. "Meanest woman that

was ever allowed to draw a breath. Rebecca and I was talkin' about her last night. Rebecca still tryin' to convince me that the woman is a motherless child. Still ain't no excuse to go through the world actin' like a hatchet, choppin' the world up with her tongue."

"Well, I looked," Kenny said. "I ain't seen no secret room."

The three of them walked to the back door of the house. Joseph stayed outside when Rose took Kenny inside. She and her son walked with echoing steps along rough dirt-covered floors. They went down the hall to the stairs and then up. Once they were upstairs, Rose showed Kenny the room that she had shared with Rabbit, the room that was the box on top of the house.

She moved the table aside with Kenny helping. She bent to the floor and lifted the cracking linoleum, and Kenny saw the board cut out of the floor. They looked around the room and found a screwdriver to pry up the loose boards. He raced downstairs and went from room to room to see how the secret was disguised.

"Wow!! It really is a secret room! But I thought you meant a place where I could jump out and scare somebody. That place is hard to get in and out of. You put my aunt down in there?"

Rose nodded.

"How you get her in? From the top?"

Rose nodded again.

"What was that Lady, my grandmama gonna whip her for?"

"Oh, my Lord, Kenny. I cannot remember."

They put the linoleum back. Put the table on top and went down the stairs holding hands. When they were back outside with Joseph, he said, "You all can come back to see me as often as you want to. Ain't got no people of my own around here now." Then Joseph asked Rose, "Don't you visit your brother and his wife in your old home place? I use to go there ever day to get water."

"Not often. We had a fallin' out over the land after my Grandmama Tab died. If Momma had a still been living, probably we'd a been able to work it out. It was like we was little again, fightin' in the same ol' pattern. And them tellin' me I was too spoiled and ruint for anybody to listen to what I had to say. And they claim Daddy want the land to go to the boys." She moved her shoulders to her ears.

On subsequent trips, Joseph taught Kenny to play checkers, explained how to know when a cow was pregnant. During the checkers games, Joseph talked about all the people who had gone to the graveyard.

One Saturday, at midmorning, Rose drove to Joseph's with Kenny sulking in the front seat, because, as he had explained during the 60 miles on the way, "There ain't no store in walking distance. It's too quiet. He don't even have a radio."

"It's your great-grandfather that you haven't seen in two months. Just a couple hours will not kill you."

In the driveway she said to Joseph, "I'll be back in a couple hours. I gone take this sewing machine to my cousin. I'll be right back."

When Kenny was getting out of the car, in those first moments, he became complacent about being there. He saw that Joseph was elated to see them. He moved with some difficulty. Even a 16-year-old could see his frailties this day.

"Old Artha is done grabbed hold of my joints. I always move better after I been up and walked a while."

"Let's walk, then, Granddad." They waved goodbye to Rose and walked to the shoulder of the road and down it to the house next door. It was not the Amos house, but in the opposite direction, a half mile away.

At the path of the neighbor's house, Kenny spotted several girls his age staring at him. It turned out they were visiting their grandparents. Joseph sat on the porch and talked to the men. Kenny sported with the girls, their brother, and their male cousin. One of the boys played a harmonica. They sang, "Open the Door, Richard," by Jack McVea and "Rag Mop" by Johnnie Lee Willis. At three in the afternoon, the parents of the girls beckoned them to the car. They put their faces in the back window of the car driving them away and waved at Kenny.

Kenny and Joseph walked the half mile back to Joseph's shed. Joseph was a good deal more limber. Kenny was invigorated by having spent time with pretty girls and was thinking that he hoped to see them again. In the meantime, he realized that the afternoon was nearly over. "I did not see my mama's car go past, did you?"

"Naw."

"She said she'd be back in two hours. It's three hours already." Soon it became four hours, then six. Both of them worried that something had happened. A car accident. Maybe she was lying in a ditch. But what could they do? Joseph remembered that he had saved the last watermelon from the garden, a giant thing elongated with stripes. He sent Kenny into the shed to find a knife to cut the last watermelon.

Kenny picked through the dirt and lint on the tiny table and found a dull knife that was already sticky from its previous use. Joseph wiped the knife along his pant leg and plunged it into the melon. Because it was ripe to perfection, it split itself, starting from the knife cut. Kenny forgot his revulsion and even his anxiety about his mother and relished the sweetness of the fruit while Joseph talked about the land and how the Black Cobbs came to own it.

"Freedom. Well. You had a Uncle. He would be your great Uncle Walter. He used his freedom to be as no count as he could be. And died in a crap game. Do you know what craps is?"

"Yeah. It's something my mama don't ever want me to do."

"Now womins. They handles freedom different. You have to ask a woman, what is freedom. But, so you don' get confused, make sure she got some age on her. Freedom. Never thought nobody would ask me about it." He smiled and sat back, looking at Kenny as though seeing him in a new light.

"Why you lookin' at me, Granddaddy?"

"I was just thinking. Tryin' to see what you will be."

"You should ask me. I'm going to be a doctor."

Rose had no way to get word that the 1949 Ford had stopped on the way back with engine trouble. When she got there the next morning, Kenny had spent the night in the narrow room that was the shed, sleeping on a bumpy cot while his great-grandfather slept in the only chair. Neither had slept well, worrying about her. But for Kenny, using a chamber pot and emptying it in the morning was undignified.

In the morning light, after the deprivation of radio and store-bought sodas, Kenny saw an old bent creaky man who looked all folded up in a room not big enough to put on his shoes. Everything in that room was the color of dirt. It had been 40 degrees outside and Joseph had piled rags that did little to warm a boy accustomed to fresh-smelling quilts and blankets. Joseph was ashen and crusty looking. Kenny smelled his own breath as well as his great grandfather's. There was no bathroom to rinse his face. He had thought the crickets at night were bad while he tried to sleep, listening for the sound of his mother's car. In the morning, the birds' chirping nearly drove him to scream. When his mother finally came, he got into the car and tried not to look back. He told her, "I don't want to go there never no more."

In subsequent trips, Rose went alone and began to take food to share with the old man after she had noticed him weakening. By the time that Kenny graduated from high school, he visited his great-grandfather maybe once a year.

In the days and weeks before Joseph Cobb went missing, he kept on living in the lean-to shed room in the yard. Rose had tried to convince him to move into the family house. On several visits over the months, she had offered to read him his mail. She offered to give him a shave. To every offer other than her food and her visits, Joseph said, "Naw. I ain't worth your while."

Finally, a man drove a truck which he parked beside the road, hopped over the pasture fence, and in the middle of the field posted a sign. Letters had started coming again. Joseph went on collecting them from the mailbox. One or two he had made an "X" for when the mailman honked. He fathomed out the words DEED. He was disgusted. He was broken, and he did not really want to know the secrets of the papers. He knew the events that created them.

In the days before Joseph went missing, an ache tore at him through his sides and ribs. It reminded him of rust. Slow. Sure. Deep. He decided it was some kind of an ulcer. What was an ulcer but a sore, a boil of some sort? He took quinine. It made him sick. He swallowed some sulfur in a glass of water.

The next day he could not get out of bed at all.

The third day, he was back up, but moving rustily. He called on Rebecca to speak. Maybe he got the dosages backward. She knew which herbs to take. How to heal. His legs swelled, just like when someone had dropsy. It was hard to get to the well to draw a bucket of water just to have some to drink. Water stood in the bucket for days and a layer of something white formed across the top. He had to rake the white topping aside and get the water beneath to ease his dry mouth.

Sleep was nice, though. His body was an adversary. He

should not have been surprised, but his thoughts stayed on in the time when he was muscled and could leap. He had lifted his bride on his wedding day and danced around with her in his arms. Now he could not lift the covers on his bed to get beneath. What had happened in between was what he could not put together, and it would seem that he had all day, many days, to figure it all out. Much of what would help him with the pieces were things he refused to remember.

Wednesdays and Saturdays he could depend on. Rose came with good food to eat. The food was still good on Thursday, but by Friday, it was getting stale. Come Saturday, more good food. That was 1962. Kenny had been in college for three years. He wrote to Joseph, and Rose insisted on reading the letters. Joseph enjoyed taking money from his leather pouch, money left from when Ida sold the tractor and the beasts. He rolled out single dollar bills a couple times a year to send to the boy, one at a time. He always got a thank-you note back. He could get so lost in the letters. He wished they were longer, wished he could read them after Rose left. In fact, he memorized them and would not have needed to look again.

On Wednesdays and Saturdays, he had to keep alert, had to keep secret why he did not just jump up and pull back the door to the lean-to. He fussed at her if she did not come when he expected her, because, when she came up on him suddenly, he had trouble hiding how long it took him to get up and slide the door latch. He liked guessing when she was coming and being ready with the latch half--cocked. He pushed with his cane popping open the door. Then, he had to constrain himself to not show how hungry he was for fresh food.

Rose paid no attention to his, "I'm doin' fine. Fine. Fine," to her questions. She knew better. She brought him aspirin tablets. She knew he was hurting somewhere. He did not tell her that the aspirin tore his stomach walls. He was not able to walk outside to pick the wild mint that grew near the fence beyond the "Auction" sign. There wasn't any need to ask her. She wouldn't know the difference between it and nettle or sage. He did tell her once that he preferred BC powders. She got right back in her car and came back with several. She took away his Watkins linaments with the coiled snake on the bottle. She suspected that he drank it, and she said that it smelled toxic.

He received a quart of milk every time she came. It soured after a day and a half. He drank it for buttermilk and got some ease from it. He expected her to fuss about the milk going bad and his not having an ice box, at least. He knew that she would fuss each week about him not going on into the house that, dirty and abandoned as it was, had some beds with mattresses, a table and chairs and real dishes, not tin cups.

He wondered if Kinchen's daughters with all their education told anyone that they had relatives down South, or if they just pretended to be the last of their line. Maybe they had married. He did not know. Maybe he had great-grandchildren other than Kenny. That house was the place they had come out of and wandered off from.

No one was quite sure when it was that Joseph stopped his trips to the store and dropping in on neighbors just to chat. He was at the King's the day that Joe King's madam got up on top of her husband's car and stomped to protest his reckless eyeballs. Mr. King had been smiling too broadly at the new pastor's wife at Pleasant Grove Baptist Church. Joseph stayed too long there with the crowd watching Mrs. King, and he wet his pants. No one offered him a ride home. A couple people slowed down next to him and saw the wet circle on his blue cotton pants.

People may not have noticed his disappearance at the time, but in the contagion of, "The last time I seen him was—" they would try to reconstruct the events of when it was that something stopped happening. Even then, they would need very specific incidents as time markers, such as before the castration of Rick's sholts, or after Mrs. Coley gave birth to the twin boys, or about the time Mrs. Nora Alston Smith's dog committed suicide on her porch. All agreed that during the fall of 1962, it rained ceaselessly. No one dropped in to see him during the rain and he probably was not seen. Then, it became winter.

Just before he went missing, he decided some things. He decided to die alone. He decided that he had no choice but to die. He decided that the final stages of the foreclosure would be more than he could bear. But Rose never knew that.

One day, Rose baked a turkey with chestnut and oyster stuffing and peach preserves on the side. It was not Easter and it wasn't Christmas. She had hit the turkey with her car. The farmer said, "Take him. Old turkey Gobbler. All the rest drowned in the rains, turned up their throats and swallowed whole rainstorms." She took a feast to Joseph. She found him sitting on the doorstep of the house.

She told him how surprised she was.

He said, "I forgot myself. But didn't no lightning strike, did it?"

She convinced him to eat at the table inside. Made him wait outside while she prepared the table in a room that had not been used in years. She stood on a chair and, as though the table was the floor, she swept it with a broom. All the dirt, insect bodies, leaves, trash, and cobwebs. She put her bed sheet over the table and served him turkey and all the trimmings. He came inside slowly, looking around, darting his big wondering eyes.

He was weak and becoming weaker. Rose had argued with herself about what was to happen to him. At least she had finally gotten him inside the house. She hurried him to the table, holding him by his elbow, not because he could not walk in his own time, but because she was afraid that he might turn and bolt. She got him to the table. He dropped into a chair that she had cleaned off. He bowed his head and muttered into his chest, then ate with his full attention. In what seemed a mere moment, his plate was a mound of bones.

Rose left him sitting at the table, looking straight ahead at a bare wall, giving her a view of a profile of a proud stiff neck, lips closed, eyes staring at something beyond that wall. He looked as though he was dreaming. He certainly did not seem concerned to have broken his own dare by setting foot inside his house.

She chuckled. "You should stay right here in this house. I brought a sack of canned foods and a can opener. I will put it right here on the floor. I'm gone to have to miss next week. That's why I brought canned goods for you to eat. I'm gone up to the university to see Kenny. You can open a can, can't you? I'm gone home now."

He sat in the ancestral home for the very first time in over 30 years. Close to 40. He looked at the other clean chair of the eight in the room, some upright, one broken. He stared at the clean chair, wanting Rebecca to come and sit before him one more time. She did. He said to her, "That's a mighty clean apron you got on. Must not have much cleaning up to do where you is."

Then a thought hit him. He had never known a time since they married when Rebecca sat down and faced him and they smiled. She was always cleaning or picking up. Even on cold winter nights in their bedroom sitting before the fire, she sewed or darned or wove. He had to take things out of her hand to make love to her. Many times. Having her face-to-face with her hands still and resting on her lap, watching her slow, even takes of breath reminded him of how people who love each other take time with each other before they are married, but almost never after. Had she known that she was what he cherished?

He didn't think much about whether she had known when he could have told her. She had become so much a part of him when she was there, he thought that her mind was the same as his. When she was blind, he missed her sighted. When she died, he missed her living. As best he could, he told her.

She sat in the other chair, the chair that Rose had swept off so that he could sit at the table and eat like regular folk. She reached her soft fingers to touch his. She took his hands in her own. He drew back. "I am so ashamed of my hands. A farmer's hands should be calloused and hard. My hands is softer than yours ever was." He tried to turn her hands over to look, but he could not manage anything physical now, now that she was dead.

She had emerged from the woods with Wilmington behind, to the relative safety of Griffinton. He had stood in the kitchen, watching and listening in this same house, which was smaller then. His mother was feeding them and Mrs. Smith had gone to her home and come back with clothes and food to add to what his mother had. Rose had been covered with the debris of flight, but the first time he laid eyes on her, his nature was stirred.

They were all gone now. Vate. Florence. Walter. Sarah. The white woman. Rebecca. He fell asleep, sitting in the chair. When he woke, it was dark outside as well as in. No sign of the moon or stars. He awoke cold in his bones. His legs were asleep. He rolled onto the floor. He did not know where he was. Something crawled over him. Sniffed him. He called out. He knew that he had died. He heard a train whistle, and there was not a train track anywhere near his place. He repented all his sins. Then, morning broke, and he was not dead.

It must have been Monday. Rose had come on Saturday, or was it Sunday, and left him in this place. It was early morning, but he was not hungry. Rebecca came in. It was Rebecca who helped him up off the floor and took him through the echoing rooms, to the foot of the stairs, and then on up those stairs that he had built. She led him to where he could look down through the floor into the secret room when he had removed the table and the linoleum and the boards. He looked down into Rebecca's room and saw no reason in the world not to climb down into it. He had built it with places to put your feet on while going down and coming back up. But, he was not coming back up. With that in mind, Rebecca helped him in.

Perhaps he recalled a day when he had been locked outside a house that contained three tiny girls who for safekeeping had been deprived of him and his stories of walking catfishes and hants and witches—three precious things sitting with skirt tails fastened to the floor beneath the feet of a bed.

Eight days later, Rose came. Something told her to go to the house first before going to the shed. She found the sack of canned goods in the same place by the door. Untouched. Inside the house she smelled a terrible odor. Nevertheless, she looked for him inside the house. She wore a thin wool coat. She climbed the stairs, and when she stood over the hold of the secret room, she saw the top of his head and caught the stench of him that nearly blinded her. She held the corner of her coat over her nose while she pressed the boards into place and put the linoleum over the hold. She let go of the coat to pull the table over the linoleum and did not breathe until she was outside, where she vomited on the ground.

She could not for the life of her figure out why her first impulse was to hide him. She could not understand why she did not run out of there, screaming for help. Help for what? He was gone. Then she thought, it was wintertime. November. Already the nights were freezing temperatures. He would probably freeze and then dry out. By spring, no one would notice the stench, if anyone even bothered to come to the house to look for him.

She felt like a thief as she sped away with Joseph's food still in the car. She went back and forth in her mind, trying to decide if she should report his death. The longer she thought, the more she was moved against sharing the news with anyone. She sobbed, washing the steering wheel. By the time she had gone the 60 miles, her eyes were dry, and she was locked in her secret.

She put a key in the door of her house and plucked a letter from the box. She opened it, barely able to see with the soreness of her eyes. Nonetheless, she read what Kenny had written.

> *Dear Mama,*
> *I have decided that I do not want to go to medical school. That was never my dream, that was your dream. I want to study history and get a Ph.D.*
> *I think I would like to chronicle Grandpa Joseph's life. Among other things.*
> *Love, Kenny*

In January, a man who said he was from Griffinton found his way into Rose's beauty shop, and he walked bashfully past customers and operators and stopped at Rose's station. After the weather and "how ye be," he asked if Rose had taken Joseph from his home to live with her without telling his neighbors.

"No. Why?"

"Then how come you stop coming?"

"Is he there?"

"'Naw. He don' seem to be. The church peoples sent me to talk to you. Even though he stopped goin' to church, he built the benches, you know. We feel obligated to him. So, we noticed that he ain't been seen and you ain't been seen comin' to bring him food. We was wonderin' if you know where he is."

She took her time unwrapping a towel about a woman's head. She took her time lighting her little stove and placing two brass combs inside. He waited in the way that someone waits for another to chew their food before answering. "Now, you say that he is not there, but you think I should be coming. Has anybody looked for him?"

"Yes. We have looked everywhere we know to look about the farm. We checked all the buildings, and even though he don' never go in the house, we looked there. So, if he not here livin' with you, did you take him somewhere else?"

"Naw. I did not take him anywhere."

"Why you stop comin'? Did he say he was going away?"

"Naw."

"Well, where is he?"

"He not with me."

Her questioner scratched his head. And started to walk backwards. Rose began to pull the smoking comb through a small bundle of hair and the room smelled of bergamot. Rose gestured to a chair. He dropped into it and said, "We talked to the sheriff. He said it was nigger business. Do you know anything?"

"About him leaving the place? I don't know anything about him leaving the place." She crossed her fingers above her implement.

"Pardon me. Did you have words with Mr. Joseph?"

Rose smiled. "Everybody know how stubborn and hard to get along with he is." She made herself say it. "He lived in the shed because he could not get along with my mother-in-law. Just a matter of time before he would fall out with me." Then a thought struck. "Has anybody checked with the relatives in Chicago?"

"Hadn' thought about that. Maybe he went there. That truly is a shame." He shook his head. "We even looked in the woods, thought maybe he fell down there and couldn' get back up."

"I'm sorry, I can't help you."

"I'm much obliged for your time. How's your family, your boy?"

"My boy is terrible. Was going to study to be a doctor. Now he want to go to graduate school to study history. Got good grades in all his science courses. But I can't tell him a thing. History. Can you understand that?"

"Yes. Yes." He put his hat on, then took it off. "It's mighty funny you stopped 'bout the same time he disappeared."

She was pulling a straightening comb through a woman's hair, the hair well below the woman's shoulders. It took a while to pull to the ends. The whole room of four beauticians and six customers waited. She lay the comb back on its little stove. Wiped her hands on a cloth for that purpose and looked up.

"Well, like I said. Grandpapa Joseph was a hard man to get along with. That's for sure." Then it hit her that she had better act sad. But when she lay the comb in the beautician's stove and made a slight stagger toward the wall, she found that the tears she felt coming were real. "I hope you all find him. And let me know." She wiped her eyes. "Is there anything the people want me to do?"

"I don' think so. Like I said, the sheriff don' even seem to care. So, Mr. Joe told you not to come?"

"Well, let's say, he made it necessary for me to stay away. Last time I was there was sometime in November." Then she thought that she needed to shift attention away from herself. "You mean to tell me, all those Christian folk in Griffinton, nobody care enough about an old man to not misplace him? I live 60 miles away. Lord have mercy."

Author Bio

Susie Ruth Powell was born in Whitakers, North Carolina, during the reign of Jim Crow to a 24-year-old mother and a 63-year-old father who was a son of slaves. The rural setting of her upbringing on a small family farm is depicted in *Beyond That Room*.

She earned degrees from Bennett College, Smith College graduate school, and Case Western Reserve School of Law. Straight out of law school, she sued the United States of America on behalf of the Garden Valley Tenants Association, which conducted a rent strike that lasted more than one year, launching her career as an anti-poverty lawyer.

Beyond That Room fictionally depicts the lives of former slaves and their families who fled Wilmington, North Carolina, in 1898, just days after Election Day and the successful overthrow on Wilmington's government in a white man's riot. The riot ushered in Jim Crow.

In retirement, Susie wrote the award-winning documentary, *The Loving Story*, with Nancy Buirski, a renowned documentary filmmaker. Susie also story-shopped work on *The Rape of Recey Taylor* by the same filmmaker.

You can email the author at qpowell@aol.com.